Rebecca was born in Chester, England and studied at Exeter University. She has had a variety of jobs that have taken her to some very interesting places, including four years teaching in a Category C male prison. Rebecca has been attempting to parent since the start of the millennium and currently lives in South-West England with her husband and three children. When not working her day job or frantically writing, she can often be found drinking prosecco.

@bexsmithwriter
/Bex Smith Writer

More Than Just Mum

Rebecca Smith

One More Chapter
a division of HarperCollins*Publishers*
The News Building
1 London Bridge Street
London SE1 9GF

www.harpercollins.co.uk

This paperback edition 2019

First published in Great Britain in ebook format by
HarperCollins*Publishers* 2019

A catalogue record for this book
is available from the British Library

ISBN: 9780008386610

Set in Birka by Palimpsest Book Production Ltd,
Falkirk, Stirlingshire

Printed and bound in the USA

For Polly.

May women everywhere have a friend as supportive, strong and bloody hilarious as you xxx

Chapter 1

The first question is stupid *and* illogical. It is also highly personal. I pause for a moment, unsure about whether I should really be doing this. But there's nobody else here, and I *am* on a break. It's not as if what I'm doing is illegal or anything.

Returning to the question, I chew the end of my pencil and mull over the multiple-choice answers.

A) Eight or more times a week. Well, that's obviously ridiculous. It's clearly been added as the amusing option. That's more than once a day. Who on earth has the time for that? Or the inclination, when it comes to it?

B) Up to five times a week. Possibly, when I was in my early twenties and didn't have anything better to be doing; like the laundry or preparing the next day's packed lunches or catching up on Netflix or sleeping.

C) Two or three times a week. Now we're moving away from the fantastical and heading into the realms of reality. But honestly, whoever wrote this question needs a good talking to. There is a world of difference between twice a week and three times a week – ask anyone. Twice a week is enough to feel smugly adequate. Three times a week is pushing it a bit, but perfectly possible if there's been a birthday or it's Christmas or a bank holiday.

D) Less than once a week. Again, this is impossible to answer without being more specific. Which week am I meant to be basing my answer on? If it's the weeks after I gave birth then the answer is a resounding D. If it's the week that Nick surprised me with a romantic trip to Devon then I can circle B with confidence. Or am I supposed to be taking a mean average over the course of one year?

I scan my eyes across the page, searching for advice. But other than the questions and the screamingly large quiz title, there's nothing.

The end-of-break bell rings and hundreds of feet start pounding down the corridor. I'm not teaching for the next hour, but I keep my eyes fixed on the classroom door, just in case a hapless Year Seven takes a wrong turn. I don't need anyone to catch me in the act of reading the magazine that I confiscated from Elise in Year Nine during the last lesson. And I am probably old enough to identify my own areas of sexual competence without taking a quiz entitled 'Are You A Sex Goddess?'. But I've started now and I'm feeling curious about what the verdict will be.

Dissatisfied with the choices, and wishing that there was a 'once or twice a week' category, I recklessly break with tradition and circle both C and D. Then I move onto the next question.

Which of these positions is your favourite?

Good god. The list of answers reads like a cocktail menu.

I haven't heard of any of them, never mind having an actual preferred position. Flicking back to the front cover, I look again at the title of the magazine. Surely Elise has got her hands on some kind of black-market, top-shelf publication and I should be handing this straight to the Headteacher? This kind of question is completely unsuitable for girls of her age.

Magazines and their content have clearly moved on from my day; this is definitely aimed at the teenage market. Or maybe they haven't moved on. Maybe it's me. I do remember poring over magazines with sketch drawings showing the 'Position of the Week' and sniggering with my friends. But that seemed more innocent somehow, like it was a serving suggestion rather than an assumption that we were all getting it on at every available moment.

I ignore the second question and move onto the next, which rather intrusively wants to know how many sexual partners I've had. Interestingly, zero is not an option – I suppose that's because the quiz writers assume that one needs to have actually had sex in order to identify whether one is, in fact, a sexual goddess. Answer A is a bit alarming though. I wouldn't have thought anyone would have the energy to have that many different liaisons, and I feel a grudging respect for the sheer work ethic that must be required. I look down the list towards the more sedate numbers, while running my own experiences through my head.

It doesn't take that long. I was a late developer, and a combination of worry about how my body looked and terror about getting pregnant meant that I waited until I'd left home and gone to university, where quite frankly, it was relief to get the whole first-time thing out of the way. And no, there were no fireworks and the earth didn't move and the sky did not fall in. Instead, I spent the entire time wondering where I was supposed to put my legs and trying to politely ask if he could take his elbow off my hair because I thought that there was a risk of me getting scalped, which wasn't really what I'd envisaged from the whole affair. And yes, it got better after that (or maybe I got better after that) and there were several longer-term boyfriends, one of whom I remember fondly and the other two who have been consigned to my he-whose-name-must-not-be-spoken list.

So, five if I include Nick, which of course I should, because we've been married forever and that counts, surely? That doesn't seem too shoddy or too promiscuous. I can live with five.

Circling answer C (which is slightly disappointing as I'd have thought five partners would place me slightly higher up the scoreboard than that) I read on.

How good are you at undoing a belt?

Ha! Now this is the kind of question that was written for me. I am the queen of undoing belts, thanks to the fact that my irresponsible family are constantly putting their dirty jeans and trousers in the laundry basket with the belts still attached. I can sort whites from darks and unbutton shirts and whip belts out from trouser loops with my eyes closed. I am an expert.

Except I have clearly overestimated my skills. The options suggest that there are women out there whose talents at belt removal far exceed my own pathetic offerings. No, I cannot undo a belt with my teeth. I can't think of a single time that I would wish to do so. Doing it with my eyes closed is actually answer B, which gives me a brief thrill of achievement – but then I read on and see that it's only eligible if I have done a sexy pole dance first. The image of me strutting my stuff as I sort through the day's washing pile makes me snort.

I whizz through the remaining questions, revealing my most personal secrets, tot up my total points and turn the page to discover my fate. And it was just as I suspected all along. I am Hannah Thompson, Ultimate Sex Goddess: all lesser mortals bow down before my sultry and provocative nature.

I'm lying. My score puts me in the bottom league. Instead of achieving the heady heights of 'Sex on Legs', I am firmly placed in the 'Could Try Harder' category. I think the pun is intended but it's difficult to know for sure.

Standing up, I head towards the door. If I'm quick I've got time to pop to the staffroom and grab a coffee before the next session of riot-control-slash-listening-to-new-and-innovative-homework-excuses.

I drop the magazine in the recycling bin as I walk past, wishing that I could abandon my slightly dented ego just as easily. Not that it matters. It's just a stupid quiz and it doesn't mean anything. I bet virtually every woman my age would get the same result that I did. There are far more important things in life than sex, and I'm sure that if I took a quiz called 'How Nice Are You?' or 'How Efficient Are You?' then I'd totally score in the top percentile.

I would on the efficiency quiz, anyway. I am very well

organised. The jury would probably be hung on their verdict as to whether I'm nice. All they'd be able to say for sure is that since I've been doing this job, I appear to be getting less nice by the day.

Chapter 2

Taylor Swift is admonishing me as I stumble into the room, my arms laden with yet another load of laundry. She informs me, in her dulcet tones, that she knew I was trouble when I walked in, which I think is fairly rude when all I'm doing is attempting to navigate from the kitchen door to the washing machine while avoiding the obstacles that my youngest child, Benji, and Dogger, the dog, have kindly put in place. Clearly they both felt that I needed the extra challenge.

'Scarlet, can you please turn your phone off and set the table?' I step nimbly over a skateboard. 'Benji! Clear your stuff away *now*.'

Taylor segues into her next song like the professional that she is, asking me why I had to rain on her parade.

It is my lot as a mother, Taylor, I tell her silently. *It's just what I do. So if you've organised some kind of parade, or perhaps a party, then you can be fairly sure that I'm not going to like it. Especially if there will be boys or alcohol involved. And judging from your song lyrics, Ms Swift, I believe that there is a high possibility of that.*

'Hello, people!' Dylan bounds into the room, throwing his arms out like Hugh Jackman in *The Greatest Showman*. 'I am here!'

'Congratulations for you,' snarls Scarlet, finally turning off the music. 'I've been here for the last sixteen years but I don't make a song and dance about it.'

She does, though. In the last six months especially, Scarlet has started behaving as if her life is some kind of dramatic theatre production. And clearly, this particular production requires a lot of tortured expressions, self-introspection and extended monologues.

Dylan strolls across to his sister and flings his arm around her shoulder. 'That's because you're just not as special as I am,' he says, pulling a sad face. 'But don't worry, little sis. I'm here for you.'

Scarlet gives him an almighty shove in the chest and he staggers backwards, narrowly avoiding Benji, who is attempting to remove his skateboard (as per my instructions) by putting Dogger on top and pushing her along.

I ram the washing into the machine and straighten up, sniffing the air. It smells suspiciously like burnt sausages.

'Has anyone checked the oven?' I politely enquire. 'Because I'm pretty sure that I asked you all to keep an eye on the cooking while I sorted out the laundry.'

'I've been revising for my Maths exam!' Scarlet's voice is laden with persecution. Nobody does aggrieved like my daughter.

'I was in the bathroom.' Dylan sits down and starts prodding at his phone.

'Again?' asks Benji, voicing what we're all thinking. 'You were in there for hours when we got home from school. Have you got diarrhoea or something?'

'Why are you so gross?' Scarlet glowers at him. 'Nobody actually says stuff like that.'

Benji glances across the room at me, his face a picture of confusion.

'I was only asking,' he says. 'Because we've been learning about germs in Science and I was just going to say that Dylan should probably wash his hands a bit better after he's been to the toilet. Then he won't keep needing to *go*.'

'The supper?' I ask, but nobody hears me. Dylan is exclaiming his disbelief that Benji could be so hypocritical as to talk to *him* about personal hygiene when we all know that Benji runs the tap and pretends to put his hands underneath but for some ungodly reason refuses to actually get them wet, and Scarlet is furiously slamming knives and forks onto the table and muttering loudly that she is the only person in this family to actually do anything helpful ever, while Benji is repeating the word 'diarrhoea' over and over again like some kind of hideous mantra.

So it is left to me to rescue the sausages and chips and heat up a tin of baked beans before screaming at them all to shut up and sit down.

'I've cooked you a delicious meal and the least you can do is have enough respect to eat it *nicely*,' I roar, slamming the charred contents of the oven onto three plates. 'I've been at work all day listening to Year Nine mutilate the English language, which is enough to send the sanest teacher over the edge, and I've got lessons to plan and your dirty pants aren't going to clean themselves and Dad won't be home until late *and* we've run out of wine.'

They all pause for a moment and I see Dylan eyeing me warily.

'It looks great, Mum,' he says.

'Yeah, thanks for cooking for us,' says Scarlet. 'We'll do the washing up.'

'Thank you for *everything*,' adds Benji, passionately. 'Like, thanks for making our food and doing the shopping and washing our clothes and making our packed lunches, and also thank you for giving birth to us and driving us to places and just for being our mum.'

He pauses for breath and gives me a big, ten-year-old beam.

'You are such a suck-up,' mutters Scarlet. 'And I think you'll find that it's *me* who makes the packed lunches, *actually*.'

'You're all very helpful,' I say, sinking down into a chair. 'It's why people have children in the first place, you know? For an easy life and for all the extra help that they get.'

Dylan laughs and starts squirting tomato ketchup copiously over his plate. I would normally make a cutting remark about the ratio of sauce to food but today I keep quiet. The sausages and chips have been cremated almost to the point of ash and I think a little extra moisture is acceptable in this case.

For a few moments, the only sound is that of knives attempting to ineffectually carve their way through several layers of pyrolysed pork. I lean back and start to relax. Nick was going out with a couple of mates after work but hopefully he won't be home too late. We'll eat pasta in front of whatever American crime series we're currently working our way through on Netflix and it's Wednesday, which means no school for me tomorrow. If I use my imagination and powers of delusion, I can almost make myself believe that it's the weekend.

'I started following Zoe on Instagram today,' says Scarlet, giving up on her knife and picking up the sausage with her fingers. Her voice is casual but the look she shoots at Dylan is distinctly shifty.

'Why did you do that?' Dylan rounds on her, his face screwed up in displeasure. 'You don't even know her!'

'So?' Scarlet shrugs, her grin stretching from ear to ear. 'That's what social media is *for*, Dylan. Getting to know new people.'

'But you know that I—' he stops and gestures wildly at Scarlet, before slamming his hands over his face.

'I know that you *what*?' purrs Scarlet. This is her favourite game. 'I know that you fancy Zoe? Is that what you were going to say?'

Dylan groans. A good mother would probably stop this but there's no chance of me doing that. This is the first thing I've heard about any Zoe character, and if Dylan is interested in her then I want to know everything that there is to know. And fortunately for me, Scarlet is an excellent source of information.

'Dylan's got a girlfriend!' crows Benji, his eyes sparkling with delight. 'Are you going to get *married*? You're allowed, you know. You can do that when you're eighteen. And you can also vote and get a tattoo and be sued.'

'I do not have a girlfriend!' snaps Dylan. 'So shut up!'

'You are not allowed to get a tattoo,' I say, but even as the words come out of my mouth, I'm wondering why *I've* never thought about having one.

Maybe something tasteful, like a small butterfly or a daisy? Maybe something that would prove I'm not old and past it. Or perhaps I could get my eyebrows shaved off and perfectly arched brows tattooed in their place? That could be worth looking into. I think I could achieve a lot more in life if I had eyebrows that were *on fleek*, as Scarlet would say. It sounds quite French. I wonder if it's actually spelt *en flique*? I must remember to ask her.

'But you'd like to have a girlfriend, wouldn't you?' says Scarlet, resting her chin on her hands. 'And fortunately for you, my Instagram stalking would suggest that Zoe is currently boyfriendless and looking for *luuuurve*.'

'You are a hideous sister,' Dylan tells her, but I can see that he's keen to hear more.

'I'm never going to get married,' Benji informs us while attempting to surreptitiously feed the rest of his sausage to Dogger. Clearly my youngest child does not have a future in espionage. 'And I'm definitely not having any kids.'

This distracts my attention from the Zoe situation for a second.

'Why not, darling?' I ask. 'Having children is wonderful and fulfilling and life-affirming and ...' I trail off, aware that all other conversation has ceased.

'Are you kidding us?' says Scarlet. 'You're constantly knackered and you're always saying that you've got no money because we're so expensive.'

'Well, yes, but you see, that's all—'

'And you and Dad are always talking about the holidays you could have if it was just the two of you,' adds Dylan. 'You could be going to Mauritius this summer and not having two weeks camping in France.'

Scarlet shudders. 'God. It's a no-brainer. Dirty nappies and crying babies and never losing your baby belly. I'm never having kids.'

I instinctively suck in my tummy. 'Those things are true, but—'

'I'm going to live with Logan,' Benji tells us. 'We're going to live in this house and go to work on quad bikes and play on the Xbox and eat pizza every night.'

'Are you both going to live with Dad and me?' I smile, momentarily warmed by my youngest child. 'That'll be nice.'

He loads up his fork and rams it into his mouth.

'No. You'll both be dead by then,' he mumbles through a mouthful of masticated beans, which takes the wind out of my sails just a little bit.

'I don't even know why you had kids,' says Scarlet. 'I've seen photos of you from before and you look way younger.'

'That's because I *was* way younger,' I retort. 'And people get older regardless of whether they've had kids or not.'

'It's not the same though, is it?' Scarlet is on a roll. 'Like, you're always moaning that you've lost all sense of your own identity and that you have no time for yourself.'

'I'm not,' I protest feebly.

I am.

'Okay.' Scarlet raises her eyebrows at me. 'So that wasn't you earlier, telling Jennifer Aniston to piss off?'

'Who is Jennifer Aniston and why were you telling her to piss off, Mum?' asks Benji. 'That was a bit rude of you.'

'Language!' I say automatically. 'And I didn't tell Jennifer Aniston to piss off.'

'You did!' crows Scarlet. 'I heard you! You were on your laptop and Jennifer Aniston was on the screen, going on about how important it is to have some "me time" every day and you said, "Oh, piss off, Jennifer Aniston and get back to me about 'me time' when you've spent all day sprinting around after other people." Or something like that.'

'I'd rather have a dog than a kid,' says Dylan. We all automatically look at Dogger who, embarrassed by the attention, starts licking her vagina.

'Well, at least none of you guys ever tried to do *that*,' I gesture towards her. 'Although Benji did once manage to wee in his own ear when he was a baby.' I remember exhaustedly cleaning him up at three o'clock in the morning and trying to sob silently so that he'd go back to sleep. Happy times.

Scarlet smirks smugly. 'I bet I never did anything as disgusting as the boys, did I, Mum?'

I smile back at her. 'Oh, sweetheart. I don't think a mealtime is the right occasion to talk about all the foul things that you got up to when you were little.' I pause. 'And also, not so little.'

Dylan and Benji laugh and Scarlet pulls a face at them.

'So, are you going to ask Zoe out, then?' she asks Dylan, retreating to safer ground.

'None of your business,' he snarls. 'And if I were you, I'd

be too busy worrying about the identity of my mystery online boyfriend to be bothered with my brother's love life.'

'What mystery online boyfriend?' I ask.

'So you're admitting that you have a love life!' screeches Scarlet. 'Ha! A *loveless* life, more like it.'

'So you're not denying that he exists, then?' returns Dylan.

'*What* mystery online boyfriend?' I repeat, louder this time. 'Will someone please tell me what you're talking about?'

'Scarlet's got a boyfriend but she's only met him online,' says Dylan, not breaking eye contact with his sister.

'He's just a friend and it's nothing to worry about,' Scarlet says, glaring back at him.

'Nothing to worry about as long as he isn't actually a fifty-six-year-old weirdo, you mean?' Dylan grins at her.

'Scarlet?' I tap my hand on the table to get her attention. 'Who is this person? Is he actually fifty-six? Because you *are* aware that would not actually be okay?'

Scarlet gives Dylan a withering look, which manages to concisely convey that she will be having words with him at a later date, before turning to me and putting on her reassuring face, which only serves to make me more wary.

'He's a friend of a friend and he's not fifty-six, Mum. He's sixteen and he lives in the Czech Republic and he's totally fine.'

I frown. 'And you know this *how*?'

Scarlet sighs dramatically. 'Because I've seen photos of him and he's a teenager, not a pervy old man.'

'What does "pervy" mean?' asks Benji.

'She said nervy,' I tell him. 'Pervy' does not feel like a word that should be in a ten-year-old's vocabulary and the last thing I want is a phone call from the school, complaining about his language. 'Go on, Scarlet.'

'I'll show you his photo,' she says. 'Then you can chill.'

'I want to see your conversations. So that I know he isn't being inappropriate.'

And also, so that I know that you aren't engaging in sexting or nudes or anything else terrifying.

Scarlet's face wrinkles up. 'That's an invasion of my privacy,' she complains. 'Those conversations are private.'

I eyeball her. 'There's no such thing as private on the Internet, you know that. The government can read anything you write online.'

'God,' she groans. 'No wonder our country is in such a mess, if politicians are spending all their time snooping at my emails and messages instead of actually doing stuff.'

'We'll discuss this again later,' I assure her, gathering up the plates. 'Now, who wants some pudding? We've got apples and bananas.'

'An apple is not a pudding,' complains Dylan. 'I need more than that if I'm going to keep my energy up.'

'And he *does* need a lot of energy,' Scarlet agrees. 'If he's going to be pursuing the lovely Zoe.'

It never ceases, their enthusiasm for winding each other up.

I think about the worries that are stacking up in my brain, like jumbo jets circling to land at Heathrow airport. Dylan and his potential girlfriend. Scarlet's online liaison with a stranger. Benji's insistence that he won't ever be having children, which makes me question whether Nick and I have done such a terrible job of parenting that it's the last thing that they want to do with their lives.

I think about all the conversations that I need to have with my offspring and I bitterly regret my decision to be self-righteous and virtuous and not drink during the school week.

Chapter 3

I gaze out across the classroom, looking at the twenty-six faces that are staring back at me. Elise has just asked me a question and I absolutely know the answer. Of course I do. I am a teacher, and therefore I possess all knowledge.

'So is it true then, miss? Did Shakespeare steal all of his good ideas from someone else?' she asks again, leaning forward and fixing me with a steely glare. 'Because that's called plagiarism, that is.'

'It's called *cheating* actually,' Brody informs her haughtily, before turning back to look at me. 'Why do we have to read his stuff, if he's a cheating scumbag?'

'I'm sure that William Shakespeare wrote all of his own works,' I say, trying to sound authoritative. I hold up a copy of *Romeo and Juliet*. 'His name is on the front, after all!'

'That doesn't mean anything,' calls Vincent from the back row. 'I once got Wayne to do my Maths homework and then put my name on the top and Mr Jenkins didn't suspect a thing.'

We all turn to look at Wayne, who is inspecting the contents of his nose. Vincent's life choices clearly leave something to be desired.

'That was stupid,' states Elise. 'There's a girl in Year Eleven who'll do your homework for five pounds *and* she puts load of mistakes in so that it doesn't look too suspicious.'

'Anyway,' I say, attempting to regain control of the lesson. 'As I was saying, *Romeo and Juliet* is a tragedy, and—'

'The tragedy is that we have to read it,' interjects Brody, earning a laugh from the rest of the class. 'I don't know why you can't just let us watch the film. That's what Miss Wallace did last year when we had to study *Macbeth*.'

A mutter of agreement spreads throughout the room and I resist the urge to groan. Not this again. I've spent the last five months hearing about what Miriam Wallace got them to do in their English lessons last year – the conclusion being that she didn't actually get them to do very much. Which means that I now have the thankless task of attempting to teach them everything that they should have learnt in Years Seven and Eight.

This is not the job I signed up for.

'I want you to get into pairs and make a mind map showing how the theme of love is portrayed in the play,' I tell the class. 'Think about Romeo first. Who is he?'

'Leonardo DiCaprio!' shouts Brandon Hopkins.

I ignore him. 'Consider how Romeo professes to feel about Rosaline right at the start and how quickly he switches his affections to Juliet.'

'Romeo is a proper lad,' calls Brody. 'Way to go, *Ro-may-o*!'

'You have twenty-five minutes,' I snap. 'And anyone who doesn't take this task seriously will be doing it as homework.'

This gets zero response. I can set as much homework as I like but I can't make them do it. We all know that.

Year Nine start organising themselves into pairs. By 'organising' I mean that they squabble and bicker and barge around the room until at least half the girls are sulking and the boys are all crowded around the back desks in one messy group.

'Ahem.' I clear my throat to get their attention. 'Brandon Hopkins! Can you please tell me how many people are in a pair?'

'Depends how large the pair is, miss.' He snorts and elbows the boy next to him who dutifully sniggers.

That literally makes no sense. These kids can make an innuendo out of absolutely anything. It is exhausting.

'Very entertaining,' I tell him, narrowing my eyes. 'There are two people in a pair, Mr Hopkins, and if you can't all sort yourselves *into pairs* in the next thirty seconds then I shall be forced to select your partnerships myself.' I pause, looking around the room. 'And they will be mixed gender.'

There is a horrified gasp and a flurry of movement as everyone scurries to find themselves a partner. I watch the clock, counting down the last ten seconds, and then, once everybody is seated, I walk around the room dispensing large sheets of paper and coloured pens.

'Ooh, felt tips,' coos Wayne. 'Miss Wallace never trusted us with the felt tips.'

This statement fills me with joy. Finally, my teaching style is being compared favourably to hers.

'Get started on your mind maps,' I instruct. 'I will be coming round in ten minutes to see how you're getting on.'

The class start pulling the lids off the pens and I return to the front, sinking down into my chair. The chair is the only good part about this job. It used to belong to Miriam and she left it behind when she got promoted to Deputy Head. I spent the entire first term having to defend it from the other members of the English department who complained that, as a part-time member of staff, my needs were less important than theirs. I'm no fool though. I set out my terms and conditions at the start of January, making it clear that the chair is the bonus for teaching Year Nine, Class C and that anyone who wished to negotiate for its extra padding and swivel seat would be expected to take on the aforementioned class along with the chair.

Unsurprisingly, nobody has come after it since then.

A superior chair is, quite frankly, the least that I deserve. In my humble opinion, Miriam could have left me a sofa and a coffee maker and my own personal water fountain and it still wouldn't have been enough to soften the blow of making me teach English.

Because I am not an English teacher. I am a Biology teacher. When I started at this school it was in the Science department, after I'd left university with a Biology degree but couldn't get a job. The choice between teacher training or moving back in with my mother was an easy one to make and things kind of snowballed from there. Teaching wasn't ever what I intended to spend my life doing but once Nick and I started having kids, the long school holidays and vaguely decent pay made it a no-brainer.

But then the inept government started making ludicrous cuts and our school became an academy and all the rules changed overnight. I didn't even see it coming, that's the humiliating part. I strutted into the Head's office last July ready for my annual appraisal, wondering whether I'd have time to pop to the shops on my way home. If I was vaguely surprised to see Miriam in there then it wasn't enough to register any thoughts of alarm. We all knew that she'd just been promoted to Deputy Head and it seemed obvious that she'd want to be involved in staff evaluations.

The panic bells only began when Miriam took the lead, telling me that sadly, financial cuts meant that the Biology department was being downsized but that I wasn't to worry, they had found a new position for me. It would be fewer hours and less pay. Worst of all, it would be taking on her old post in the English department.

I had stutteringly queried my suitability for such a job, but Miriam had glossed over my concerns.

'We've been looking back over your curriculum vitae,' she told me, brandishing a file with my name on the front. 'And it states quite clearly that you are an avid reader of books and an aspiring writer. If anything, you are overqualified to teach the students at this school.'

I tried to tell her that the phrase 'aspiring writer' referred to my one attempt at writing a collection of short stories, after I took a creative writing module as part of my teaching course. When I presented my efforts to the tutor, he informed me that my writing was too try-hard and that it lacked any sparkle. My CV was the last fictitious work that I ever wrote.

I also attempted to explain that my life has changed quite dramatically since then. Not least with the addition of three children, which hasn't left me with a lot of spare time for pursuing my own hobbies and interests. But Miriam is like a very efficient bulldozer, and before I knew what had really happened I had agreed to a one-year temporary contract, teaching English, three days a week.

'We will review your progress on a regular basis,' Miriam assured me. It sounded like the threat that it was meant to be.

And so, for the last six months I have faked my way through agonising grammar lessons and un-creative writing lessons and lively debates where nobody says anything remotely linked to the topic at hand. I have diverted and distracted and downright lied when asked a question to which I do not know the answer and I have stood at the front of the class pretending that I am not an imposter, a charlatan and a complete and utter con artist.

It has been the most exhausting six months of my life and I have hated every single second of it. But I can't afford to lose this job, and Miriam knows it. If we were playing a game of poker, she would have the entire royal family and I'd just be left with a few twos and a three, and maybe the joker.

The noise in the room has escalated to uncomfortable levels so I bang my hand on the desk.

'All that talking had better be about the theme of love,' I warn. 'Vincent. What have you got so far?'

Before Vincent can reply, the door swings open and Miriam Wallace walks in, as if my thoughts have magically summoned her from whichever dark corner she'd been lurking in. She casts a beady glance around the desks, her eyes narrowing.

I stand to attention and resist the urge to curtsey. Or salute.

'You've given them felt tips, Mrs Thompson?' she asks, her voice frosty.

And that, Year Nine, Class C, is a perfect example of a rhetorical question. Beautifully executed with a hint of power play. Round One to Ms Wallace.

'Yes.' I attempt a smile. 'I always find that mind maps are much more powerful if the words stand out in a vibrant colour.'

Round Two to me. I am taking control of my choices. This is my classroom now.

Miriam sneers at me. 'It's the "vibrant colours" that cause me concern,' she says. 'We are encouraging a professional, corporate look here at Westhill Academy and that includes crisp, white shirts that are unadorned with childish scribbles.'

'Oh, I don't think we need to worry about that,' I laugh. 'This is Year Nine, Ms Wallace. They're quite capable of—'

'It's Year Nine, *Class C*, Mrs Thompson,' she snaps back. 'Wayne! Stand up!'

'Honestly, Miriam,' I murmur. 'I'd have noticed if they were doing anything untoward. Look. His shirt is fine.'

Wayne is standing in the middle of the room, a large smirk on his face. I smile at him reassuringly and turn back to the Deputy Head.

'We've been doing a lot of work on responsibility and appropriate behaviour,' I tell her, not wanting to lose this opportunity to brag about my teaching. 'I really do think that

I'm getting somewhere with them. I've seen a real improvement in their levels of maturity and their ability to focus. For example, this lesson is all about identifying the way that the theme of love is addressed in *Romeo and Juliet* which, I think you'll agree, is a complex and highly nuanced topic.'

Miriam ignores me, choosing instead to direct her full attention at Wayne.

'Turn around!' she barks. 'Now!'

At the back of the room, I see Brody and Vincent start to laugh. An icy droplet of dread trickles down my spine, but I am powerless to do anything except watch as Wayne raises his hands in the air like he's being arrested and slowly, slowly turn so that his back is facing towards us.

How did she know? She can't possibly have known.

'What do you have to say about *that*?' Miriam enquires. There is silence for a moment before I realise that the question is aimed at me, not Wayne.

I stare at his shirt for a second and then I walk closer, weaving my way in between the desks until I'm standing right behind him, reading what is written in very bold and very permanent pen.

Love is beautiful like #nofilter.
Love is precious like an iPhone X.
Love is sex and drugs and rock and roll.
Love is chaos and death.

'Who was working with Wayne?' My voice is quiet and nobody speaks. I do a slow one hundred and eighty degree turn, looking at every single member of the class. 'Who was working with Wayne?'

Very slowly, three sets of hands rise into the air.

So much for working as a pair.

'I said that we—' starts Elise but Miriam sticks her hand out, palm towards the class. Elise wisely shuts up.

'Stand up, all of you,' I snap. Brody, Vincent and Elise all move to stand beside Wayne. 'Whose idea was it to write on Wayne's shirt?'

More silence, but I am not surprised. These kids would rather chop off their own arm than risk looking like a snitch; even Elise, who is currently chewing on her bottom lip and looking slightly pale.

'If they aren't prepared to tell the truth then they must all suffer the consequences,' intones Miriam. 'Destruction of property is a serious offence.'

I nod at the four delinquents to sit down and gesture Miriam to the side of the class.

'Have you read their mind map, though?' I whisper. 'It's actually pretty good. They've really considered the complexities of love as it's portrayed in the play.'

She stares at me like I've just grown devil horns.

'They drew on Wayne's *school shirt*, Mrs Thompson. The quality of the work is absolutely irrelevant here.'

No. It isn't. This is the first time that I have seen any member of Year Nine, Class C exhibit even a modicum of intelligence. I could give literally zero fucks about the method of display. They could have smeared it in lipstick across the wall for all I care – the entire point is that they have clearly, despite every single piece of evidence to the contrary, been listening to my lessons.

It is an actual miracle. I refuse to let Miriam Wallace and her stupid rules take this away from me.

'I expect to see all four pupils in after-school detention for the rest of the week,' she says, raising her voice. 'You too, Mrs Thompson.'

'You're putting me in after-school detention?' I say weakly.

She's gone too far now. She might think that I'm doing a crappy job but she can't treat me like one of the kids. I will not be sent to after-school detention – it's a complete violation of my rights.

Miriam nods. 'I've been revising the rota and you are now down to cover after-school detention duty today, tomorrow and Wednesday.' She pinpoints her laser focus onto me. 'Is that going to be a problem? It *is* part of your *temporary* contract.'

Of course it's a problem. And it's completely unfair. She's punishing me and there's nothing that I can do about it if I want to keep my job. The job that she takes great pleasure in reminding me is only guaranteed until the end of the year. I'm putting my foot down over this. She's pushed the wrong woman this time. Brace yourself, Miriam, and prepare to witness my wrath.

'No problem at all, Ms Wallace,' I trill brightly, through gritted teeth. 'I shall be there.'

Miriam nods at me and with a last glower at Year Nine, Class C, storms back out of the door.

I stagger to my desk and sink back into the chair. I am not living my best life right now. Not in the slightest.

'We told you that she never let us use the felt tips, miss.' Vincent's voice rings out loud and clear. 'She thinks we're too thick to be let loose on anything permanent.'

'You and me both, Vincent,' I mutter under my breath. 'You and me both.'

Chapter 4

There's no questioning the facts. It is one hundred per cent there and I have one hundred per cent got to deal with this situation immediately. Part of me was hoping that it was a joke, but the more that I stare into the magnifying side of my mirror the more the evidence stares back at me.

Brandon Hopkins was correct, which must surely be the first time since I started teaching him that such an event has actually occurred. I would find this cause for celebration if it weren't for the fact that on this particular occasion, I would be happy to prove him wrong.

But as he so accurately and loudly pointed out during period six on Wednesday afternoon, I have a lady-moustache.

And I am about to do something about it.

The instructions on the packet are pretty basic but the page of safety precautions goes on forever. I start to read, squinting to see the tiny words.

This product is suitable for upper lip, cheeks and chin.

Chin? Brandon Hopkins didn't mention anything about

me having a lady-beard, but I'd rather be safe than humiliated in front of Year Nine, Class C next week. Grabbing the mirror, I scrutinise the skin below my mouth, searching for errant hairs. Fortunately for me, the majority of my facial growth appears to be confined to the area between lips and nose; I breathe a sigh of relief. I'm pretty sure I didn't buy enough product to deforest my entire face.

I keep reading.

This item is NOT SUITABLE for the rest of the face, the head, the ears, or around the anus, genitals or nipples.

What now? Why would anyone in his or her right mind want to put wax *there*? What would be the purpose? Are there really people in the world who care about whether they have a hairless arse? And who would even know if they *did* have the odd hair or two in the vicinity of their rectal opening? I mean, I've never thought to check but now I'm wondering if I need to have a quick look.

Shuddering, I shove the instruction leaflet in the bin. It lost me at *anus* and I don't care to read one more word. Not that I need instructions, anyway. The wax strips are laid out in front of me and it's obvious what I need to do. I have two X chromosomes after all. The skills that I need to complete this task are inherent in my DNA. It's genetic memory – I have inherited the knowledge that I need to remove my excessive and unwanted moustache from my mother, and her mother before her, and *her* mother before her, and – well, I'm not sure how long waxing your upper lip has been a thing, but it's not as if candles are a new invention, so the craft probably goes back for many generations.

I pick up a strip and warm it between my hands before peeling off one side. Then I apply it to my skin, pressing it into place to make sure that it's stuck down really firmly. And now it is the moment of reckoning. I'm quite looking forward to this bit. I'm not stupid – I'm aware that there may be a small degree of pain involved – but surely it won't be worse than pulling off a plaster? And these things can often be quite satisfying, in their own way.

I take a deep breath and yank the wax away from my upper lip in one smooth movement.

'Fuck it, that hurts!'

On the floor, Dogger gives me a baleful look. I ignore her and peer eagerly at the wax strip, keen to see how much hair I have managed to remove.

There is bugger all there. Not one single strand.

I am not feeling satisfied in the slightest.

I lean towards the mirror again, trying to ascertain the current status of my moustache, but the skin is tingling and slightly pink and I can't tell if the hairs are still there. But it's okay because this is my first go and sometimes it takes a while to get the knack of doing something technical like this. Otherwise, beauty technicians wouldn't need to exist, would they? And I have loads more wax strips left. I'll just keep going until I've got rid of them all.

The next fifteen minutes are not the best fifteen minutes of my life. On a scale from stubbing a toe to giving birth, I would say that the pain threshold hovers somewhere around the time I accidentally shaved off an entire strip of skin from my ankle to my knee. Both the bath and I looked like we'd been involved in a particularly gruesome episode of *CSI: The Shires*. At least this time there isn't any blood.

Finally, when I have waxed over the same piece of upper lip with every wax strip that was in the box, I admit defeat. I haven't seen a single hair come out and my lip is sore and suspiciously red.

There are worse things than a slight smattering of hair on my face, I tell myself. I am a grown-ass woman and I do not have to conform to the stereotypes imposed upon me by society. In fact, it is my duty as both a parent and a teacher to educate the next generation and show them, by my example, that it is possible to be successful and professional and intelligent and a worthwhile member of society while sporting a tiny lady-moustache. These things are not mutually exclusive.

Glancing at the time, I realise that unless I get moving then I'm going to be seriously late. I am experimenting with trying to keep as busy as humanly possible on Thursdays and Fridays, in a pathetic attempt to convince myself that not being at work is a treat and basically *a good thing*. My plan for today is to pamper myself. I have a lovely, relaxing appointment at the hair salon – which I probably can't afford, hence the DIY hair removal, rather than paying an extortionate amount for someone else to get up close and personal with my lip-fringe.

Coaxing Dogger downstairs, I shoo her out into the back garden, so that she can take care of her own personal hygiene, before grabbing my coat. I call her back inside, give her a biscuit, dash out to the hall and pause briefly to appraise myself in the mirror. My face isn't looking too exhausted, and while my hair is a bit of a state, that's okay – it would be a complete waste of a salon trip if it weren't.

The drive across town is slow due to it being market day. It's freezing cold but the sun is shining; there is an optimistic sense of spring just around the corner. Despite this, as the minutes tick by, I become increasingly aware that something is wrong.

Hideously, badly, catastrophically wrong.

On my face.

The tingling sensation that I had from the moment I yanked off the first wax strip has increased. In fact, it would be highly inaccurate to even describe it as tingling anymore. It is more an agonising, burning, stinging, throbbing torment that is making it difficult to think about anything else. I brake for a red traffic light and risk a glance in the rear-view mirror.

Fuckety fuck. My lip looks like I've been stung by a thousand bees, and not in a good way.

Now I come to think of it, who ever thought that 'bee-stung lips' could be a positive thing? Nothing good can ever come from being stung by a bee *on the mouth*. It's utterly ridiculous.

A honking noise from behind alerts me to the now-green traffic light. I drive carefully down the road, trying to focus on parking the car safely, all the while wondering if I require immediate medical attention. The sign for the car park is up ahead and I take the corner, gently easing into a space and then turning off the engine before pulling down the sun visor so that I can examine the damage more closely.

The skin above my mouth is swollen, stretched so taut that it is shiny. But worse than that are the weeping, oozing spots that seem to have appeared from nowhere.

And I was wrong earlier. There is a little bit of blood.

On a scale from terrible to fucked up, this is very, very bad.

And I'm late for my appointment.

Grabbing my bag, I leap out of the car and race across the car park, my hand held defensively in front of my face as a precautionary measure. I don't want to upset any small children who may catch sight of me. Dodging between little old ladies with pull-along baskets and mums with prams, I speed down the street and then, with a huge sigh of relief, push open the door and fling myself into the sanctuary of the salon. I will be safe here. They are professionals and their business is to take the lame and make them beautiful again. I am among friends.

'Morning!' Caroline emerges from the staff area as I catch my breath by the front desk. 'How's it going, Hannah? How are your kids? I saw Scarlet in town yesterday afternoon – I can't believe how tall she's getting!'

'It's going really well,' I mumble, from behind my hand. 'And the kids are fine, thanks. How about you?'

What does she mean, she saw Scarlet in town? Scarlet was at school yesterday. Caroline must be confusing her with someone else – maybe she's got a doppelganger, or a clone. God, what a thought – I love my daughter deeply but two of her is a bit of an overwhelming possibility.

'I'm good, thanks. Shall I take your jacket?' She reaches

towards me for my coat and I realise that I'm going to have to move my hand.

'Thanks, Caroline.'

I turn my back on her and hastily lower the zip before shrugging the jacket off and turning back to face her, my hand once again in place across my mouth.

Caroline gives me a slightly weird look but says nothing as she takes a gown from the row of hooks by the door and hangs my coat in its place.

'Just pop this on,' she tells me. 'And then come on through.'

I repeat the performance with the gown and then follow her into the main part of the salon, sitting down at the seat that she is pulling out for me.

'So, what are we doing today?' she asks my reflection in the large mirror. 'Same as normal?'

I smile in agreement and then realise that she can't see my mouth behind my hand. 'Yes, please. I need my grey roots sorting out and a quick trim on the ends.'

'No problem! I'll just mix the colour and then we'll get started. Can I get you a cup of tea while you're waiting?'

A cup of tea would be lovely. It's exactly what I need to calm myself down after all the stress of the morning. I would kill for a cup of tea right now. But they bring the milk in a little jug here; I will either have to drink black tea or move my hand from my face. Neither of those is an acceptable option right now.

'No thanks,' I mumble. 'I'm fine.'

Caroline shoots me another look before retreating to the staff area and I stare bleakly at my reflection, my hand pressed tightly across my mouth. It seems very unfair that I am sitting in front of the world's largest mirror, today of all days.

'Here we are then.' Caroline is back with the tiny amount of dye needed to eliminate my barely-existent grey hair. 'Shall we make a start?'

'Let's do it,' I mutter. 'Work your magic.'

She places the bowl on top of her hairdresser trolley and swivels my chair round so that she can begin with the front of my head. I give her an encouraging smile with my eyes and hope that she's not in a chatty mood.

'Erm, Hannah?' Caroline looks awkward. 'I'm going to need you to move your hand. I can't reach your hair with your arm blocking the way.'

Bugger.

I spend three seconds debating the pros and cons of asking her to just dye one side of my head before coming to the harsh realisation that there is nothing for it. I am just going to have to lower my hand and hope for the best.

And I'm probably being totally melodramatic, anyway. I haven't actually looked at the stricken area since I left the car. The biting winter wind will no doubt have done a lot to bring the swelling down. Caroline probably won't even notice anything wrong.

I lower my hand.

'Bloody hell!' Caroline's shriek gets the attention of the rest of the salon; I feel five pairs of eyes turn to gaze upon my terrible form. 'What have you done?'

'I was trying to wax my upper lip,' I whisper. 'It's not *that* bad, is it?'

'Not that bad?' howls Caroline. 'I've never seen anything like it, Hannah! And we've seen most things in here,' she turns to the gawping audience, 'haven't we?'

'We've seen some shocking things,' agrees her colleague from across the room. 'But none as awful as that.' He's new since the last time I came here and I don't know his name but, from the sneering look on his face, I suspect it's something mean.

Caroline pats my hand in what I think is an attempt to be reassuring.

'Maybe you're allergic to the hair wax?' she suggests. 'I can't think of any other reason you'd get a reaction like that. You did do an allergy test first, didn't you?'

I shrug. 'I didn't know that I was supposed to.'

Caroline looks shocked. 'Hannah! You must always test out any new product. You can't just go playing life and death with your skin.'

I allow myself a small laugh. 'I hardly think this is a life and death situation, Caroline. Let's get it into perspective, shall we?'

Her response is to spin my chair so that I'm facing the mirror.

Oh, for fuck's sake. This is so not okay.

I look like I've dipped my top lip into a raging inferno. I wonder if I will forever bear the scars of vainly trying to remove the tiny bit of hair that nobody except that little maggot, Brandon Hopkins, ever noticed in the first place.

The new hairdresser wanders over, his scissors in one hand, an industrial amount of mockery and contempt in the other.

'You know, it looks to me like you've removed several layers of skin,' he tells me helpfully, peering closer. 'Did you wax the area more than once?'

'That is a potential possibility,' I murmur, closing my eyes for a second so that I can avoid seeing the horror on Caroline's face and the amusement on his. 'I thought it wasn't working so I used each strip several times.'

'And how many strips did you use?' he enquires.

'All of them.' I swallow loudly. 'Was that wrong?'

There is a brief moment of silence while everyone takes in my words.

'You waxed your upper lip using *all* the strips?' breathes Caroline. 'How many strips were in the box?'

I think back. 'Maybe six?'

'Didn't you read the instructions at all?' She is literally incredulous that anyone could be so stupid.

I think we can all agree, Caroline, that it is quite clear that I did not, in fact, read the instructions. Not after the word 'anus', *anyway.*

I nod my head vigorously. 'Of course I read them. I'm not a complete idiot, you know.'

'Hmmm.' The new hairdresser looks at me appraisingly. 'Then you'll know that absolutely, under no circumstances, are you supposed to wax the same bit of skin more than once. You've given yourself a first degree burn.'

'Will it take long to heal?' I think about the fact that I am due in the classroom on Monday morning. I will never live it down if I walk in looking like this.

Caroline tilts her head to one side. 'It'll probably take a few days if you treat the burn and stop it from getting infected.'

'How do I do that?'

The new hairdresser grins at me wickedly. 'You need to get some of those burn pads from the supermarket and cut one down to size,' he tells me. I sense that he's enjoying himself. 'And then stick it to the affected area.'

I look at him in disbelief. 'You want me to walk around with a massive pad stuck to my top lip? Are you serious?'

'I don't care what you do, lady.' He puts his hands on his hips and raises his eyebrows at me. 'It's your call. Do you want a permanently scarred lip or are you prepared to suffer in the short term?'

He struts back to his client who has been watching the whole thing as if she's never seen a woman with a mutilated lip before. The rest of the salon resumes their business and Caroline gently spins my chair so that I am once again facing her and not my evil nemesis, the mirror.

'Let's get rid of these grey hairs, shall we?' Her voice is shaking as if she's trying not to laugh, but I don't care. I've got bigger things to worry about than whether I've just made myself a complete laughing stock.

I care. I really, really care.

I sit in silence while Caroline starts slopping hair dye onto my head. I have three choices that I can see.

One: ignore the entire situation. Act normally and pretend that it never happened. If I don't mention it then maybe nobody else will and my lip will heal before I have to walk into school on Monday.

Two: take the new hairdresser's advice. Buy a burn pad and walk around looking like Groucho Marx all weekend. Hope that anyone I encounter, including my loving family, doesn't mock me too enthusiastically.

Three: Wear a balaclava. It is still February, after all. People wear all manner of headgear during the arctic winter months here in southern England.

Okay, so option two is out straight away. Wearing a burn pad is going to look almost as ridiculous as my current appearance. And I don't think much of option three. I can't go into the supermarket wearing a balaclava – they have a very enthusiastic security guard who spends his days ensuring that nobody tries to steal the trollies. I'll be rugby-tackled to the floor and put in a deadlock before I can say 'lip trauma'.

Not that I can see the first option working too well for me either. I might be able to pretend that this hasn't happened but there's no way that my darling children will ignore it.

Which means that I'm going to have to choose door number four.

'Is Laura in today?' I ask Caroline. 'And can you ask her if she has any spare appointment slots.'

And so it is that two hours later, I am sidling down the frozen food aisle with my beautifully manicured hands held out in front of my face. I have chosen a particularly zesty shade of azure blue and my nails are sparkling like the Mediterranean Sea. They will surely distract even the most observant of viewers from the car crash that is going on in the vicinity of my mouth.

And if that fails, then the very teensy bottle of Prosecco that I am currently purchasing will mean that I really don't care.

Chapter 5

The bottom falls out of my car as I pull into the school car park. I know this because the accompanying noise is enough to attract the attention of the teenagers who loiter by the gates; they won't draw their gaze away from their phones for anything but the direst of emergencies. And from the look of delight on their faces, my ancient old car is breathing its last, fume-filled breath. I won't hear the end of it when I'm attempting to teach them the finer points of passive voice on Monday morning.

'Maybe it's not that bad,' I tell myself, closing my eyes briefly and clutching the steering wheel. 'Perhaps I just went over a pothole or a small cat? Maybe this isn't actually a complete, unmitigated disaster?'

I inhale deeply, trying desperately to remember the mindfulness training that we had to endure on the last Inset day at work.

Be in the moment. That's what the infuriatingly calm woman leading the course told us. *Make sure that you have times of peace and serenity throughout your day.* It was tricky enough finding peace and serenity in the comfort of the school staffroom; I am unconvinced about my ability to bring forth my inner tranquillity right now. However, I refuse to be deterred. Desperate times and all that. I rack my brains for any of the other words of wisdom that fell from her calm and composed lips.

FOFBOC. That's what she told us we had to do when things felt overwhelming. We are supposed to ground ourselves in the here and now, which ironically is also what my car appears to have done. Clenching the steering wheel harder, I run through mindfulness lady's instructions.

Feet On Floor? Check.

Bottom On Chair? Also check. If by 'chair', she meant slightly fraying and tatty car upholstery that has seen better days.

I am making a concerted effort to step away from my worries and towards my happy place when a rapping sound on the glass distracts me. I open my eyes and see that Elise from Year Nine is frowning at me through the window while simultaneously gesturing at the car and furiously stabbing away at her mobile phone.

I open the door. It's not like I could have stayed in here indefinitely, no matter how appealing a prospect that might be.

'Hello, Elise.' I plaster on a big smile.

'You do know that your car has just fallen apart, don't you, miss?' Elise punctuates the end of her proclamation with a smack of bubble-gum. 'And also, there's something wrong with your lips. Looks like stubble rash to me.'

'I was aware that something was amiss, yes.' I feel that my reply is sufficient for both observations. Sighing, I step out of the car and then crouch down to peer underneath. Something large and dirty and metallic looking is hanging down onto the road. It looks like it's a vital component and probably fairly necessary for actually driving. 'Oh, shit.'

Behind me, Elise gasps dramatically. I do not for one second believe that she is genuinely shocked to hear an adult swear, but still, I suppose I am on school property.

'I'm sorry, Elise,' I say, standing up. 'That was unprofessional of me. But my car appears to have died and I'm feeling slightly upset.'

Elise is saved from having to answer by the appearance of Scarlet who instantly forms the impression that the car has broken down to shame her.

'Mum!' she hisses, standing several feet away as if she can't be seen talking to me. 'Why is the car in pieces? Why are you standing in the car park? You know the rules if you must insist on collecting us. Stay. In. The. Car.'

'It's broken down,' I hiss back at her. 'And I'm standing here because I'm going to have to sort this mess out.'

'God!' Scarlet's shoulders droop down and her bag slides onto the floor. 'This is so embarrassing. I told you we should get a better car.'

I am not in the mood. Not today. My brain is whirring with everything that I've got to do and I can't even begin to figure out how we're going to pay for the repairs, if it can even be repaired in the first place.

'What's going on?' Dylan lopes up to us. 'Has the old rust-bucket finally died, then?'

I leap into action. 'Right, you two need to get over to the

primary school and collect Benji,' I pull out my phone. 'Then bring him back here to me.'

Scarlet grimaces. 'Can't I just get the bus home?'

Both she and Dylan get the bus home on the days that I'm at work. Benji goes to the after-school club at his school. I had fondly imagined, back when Dylan started in Year Seven and later when Scarlet joined two years later, that they would hang around in my classroom at the end of the day and we would swap witty anecdotes about what we'd been up to while I got my marking done. The reality is that neither teenager will even acknowledge my existence when they pass me in the corridor and I suspect that they would far prefer to get the bus home every day. But on Thursdays and Fridays, when I'm not at work, I like to collect them myself. It gives my days off a sense of purpose.

Scarlet reaches out her hand and grabs Elise's arm. 'We've got loads of homework to do, haven't we?'

Elise nods her head earnestly. 'It's true, Mrs Thompson. So much homework.'

I glance at my phone and see that Benji's class will be coming out in ten minutes. I do not have time for this.

'You aren't even in the same year group as Elise,' I snap at my daughter. 'Stop trying to drag her into your web of deceit. Now go! Get your brother and bring him back here. I'll ring the breakdown people and they'll fix the car. And run!'

Dylan launches into action, flinging his bag to the ground and setting off at a run. Scarlet hesitates for a brief second but the thrill of the competition is too much for her to resist.

'Good luck with all that homework,' she yells at Elise and then she's off, sprinting after Dylan with a determined look on her face.

I scroll through my phone and find the number for the breakdown helpline.

'I hope your car gets sorted, miss,' says Elise, giving me a wave before plodding off in the direction of the buses.

'Have a good evening!' I call back, and then a nice lady answers the phone and reassures me that all of my problems are about to be solved because I had the magnificent foresight to join the nation's most elite breakdown service.

I might ask for advice about how to handle being forty-three years old, permanently strapped for cash and doing a job I hate while trying to deal with three exhausting kids. That's the kind of breakdown service for which I would happily pay a monthly premium.

The nice lady lied. I'm sure that she didn't mean to – she was probably just trying to bolster me with her calming and encouraging words – but all the same, she told me a massive fib. All my problems have not been solved. The evidence for this is the fact that we are making the three-mile journey from school to home in the crew cab of a breakdown lorry while my poor, geriatric car rides in regal splendour on the back of the truck.

Scarlet is sulking about the time wasted when she could be revising and muttering about the ridiculousness of not just getting the bus home. I really am going to have to speak to her about her attitude. Dylan can tell that I'm worried about the car and the money and is helpfully attempting to distract me by explaining an idea he's had for an amazing app that will make him thousands of pounds. I'd be more enthusiastic if I hadn't already heard this speech about fifty times. Benji is bouncing up and down in his seat, excitedly pointing out familiar landmarks even though we make this journey at least twice a day. Clearly, seeing the world from a higher perspective is pretty fabulous when you're ten years old.

And me? I am frantically doing sums in my head, trying to work out how I can get the car fixed and pay the mortgage and buy food and get the oil tank filled up yet again because our ancient old radiators seem to guzzle fuel like it's going out of fashion and apparently it's going to snow next week and we're all likely to get hypothermia; but it will definitely be all right.

I'm sure it will be all right.

There's a remote chance that it will be all right.

The mechanic drops us off at home and we wave goodbye as he drives off up the road, taking the car to the local garage where they are primed and on standby, ready to try and revive it. Then we go inside and Scarlet puts the kettle on and Benji unpacks his school lunchbox without me even asking and I start to relax, just a little bit.

'There's a school trip to the theatre coming up.' Scarlet turns to look at me. 'It costs fifteen quid and I have to pay by tomorrow – can I go?'

I wearily reach for my purse and open it up. Of course she needs money today of all days, when I'm already haemorrhaging cash.

'I've only got a twenty-pound note,' I tell her. 'You're going to have to wait until I can get some change.'

Scarlet reaches her hand into her pocket and pulls out a wodge of five-pound notes. 'No worries – I'll swap you for one of these.'

She swipes the twenty out of my hand and hands me one of her notes in return.

'Where did you get all of that from?' I ask, easing my shoes off. 'And can you pass the biscuit tin?'

'Oh, you know – birthday money and stuff.' She hands me a cup of tea. 'Also, Mum, I was just wondering how illegal it is to do other people's homework and charge them money for doing it?'

I nearly splutter out my drink. 'What? Why are you asking that?'

Scarlet assumes her most innocent expression. 'I'm just asking, that's all,' she says. 'For a friend.'

I frown at her. Is it possible that she knows the Year Eleven girl mentioned by Elise? Is my daughter hanging out with the kind of racketeer who would run an illicit homework ring at Westhill Academy? Oh my god, maybe she's being forced to launder the dirty money and I'm now in possession of a hot five-pound note.

'Scarlet—' I begin, but I'm distracted by the sound of the front door opening. As Nick walks into the kitchen, Scarlet takes the opportunity to make her escape. Before I can yell at her to come back, Nick tells me that he popped into the garage on his way home and the car will be fixed by tomorrow afternoon. And then he quotes an eye-watering price and I forget about everything except the spiralling panic in my stomach.

'We can't afford that,' I tell him, shaking my head. 'That's a stupid amount of money.'

'I do keep saying that we need a car fund,' he says, pouring me a glass of wine. 'It'd help when we have emergencies like this.'

'Well, it's all very easy to be sensible in hindsight, isn't it?' I snap. 'I don't see you holding back on the spending.'

Nick holds his hands out in self-defence. 'What spending? I'm at work all week. I don't get the chance to spend any money! And anyway, I've got something to tell you.'

Unfortunately for my argument, he's right. Every penny we earn (and he earns more than I do now that I'm on a three-day working week) goes straight into our joint account and it's almost all accounted for with the mortgage and food and electricity and oil and insurance and taxes and petrol – and that's before we've paid for music lessons and vet bills and driving lessons and new school shoes (because Benji's feet seem to have a dedicated growth mindset all of their own). Nick never has any spare cash and he rarely complains about it, even though he works so hard.

Not that any of this makes me feel any better.

'You could always sell Betty,' I suggest, feeling like a bitch the instant that the words are out of my mouth. Nick's old Land Rover is his pride and joy and after a challenging week at work, tinkering about on it is one of the only things that helps him unwind.

'You could always go back to work full time,' he counters and for a second, the air is heavy.

Then he gives me a grin. 'But I told you, I've got some news.' He pauses, milking the moment. 'I got that contract that I was after. You are now looking at the new head tree surgeon for Urban Tree Surgeons Limited!'

'That's fantastic!' I leap off the stool and fling my arms around him. 'I'm so proud of you. You didn't think you'd get it!'

'Head Office called me in at the end of the day and told me.' Nick's arms tighten around me. 'It means a bit of a pay rise, Hannah.'

I squeeze his waist and close my eyes. I love this man as much today as I did when we first got together, twenty-two years ago. Probably more, actually, because he was a bit of a knob back then and neither of us had a clue that our first drunken kiss in a tacky nightclub would end up with the life we have now. And the life we have now is manic and constantly changing and filled with adventures but never, ever boring.

His pay rise will probably cover the cost of two driving lessons for Dylan and we both know it. Consultant arborists are never going to be living a champagne lifestyle, even with a new contract like this one. But it would be a criminal shame to waste an opportunity for a celebration, and it isn't about the money. Not always, anyway.

'Fish and chip supper?' I ask him, pulling away and giving him a grin.

'Only if we've got some raspberry ripple ice cream for pudding,' he says, smiling back at me.

We are the epitome of classiness.

Later, lying in bed, I think about what Nick said. He's been mentioning me going back to work full time more and more recently, although we've yet to have a serious conversation about it. Mostly because I can't decide how I feel. Next to me, Nick snores and rolls over. It doesn't seem to matter how stressed out he is, he's always fast asleep the instant that his head hits the pillow.

I get up and tiptoe to the bathroom, hoping that a drink of water might help me settle. But getting out of bed was a mistake; now I'm wide awake, mulling over the pros and cons of trying to apply for a new full-time teaching job.

Pros:

1. We need the money. Urgently.
2. I never intended to be working part time. And I have discovered to my cost that teaching three days a week usually ends up meaning that I have to work twice as hard when I'm in school and I still end up doing all my planning and marking at home. It's not really half a job.
3. I can reinvent myself. I can present Hannah Thompson in whichever way I choose to my new colleagues and they won't know any better. Like, I can become a fitness fanatic or an ambitious career woman – basically, as someone who has got their shit together. You can't do that when everyone knows that you last exercised in 1999 and your only ambition is to make it through the school day without crying and/or swearing.
4. I can escape from Miriam Wallace's power-mad clutches and go back to teaching Biology. She's never going to renew my contract for next year anyway so I may as well get ahead of an inevitable situation.

Cons:

1. There aren't any jobs out there for Biology teachers. I know this because I check the *Times Educational Supplement* every week.
2. Since I've been spending more time at home, I've been amazed by how much the kids still seem to need me. I thought it would be different when they weren't tiny but I was wrong. And their issues and worries are way more intense now than when they were toddlers.
3. I will have to actually apply for a job. I'll need to dust off my ancient CV and write an application letter and then go to an interview and talk about all the recent developments in schools and honestly, the thought of all that fills me with dread. The bloody Education Secretary can't keep up with all the changes so how on earth I'm supposed to I have no idea.
4. I am scared. I am scared that I am going to disappear completely. Just another forty-something woman with a list of predictable and unimaginative titles. Wife. Mother. Teacher. Daughter. Friend. And I love that I am all of those things and I try not to take them for granted – but they aren't exactly unique. They aren't the sum total of who I thought I would be.

The facts are irrefutable. I need to work. I want to work. But I don't want to lose my soul in the process. Which means that it might be time to begin a whole new chapter of my life. A chapter where I get to play the starring role for a change.

I clamber into bed and spoon into Nick's back, feeling a

frisson of excitement. I will find something that allows me to explore my own interests and challenges me and reminds me that I am more than just a forty-three-year-old wife and mother with a part-time job. And I will be a fabulous role model for Dylan, Scarlet and Benji and they will all see me with new eyes and respect me as Hannah, not just Mum.

And while I am pushing my boundaries and learning new things about myself, and exploring my hidden talents, I will also make a shitload of money and everything will be great.

I drift off to sleep feeling more content than I have done in ages. This is going to be the start of a whole new me.

Chapter 6

I look again at the computer screen and try to resist the urge to throw it onto the floor. Surely there must be some kind of mistake? This can't actually be right; the figures just don't add up.

Sighing, I press the back arrow and go back to the start of the online form.

'Maybe we entered the details in the wrong place,' I say to Nick, who is sitting next to me and looking as stressed as I feel. 'Let's do it again, really slowly this time.'

'We must have done,' agrees Nick. 'That amount of money isn't enough to feed a newborn baby, never mind a teenage boy.'

We both lean forward and read the instructions on the screen for the student finance calculator. Behind us, Dylan cranes over our shoulders.

When does your course start?

That's easy. I click the option for this September and move onto the next page.

What type of student are you?

'A lazy one?' suggests Nick. 'A student who needs to get a job?'

'Hey!' protests Dylan. 'I have a job, thanks very much. And I'd like to see you dealing with stupid customers who are asking you for the gazillionth time if they can have an item for free when it won't scan through the till.'

'He's going to be a full-time UK student,' I say, clicking the box. 'Next question.'

How much are your tuition fees per year?

'Too much,' snaps Nick. 'Honestly, is he really going to be getting nine grand's worth of education? I don't think so!' He turns to me. 'We spent most of our time either in bed or in the student bar, remember?'

'You might have done,' I reply, primly. 'I seem to recall that I attended virtually every lecture and handed in every assignment on time and took my higher education incredibly seriously.'

Nick laughs. 'In what alternate universe? You were as slack as I was, Hannah – don't try to rewrite history!'

I pause, thinking back to my student days. 'I do remember a fair bit of shopping for clothes,' I say. 'And nights out. And afternoon naps to recover from the nights out. And sitting around watching kids' television – we seemed to do a lot of that.'

'Well, it isn't like that now,' Dylan tells us. 'Not now we're all going to be leaving university with sixty grand's worth of debt.'

I pale. 'We bought our first house for sixty thousand pounds.'

'I'm not going to be wasting time watching television and partying, am I?' Our son is sounding suspiciously sanctimonious. 'Oh no. It's not like the olden days, you know. Back in the nineties, you guys had it made. Everything cost five pence and there were no pressures. Not like it is for us.'

'Less of the *olden* days,' grunts Nick. 'And we had our fair share of pressure.'

Dylan smirks. 'Yeah, right.'

'Anyway,' I say, getting their attention back to the task at hand. 'Can we just get on with this, please? I do have things to be doing today, other than freaking out about how we're going to afford for you to ever leave home.'

Where will you live while studying?

'Who would choose to live with their parents?' asks Dylan in disbelief, reading the options over my shoulder. 'Surely that's the entire point of going to uni in the first place? To get away from you lot.'

'In that case, we can stop worrying,' says Nick, his face brightening. 'There's plenty of things you can do in September, if leaving home is your main priority. You can join the army, or emigrate, or move in with Granny, or—'

'He isn't doing any of those things,' I interject. 'He's going to university and he's going to get a good degree and then he can get a decent job doing something that he loves and he'll be able to afford to be an independent, fully functioning and worthwhile member of society who is capable of giving back to his community while also not forgetting that it was us who gave him such an excellent start in life and he therefore needs to spend every Christmas and holiday here at home with us and not with anyone else.'

Nick and Dylan stare at me as I stop for breath.

'That's asking quite a lot from a degree, Hannah,' Nick tells me. 'If it can do all that then maybe it is worth nine grand a year, after all.'

I click the correct option and we move on to the next page. And this is where my heart rate starts to race, because now we're getting down to business.

What is your annual household income?

I pull two pieces of paper towards me and once again look at the figures at the bottom of each page. Then I pick up my phone and for the third time today, add up our total salaries. Nick does the same and when we are agreed on the amount I type it onto the screen. We go through the remaining questions about dependents and additional income and then we arrive at the final page, which gives us two numbers. And despite the fact that I am crossing all my fingers and toes, it is the same two numbers that we had last time.

There is no mistake. Dylan will get a loan for his tuition fees, but his maintenance loan isn't even enough to pay for his accommodation.

I drop my head into my hands.

'How do they think kids are supposed to go to university when they literally can't afford to eat?' I moan. 'It's beyond ridiculous.'

'They expect them to work,' says Nick. 'And they expect parents to pay up.'

'I know I'll need to get a job when I'm there,' says Dylan, his voice quiet. 'I'm not expecting you to give me any money.'

I look up at him and smile. 'Of course we'll help you out,'

I say. 'But you're right. You're going to need to fund some of this too.'

There is silence for a moment as we all consider the facts. I've been talking to Nick about this for a few weeks, ever since Dylan firmed up his university place on UCAS and we could see how much his accommodation is going to cost. The deficit between income and outgoings is much bigger than I anticipated, though, and there's no way that Dylan can find it all by himself.

'Maybe he'll fail his A Levels and won't be able to go?' suggests Nick eventually, trying to make his voice light.

'I'm standing right here!' Dylan tells him. 'Thanks for the vote of confidence, Dad.'

Nick twists round and puts his hand on Dylan's arm. 'I'm kidding,' he tells him. 'You let us worry about the money and concentrate on passing those exams, okay?'

Dylan nods slowly. 'The uni has got a Facebook page. I can probably use that to start figuring out where the best jobs are. That way I'll be ahead of the rush when we all start.'

'That sounds like a great idea,' I say, forcing myself to smile. 'And in the meantime, Dad and I will look at our budget and let you know how much we can give you each month.'

Dylan steps forward, giving me a quick hug before loping out of the room. His phone is already out of his pocket, his thumbs speeding over the screen.

'Oh my god.' I flop down onto the table as soon as he's left the room. 'This is a genuine, arsing disaster. Everything just seems to be going wrong at the moment.'

Although on the plus side, my lip has almost cleared up

and the scarring appears to be minimal. Dr Google has reassuringly informed me that the numbness will almost certainly pass with time and at least I'm not going to have to find the money for plastic surgery, which is definitely something to celebrate.

'Calm down,' Nick says, standing up and moving across the kitchen. I watch as he fills the kettle and pulls two mugs off the shelf. In a crisis, we drink tea, just like the rest of the population of the British Isles. And if we're out of tea then we just have to make do with wine. 'It can't be that bad.'

I raise my eyebrows. 'Were you even listening last week when I told you how much he needs for food and stuff? And that was before we knew how pathetically small his loan was going to be.'

Nick turns to face me, looking a bit sheepish. 'Was that when I was watching *Game of Thrones*?' he asks. 'Because you started talking just as it got to a good bit and there's a remote possibility that I wasn't listening.'

I glare at him. 'Well, let me outline our financial situation once more, for those of you in the back who were too busy fantasizing about scantily clad women riding dragons.' I stand up and rest my hands on the table. 'We need to give Dylan at least three hundred pounds each month. Plus, in two years' time, we're going to have to do the same for Scarlet. And as it stands, I do not know where that extra money is coming from because we don't have a secret stash of savings hidden under the bed and every time I think we might be able to put some money away, we seem to have a new disaster.'

I hold up my hand and count off on my fingers. 'The car

breaking down. The oven deciding that it didn't feel like actually heating up. Dogger hurting her leg and needing the emergency vet, which cost us the equivalent of two week's food shopping. The school trip that Benji needs to go on unless we want him to be the only child in his class who doesn't attend.'

I pause for breath while Nick gawps at me. 'Winter is coming, Nick,' I tell him, as dramatically as I can. 'Winter is coming and we don't have any warm coats.'

There is silence while my husband digests my words.

'Three hundred quid a month?' he says eventually. 'Are you sure?'

I nod and we stare at each other across the kitchen.

'We're going to have to rethink a few things around here then.' He hands me a cup of tea, his fingers brushing against mine. 'We knew that this day was coming, Hannah. You said it yourself a few weeks ago. We need to increase our earnings.'

He means *my* earnings, and he's right. I need to earn a full-time wage.

I need a plan.

Chapter 7

I spend days brainstorming ideas for a new career path, letting my mind explore the sensible, the wild and the downright obscure. On Saturday night, Benji has a sleepover at Logan's house and Dylan is in his room watching god-knows-what on his laptop and talking to god-knows-who on his phone. Scarlet is diligently ploughing on with the ever-increasing amount of homework that she's been given (I really think I might need to have a quiet word with her teachers; it's unacceptable how much work that child is getting at the moment). So Nick and I have the kitchen to ourselves, which is a rare event. I'm intending to wait until after we've eaten to talk to him about my new plan, but just as we clear away the plates, my mobile pings with a text from Logan's mum.

That's her genuine contact name on my phone, along with Nina's mum and Franco's mum. And I am very aware that I don't exist as Hannah in the lives of these people – I am Dylan/Scarlet/Benji's mum, despite the fact that I have shared some of my most traumatic parenting situations with them while waiting in the school playground at the end of the day. We are all women who have been relegated to the status of 'someone's mum' from the moment that our children started making friends with other kids.

Benji wants to come home. His teddy's arm has fallen off & I think it's upset him a bit x

'Are you kidding me?' I read the text aloud to Nick and we stare at each other for a moment. 'Teddy's arm?'

Nick shakes his head. 'I sewed it back on after the last time. It must have come loose.'

I slam the dishwasher closed and wait for a second to hear the tell-tale gushing of water. A new dishwasher is not in my budget right now.

'I think you're missing the point,' I tell Nick. 'He's going into Year Six in September and then he'll be starting at Westhill Academy before we know it. How is he going to cope in a world of constant fights and drug-dealing and rampant sex when his teddy's arm falling off sends him into a meltdown?'

Nick raises his eyebrows at me. 'I think you're being a little bit dramatic there, Hannah. He's got a whole year to grow up and anyway, it's secondary school, not prison.'

'You don't know what it's like,' I mutter darkly, pulling my shoes off the rack next to the door. 'You're not there all week.'

'Neither are you,' Nick points out, slightly unreasonably. 'I'll drive – I want to check if Betty's new windscreen wipers work.'

He hasn't got a clue. He doesn't see the kids scurrying down our school corridors like there's a herd of zombies hot on their heels. He isn't the one who has to lurk outside the girls' toilets, ready to catch the smokers red-handed. He isn't here after school when Scarlet and Dylan (although mostly Scarlet, to be honest) regale us with terrifying stories of crime and punishment that never make it as far as the staff room. And Benji is our *baby*. It was only two minutes ago that he couldn't wear shoes without Velcro.

I yell up the stairs, telling the older two that we'll be back soon, and then we head out into the dark. It's a clear night without a cloud in the sky and the stars are out in force. I stand for a second, wondering when the world got so big.

The sound of Betty roaring to life jolts me back to the task in hand. I clamber into the Land Rover and we rattle our way up the road, the heater making a complete song and dance about being turned on full. It clearly has little man syndrome because it certainly isn't producing anything even vaguely warming. Nick flicks the wipers on and they manage two half-hearted swipes of the glass before freezing in position across the windscreen and I have to endure the rest of the journey listening to him mutter about how he just can't understand it and he fitted them perfectly and he read the instruction manual *and* watched a YouTube video and there's no reason at all why they shouldn't be working.

I love my husband very much but when he gets started on the topic of Land Rover maintenance I am sometimes tempted to shove his diff lock where the sun doesn't shine.

We get to Logan's house and his mother opens the door, depositing a teary and rather subdued-looking Benji onto the front step.

'I'm sorry, Mum!' he says, the instant that he sees me. 'I just felt weird and you said to call you if I wasn't okay.'

I pull him into a hug and Logan's mum nods understandingly at me over the top of his head.

Oh god. He should be sorry. She probably thinks that he's a complete wimp and that I have failed in my duty to provide him with the life skills that he should have acquired by the ripe old age of ten. She'll tell all the other mums and they'll mock me behind my back, saying that I baby him because he's my last child and I'm incapable of letting him grow up.

'It's fine,' I tell him. 'And you don't need to be sorry.'

Logan's mum hands me his rucksack. 'I think all his things are in there. We've put Teddy's arm in a sling but it's possible that he's going to need a bit of surgery.'

I look gratefully at her and raise my eyebrows. 'Kids, hey?'

She smiles. 'I know – and we haven't even started on the teenage years with Logan yet! Speaking of which, I saw your Scarlet walking out of the park yesterday morning when I was coming back from yoga. She's a beauty, isn't she? Have you thought about sending her photo off to one of those modelling agencies?'

'I'm not sure that would be a good idea,' I tell her, shuddering. 'She's difficult enough to handle as it is, without getting any big ideas from a bunch of supermodels.'

Logan's mum laughs gently. 'And you must join us one of these days. Honestly – one hot yoga session with Orlando and you won't ever look back!'

I open my mouth with the intention of making a hilarious quip about the fact that yoga is supposed to aid flexibility, and therefore surely my ability to look back would only be improved after a session with hot Orlando, but then I pause. Some of the mothers in the school playground take their exercise regimes incredibly seriously and the last thing I need right now is to piss off the PTA.

'Maybe one day!' I trill, trying to look like attending a yoga class isn't my definition of hell.

I usher Benji towards the garden gate where Nick is waiting. And then a thought hits me and I spin round.

'Actually,' I say, 'it can't have been Scarlet who you saw, because I dropped her at school myself yesterday.'

But Logan's mum has closed the door. Benji trips over his own feet and starts to wail.

When we get home, the fairy lights are on outside the front door. I always put them on if Scarlet or Dylan are coming home late but I was in too much of a rush to think about doing it tonight. One of them must have come downstairs and switched them on while we were getting Benji.

We get inside and I'm intending on scooting him upstairs to bed, but as we walk into the living room, I see Scarlet and Dylan draped across the sofa.

'Hey!' calls Scarlet. 'We heard you were coming home. It's just as well – the house was too quiet without you here.'

'Get over here, little dude,' says Dylan, opening his arms.

Benji dashes across the room and flings himself down between them, snuggling his feet onto Scarlet's lap and his head against Dylan's shoulder. Nick and I sit down, and we spend the next fifteen minutes watching our teenage children comfort, reassure and finally get a smile out of their little brother.

It isn't until Sunday lunchtime that I finally get to discuss my new plan with the rest of the family. Nick cooks a roast dinner and I wait until everyone's plate is full before clearing my throat and getting their attention.

'I have an announcement to make,' I say, hitting my water glass with my fork.

Nick cringes and puts out his hand to stop me. 'Don't do that, Hannah. Those glasses are only cheap. They'll shatter if you look at them the wrong way.'

'An announcement!' Scarlet's reaction is far more satisfying than my boring health-and-safety-conscious husband, so I turn to her, a big smile on my face. 'Are you finally going to let me change my name to Scarlett with two ts, which is *obviously* how it was supposed to be spelt in the first place?'

I squint at her, wondering what she's wittering on about now.

'No, and I have no idea why you would think *that's* what I'm about to say. Anyway, I'm really excited to be talking to you guys about this. So, the thing is—'

'We're going somewhere amazing on holiday, aren't we!' squeals Scarlet. 'Oh my god, Mum! Where is it? Is it America?'

'Is it Disneyland?' yells Benji. 'Logan went there last year and he said it was fantastic. You can go on rides and eat candy floss and meet Mickey Mouse and—'

'It's not Disneyland, numbnuts.' Scarlet waves her hand,

dismissing Benji's suggestion. 'Can you imagine Dad somewhere like that?'

We all turn to look at Nick, who is staring at us all like we've grown three heads.

'What are you going on about?' he asks. 'And can you please eat this roast before it goes cold.'

'We're just saying that you wouldn't be seen dead at Disneyland,' Dylan informs him, ramming a huge piece of chicken into his mouth. 'You know. Not with all that expectation that you might actually have a good time.'

Nick frowns. 'You're damn right I wouldn't. What a waste of money! I don't need some wet-behind-the-ears, spotty juvenile in a mouse costume telling me that it's time to enjoy myself, thank you very much.'

Scarlet groans. 'Well, not everyone is a killjoy like you, Dad.'

Nick looks hurt at this accusation.

'I am not a killjoy. I just can't stand *organised fun*.' He spits out the last two words like they're putting him off his food. 'I don't need permission to have a good time.'

It is for this very reason that the Thompson family will never step over the boundaries of Center Parcs or anything Disney-related or indeed any campsite that has the audacity to offer entertainment of any kind. We did once visit Legoland when Dylan was younger, mostly because Nick was under the innocent illusion that it would just be about Lego bricks. The car journey home was mostly spent listening to him bang on about the ratio of activity to queuing time and the cost of a can of coke. The day only managed to avoid being a complete disaster because Dylan had quite a lot of birthday money to spend and Nick convinced him to buy a box that consisted of boring, grey Lego, which he then spent three solid days turning into a replica of something from Star Wars that Dylan wasn't allowed to play with.

'I think we're going to Morocco,' says Dylan, having finally swallowed his chicken. 'That's on your bucket list, isn't it?'

'We're not going to Morocco,' I say. 'And what I actually wanted to—'

'Not with any of you, anyway,' adds Nick. 'We're going to wait until you've all left home and then me and your mum are going to have the holiday of a lifetime.' His eyes glaze over slightly. 'We're going to shop in the souqs of Marrakech and hike in the Atlas Mountains and drink funky cold medina.'

He sings the last three words, wiggling his shoulders in what I can only assume is his interpretation of a hip-hop dance move.

Scarlet's eyes narrow. 'You *do* know that song is talking about date rape, don't you? Medina was a drug that the guy put in people's drinks to make them have sex with him because they didn't like him.' She holds up her hand and starts counting off on her fingers. 'It's all there in the lyrics, Dad. He thinks that girls should be with him just because he has nice clothes *and* it condones animal testing *and* it is totally transphobic.'

We both stare at her and I run through the song lyrics in my head. The dog doing the wild thing on his leg. Sheena. The comment about making sure that the girl is pure.

'Scarlet's right,' I tell Nick, feeling shocked. 'He drugs them. And we've been playing it to the kids since they were tiny.'

'Exactly.' Scarlet smacks her lips with relish. 'What kind of parent forces their kids to listen to lyrics like that?'

'And anyway, the medina that you're thinking of is a part of some cities in North Africa,' Dylan informs Nick. 'The streets are like mazes and it's really easy to get lost.'

'Thanks,' says Nick, nodding. 'I'll try to remember that.'

'That song is ruined for me now,' I mutter. 'Forever.'

'So if we're not going to Morocco and we're not going to Disneyland then where *are* we going?' asks Benji, waving his hand to get our attention back on the topic.

Which is absolutely *not* the topic that I actually want to discuss.

'We're not going anywhere,' I say firmly. 'The announcement that I want to make has nothing to do with any holiday.'

'Bloody hell, you're not pregnant, are you?' asks Dylan and there is silence as four pairs of eyes bore into my stomach.

'No, I'm not!' I snap. 'And Nick, you shouldn't be looking so panicked, for god's sake.'

'So – if you're not having a baby, which I'm glad about by the way because babies are annoying and Dogger wouldn't like it, and we're not going on holiday, then what are we doing?' asks Scarlet.

'It's not what *we're* doing, it's what *I'm* doing,' I tell her and everyone puts down their knives and forks and I finally have their unadulterated attention. Because I don't do anything without any of them. Not ever.

'I feel like we should have a drum roll.' Scarlet raises one eyebrow. 'You're really building this up, Mum. I've got places to be this afternoon.'

I frown. 'What places? And speaking of which, have you been bunking off school? Because I've been told by two different people now that you've been spotted out and about in *places* that you shouldn't be.'

Scarlet inhales sharply and turns to glower at Dylan. 'What people? As if I can't guess.'

Dylan shrugs. 'Wasn't me, so you can stop giving me the evil eye,'

I bang my hand on the table. 'Scarlet! Have you or have you not been hanging out in town when you should be at school? This is incredibly serious, you know. You're supposed to be getting an education, not wasting these precious years shopping and lazing about in the park.'

'I'd probably get more of an education in the park than I would at our crappy school,' she mutters.

She does have a point. Not that I'm prepared to concede it.

'Scarlet's not daft enough to skive school,' states Nick. 'So it must have been someone else who looks like her. Anyway, about this big announcement, Hannah.'

'God. Imagine looking like Scarlet.' Dylan rocks back on his chair and smirks at his sister.

'At least I've got all my own teeth,' she snarls back.

Dylan laughs. 'So have I. Is that the best you've got? You're slacking, Scarlet – maybe you should start attending school a bit more.'

Scarlet's growl of anger is drowned out by Nick's voice. 'Your mother is trying to tell us something and I for one am very keen to hear what she has to say. So either be quiet or you can leave the room.' He turns to face me. 'Hannah. Please ignore our horribly behaved offspring and tell me about this announcement.'

I clear my throat, making sure that I have the full attention of the room.

'What I want to talk to you all about is the fact that I have made a big decision,' I declare, rather grandly. 'And my decision is that I am going to be getting a new job, which I'm really, really excited about.'

'Thank god for that,' murmurs Nick and when I look across the table, he is holding his hands together and looking up at the ceiling, as if he's praying. With any luck he'll notice that two of the spotlights are out and finally get around to changing the bulbs.

'I'm not going back to full-time teaching,' I say, just to clarify the situation. 'Probably not, anyway.'

Nick's face falls. 'What *are* you going to be doing then?' he asks. 'Do you actually have a new job or is this whole thing still in the let's-talk-about-it-for-the-next-six-months stage?'

I frown at him. 'Don't be like that, Nick. This is a fledgling idea and I don't need your negativity to squash it before I've even begun.'

He gives me a firm look. 'So it's not going to be like the time that you watched a television programme about being a paramedic and decided that you could retrain during your maternity leave?'

It's unfair of him to bring that up. Dylan was a few months old and I was sleep deprived and the fact that I can't stand the sight of blood seemed like a trivial point. I attended one first-aid training session and had to leave at the coffee break. And right now, when I am flushed with the excitement of a new project, I do not need reminding of my past mistakes. Besides, this is going to be nothing like that.

'This is going to be nothing like that,' I inform Nick, haughtily. 'This is going to be an actual serious venture.'

'So what are you going to do, Mum?' asks Dylan. 'Are there seconds of potatoes?'

Nick passes him the bowl. 'Help yourself. And yes, what *are* you going to do, Hannah?'

'That's what I want to talk to you all about,' I say, trying to keep the exasperation out of my voice. 'I wanted to see if you have any ideas.'

In my head, they all take a moment to consider my talents and attributes before offering helpful and exciting job suggestions.

In reality, they react before the words are barely out of my mouth.

'You could work at the supermarket,' says Dylan. 'You're always saying that it's your second home.'

'One of my friends has started doing Saturday shifts at Nando's and he gets free chicken,' Scarlet tells me. 'You could see if they've got any vacancies there.'

'Mmmm,' groans Dylan appreciatively, in his best Homer Simpson voice. 'Free chicken.'

I force a smile. 'I was rather thinking of a job that would utilise my years of experience. You know, something where my transferable skills will really come into their own.'

'So we need to identify your transferable skills,' says Nick, looking thoughtful.

The room goes silent.

'Oh, come on!' I break after thirty seconds. 'I've not exactly spent the last twenty years sitting on my backside. I have tons of expertise.'

The faces in front of me are now demonstrating their best thinking poses. Nick's eyes are looking up and to the left as he tries to retrieve memories of my brilliance. Scarlet is biting her finger and staring at me while Dylan is scratching his head and scrunching up his mouth. Only Benji looks confident and that's because he is making the most of their distraction to load his plate with more food.

None of which is particularly reassuring or complimentary.

Eventually, after an interminable hush, Dylan speaks.

'You could always be a party planner?' It's more of a question than a statement.

'What does a party planner do?' asks Benji, looking up from his plate.

Scarlet rolls her eyes. 'They clean toilets,' she tells him.

'Seriously?' Benji looks puzzled. 'So why are they called—'

'Oh my god! Why are you so retarded?' groans Scarlet, slapping the palm of her hand against her forehead.

'Don't call your brother retarded,' growls Nick.

'The clue is in the name,' Dylan tells Benji. 'They plan parties, genius.'

'Don't call your brother a genius,' I snap, not really thinking about what I'm saying. 'And becoming a party planner isn't really the direction that I'm thinking of going in.'

'You *are* good at organising things,' says Nick. I stare at him suspiciously to see if this is a roundabout way of saying that I'm bossy, but his smile seems genuine enough so I let it go.

Maybe I should consider it, as it's the first vaguely sensible suggestion that I've been given. I let the possibility percolate round my brain, imagining myself floating around a fancy venue, ensuring that the champagne fountain and the table decorations are all in place. I could do that, no problem. But I bet the party planner doesn't actually ever get to enjoy the festivities. I'll probably be in the back, sleeves rolled up and doing the washing up or sorting the blocked toilets or dealing with rowdy partygoers who don't know when they've had enough of a good thing. So basically doing what I have to do at home.

'How illegal is it to punch someone in self-defence?' asks Scarlet casually, whipping my thoughts away from my doomed party planner career. 'Is it okay if they start it?'

I put down my cutlery and give my daughter a concerned look. 'Why do you want to know? Has something happened?'

Scarlet shrugs. 'Just wondering,' she mumbles around a mouthful of potato.

And then Benji knocks over the gravy jug and in the ensuing carnage, I push any ridiculous thoughts of party planning or new careers to the recesses of my mind.

Chapter 8

Benji has a football match today and my mother has kindly agreed to go and stand on the freezing cold touchline and cheer him on. This has the added benefit that when I finally stagger into the house, laden with twenty thousand books that need marking by next Monday, she is sitting at the kitchen table and the house has an air of calm that is non-existent whenever Dylan and Scarlet are here on their own.

'Good day, Hannah?' she asks, grimacing as I dump my bags onto the floor. 'You should get yourself one of those tartan shopping-trolley things. You're going to give yourself a hernia, going on like that.'

I give her a look and plonk myself down into the seat opposite her.

'Have you got one, then?'

Mum shudders. 'Good god, no! They're for pensioners. I wouldn't be seen dead dragging one of those round with me.'

'Yet you think I should get one.' I start massaging the back of my neck in a pathetic attempt to ease out some of the knots. 'How was the football match?'

'Bloody arctic.' She looks around, checking that we're alone.

'You are aware that Benji is totally abysmal at sport, aren't you?'

I nod. 'Yep.'

He takes after me, bless his two uncoordinated left feet. I am still waiting for the right sport to present itself to me. I had a brief moment of hopefulness when Nick bought me flashy new trainers and some spanx-like running shorts for my last birthday, but sadly it seems that having all the gear does not counter the fact that I am not built for aerobic activity.

'Which raises the question: why was he chosen to participate in the match in the first place? You can't be telling me that he's the best that the school has to offer?'

'Of course he isn't,' I tell her, slipping off my shoes and wondering if it's too early to open the wine. 'It's equality, isn't it?'

Mum looks confused. 'What is? Letting the rubbish kids play instead of the good ones?'

I wince. 'Don't let him hear you say that. And it's just how it is these days. There'd be an uproar if teachers only ever chose the talented kids to represent the school.'

'Why?' Mum seems genuinely interested, so even though I'm tired and I really can't be bothered to talk about anything even remotely related to education, I try to explain.

'It's different to how it was when you or I were at school,' I say. 'Everything has to be fair. Benji has a right to play football, even if he is a little bit crap.'

Mum frowns. 'Well yes, he should be allowed to kick a ball around in the privacy of his own garden, where nobody else has to witness his lack of skill. But is it actually fair to let him play in a match? If anything, I'd say the kindest thing would be to keep him as far away from a football pitch as humanly possible.'

'You're probably right.' I let my gaze wander around the kitchen, hoping to solve the conundrum of what we're supposed to be having for supper. 'But it's a moot point now anyway. He won't be chosen again until next season.'

Mum tuts. 'Well, I think it's absolutely ridiculous. All this pretending that anybody can do anything. It'll only lead to disappointment in later life. Kids today need a few home truths.'

The kitchen door crashes open and a ball comes flying into the room, followed seconds later by an exuberant Benji.

'He shoots! He scores!' he yells, skidding to a halt by the table. 'You should have seen me today, Mum!'

'Here he is!' My mother beams at her youngest grandchild. 'The Player of the Day himself!'

I stare at her. What happened to *a few home truths*?

Benji giggles. 'It's not Player of the Day, silly,' he tells her. 'It's Man of the Match.'

Then his face falls. 'Only I didn't get it. I never get it.' He turns to me. 'Jasper McKenzie was Man of the Match *again*. For like, the gazillionth time. It's not fair.'

I shrug, thinking about what Mum was just saying. 'Well, it probably *is* fair,' I tell Benji. 'If he played really well then he deserves to get the title.'

'That football coach wouldn't know talent if it kicked him in the face,' protests my mother. 'Honestly. I thought that Jasper McKenzie child was nothing but a glorified thug. And what's more important? Being able to kick a ball in a straight line or being a nice person?'

'In this particular context, I'd say that kicking a ball is probably what they're looking for,' I venture, but Mum has already pulled Benji towards her and is murmuring platitudes and reassurances about how, if it were up to her, he'd be Man of the Match every single time he set foot on the pitch.

Once Benji has been placated and sent off to finish his homework and I have managed to find some tins of tomatoes lurking at the back of the cupboard, Mum stands up and reaches for her bag.

'Thanks for helping me out today,' I say. 'I really appreciate it, Mum.'

She walks across the kitchen and gives me a hug. 'I'm worried about you, Hannah,' she tells me. 'Is everything all right?'

And I want nothing more than to sink my head onto her shoulder and tell her that no, I am not all right. I feel like I'm splashing about in the middle of the ocean, searching desperately for a life raft while just behind me is a luxury cruise liner where everyone I know is relaxing and laughing and drinking exotic cocktails with those little paper umbrellas that I really, really love.

But I can't tell my mother that I am miserable and all at sea because I want a cocktail umbrella. It's self-indulgent and stupid and utter, utter middle-class angst. I cannot tell the woman who brought me up all on her own, sacrificing her own wants and needs to ensure that I had good Clarks school shoes, that I feel adrift.

Instead, I give her a squeeze and plaster a big smile on my face. 'I'm fine, Mum. Just a bit tired, that's all.'

She gives me a piercing look and I know that she isn't fooled.

'It's okay to ask for some help, now and again,' she says. 'I know how hard it can be when your kids start to get older and you're trying to juggle several hundred things all at once. It makes your brain hurt!'

'I don't mind the juggling.' It's true, I really don't. I'm an expert juggler. My skills are so brilliant that I could run away and join the circus, if I so desired. 'I just wish that at least one of the balls had my name on it.'

Mum laughs. 'Well, that's not so difficult,' she tells me. 'If you really want to juggle your own ball then you're going to have to write your name on it yourself!' She takes her coat off the back of the chair. 'And my advice? Use an indelible pen then the buggers can't rub it off when you're not looking.'

It is freezing cold and bleak outside, which matches my mood nicely.

I haven't given up on the idea of a new job, but there's just a lot going on at the moment and it's not appropriate for me to be thinking about changing my life. I suppose I have to accept that we all have a time, and that right now, it isn't mine. I have just got to make the best of a crappy situation and ensure that Miriam keeps me on next year.

I have pushed the entire plan to the very back of my head and I'm pretending that I don't feel a little bit sad, slightly pointless, and also mildly terrified that I may not have a job in September.

'Can I help you with anything, Mum?' Dylan walks into the kitchen and sidles up to me, wrapping one arm around my shoulder. This is a sure sign that he wants to talk. 'Do you need a hand with cooking supper?'

'You can open the tomatoes,' I tell him. 'And then find some tuna. I'm making my specialty, haute-cuisine pasta bake, tonight.'

I pass him the tin opener and get on with chopping some onions. I learnt a long time ago that if teenagers want to tell you something, then it's best not to look them in the eye. They're easily spooked, a bit like ponies. Or Medusa.

'So, I wondered if you could give me a lift to the station on Saturday?' he starts.

I play it as cool as I am capable. 'Sure. Going anywhere nice?'

'Not really.' He shrugs. 'Just thought I might go to the cinema.'

'Nice.' I nod thoughtfully, like he's just said something incredibly intelligent. 'Who are you going with?'

Dylan takes the lid off the first tin and pushes it across towards me. 'Just a friend.'

'Cool.' Nobody says cool anymore. Nobody except people in their forties who can't quite bring themselves to believe that they are possibly middle-aged. 'That's totally cool. Anyone I know?'

Dylan busies himself with the complex task of opening the second tin. 'Nah.'

This is your chance, Hannah. Your chance to be the liberal, non-interfering mother that you always thought you would be. The mother who allows her children to have privacy and respects their decisions because she trusts them and she knows that she cannot control their entire lives forever more.

I take a breath and tip the onions into the warming oil. 'Oh. That's fine. I can take you to the station.'

There is silence for a moment and I'm fairly sure that Dylan is wondering, just as I am, if the conversation is really over.

'But just tell me who you're going with,' I say, as casually as possible. 'In case there's an emergency.'

The conversation isn't over. It has barely even begun.

'What emergency?' Dylan looks at me, one side of his mouth twitching like he's trying not to laugh. 'I'll have my phone, Mum. You can text me any time.'

Is it a girl? Is it that Zoe who Scarlet was talking about? Does she go to our school? Why don't I know who she is?

I have ransacked my brain but I can't recall ever teaching a Zoe, so maybe she transferred to us for Sixth Form.

Is she nice? Will she fit into our family? Are her family more fun than us? Am I going to lose you?

I stare at him, clamping my mouth shut in a desperate attempt to stop the words shooting out.

'I'll let you know what time when I've spoken to her,' Dylan tells me. He's doing it deliberately now, dangling tempting morsels of information right in front of my nose. 'I think your onions might be burning, Mum.'

I can do nonchalant.

I can be easy-going and chilled out.

'I don't care about the arsing onions. You just said "her", so it's obviously a girl. Just tell me!'

There goes my nomination for Mother of the Year.

I grab a wooden spoon and scrape the onions off the bottom of the pan. I do care about them a little bit. Nobody likes burnt onions in their pasta sauce. Then, smiling as sweetly as I know how, I turn to face my first-born child.

'Dylan. It is not me being nosy.' Actually, I suspect, deep down, that this counts, completely and utterly, as nosiness. 'It's just that, as your mother, I don't think it's unreasonable for me to casually enquire about the company that you will be keeping.'

Dylan grins. 'Is that what you're doing? Casually enquiring?'

I nod and tilt my head to one side, in an attempt to look wise and sage-like. 'It is. And you know, some people do find it helpful to talk about how they're feeling and what they're up to and whether they're intending on asking someone out. Or not.'

'Some people might prefer to keep that information to themselves,' agrees my son. 'Luckily for you, Mother, I have no problem in telling you that I'm going to the cinema with Zoe and that yeah, I'm thinking about asking her out.'

'You could have just told me that in the first place,' I mutter. 'It would have saved me a lot of effort.'

'It would. But it wouldn't have been so entertaining.' Dylan walks across the kitchen and starts randomly opening the cupboards. 'Where do we keep the tuna?'

'Not in with the cereal,' I tell him. 'Honestly, it's hard to believe you actually live here sometimes.'

'Well, I won't be for much longer,' he says, trying a different cupboard. 'It's only seven months until I go to uni.'

My stomach flips a bit, like it always does when this subject comes up. Nobody warns you, when you hold that tiny baby in your arms and promise them that you'll do whatever it takes to keep them safe, that one day you'll have given them enough skills that they can walk out of the door and leave you behind – and that you'll have to plaster a great big smile on your face while you watch them do it. Nobody tells you that you won't feel a single bit less love or any less need to protect them than you did when they were helpless babies. If you do your job right, then your teenager will break your heart. It's a difficult truth to deal with sometimes.

'You'd better finish off the pasta bake then,' I say. 'Then at least you'll be able to cook one meal when you go.'

We potter around each other in silence for a minute or two and then, once the cheese is grated and the tuna is stirred into the sauce, I throw a tea towel across the kitchen at Dylan.

'You can go now,' I tell him. 'Thanks for the help.'

'I don't even know if she likes me,' he says in a rush. 'How am I supposed to know?'

He stands there, this man-child who can be so grown-up one moment and then remind me of the little boy that he once was in the next.

'How could she *not* like you?' I tell him, because it's the truth. She *might* not like him, but I cannot begin to understand how anyone *could* not and that's the best that I can give him.

'And you'll know. If you listen to her, she'll tell you if she likes you. Just don't be in too much of a hurry.'

He darts across the room and gives me a quick hug before heading out of the door. 'Don't tell Scarlet!' he yells back over his shoulder.

He's wasting his words. She'll know by breakfast time. She always does.

Chapter 9

I am slumped in the staffroom in my usual seat, crammed in between Peter, who runs the English department, and Isobel, the unfeasibly young and trendy PE teacher. Opposite me, in a similarly depressed state, is my best friend, Cassie, who teaches Chemistry. She's sitting next to Mrs Knight from Home Economics who, as ever, is unnaturally chipper for Monday lunchtime.

'Challenging morning?' asks Peter, eying me sympathetically as I mainline my coffee.

'Year Nine,' I tell him. 'Class C.'

He grimaces and nods understandingly. 'I taught them last year. I knew things were bad when Brandon Hopkins asked me if I was planning anything nice for my retirement.'

I wince. Peter is the same age me.

'It'd be fine if they'd just leave the melodrama at the door for *one* lesson now and again,' I say. 'The theatrics – god, it takes over everything.'

'Which is ironic when you consider that they're the worst class I've taught in years,' throws in Adele, the Drama teacher, from across the room. 'Not one single brave, creative soul among them. Last lesson I asked them all to re-enact the process of being born through the medium of mime and it was a complete and utter shambles.' She tuts loudly and throws her hands in the air. 'They're too concerned with being *cool* to let go and throw themselves into the unknown.'

I shudder, trying to imagine Brody and Vincent performing the scene of their own birth.

'I can't imagine any pupil failing to be inspired by one of *your* lessons,' Danny tells her, walking across from the kitchen area. Danny teaches Physics. Danny is new to teaching. Danny is still perky and enthusiastic and keen.

None of us really like Danny.

'But what a fascinating activity, Adele,' says Miriam, prowling towards our part of the room. I hadn't even realised that she was in here – but that's one of her super-talents. Popping up when you least expect her.

I groan silently and brace myself. Miriam is the kind of person who fails to understand that a school staffroom is no place for a serious discussion about education.

She leans forward now, fixing Adele with her beady eyes. 'So what was the objective of that lesson?'

Adele puts on her 'earnest educator' face.

'It's all about reimagining your own story,' she explains. 'By acting out our own birth, we are able to relate to the innocence and naivety that we once possessed and then bring that into our everyday lives.' She pauses. 'It's incredibly therapeutic and highly intense and, done correctly, it can help a person address their weaknesses and faults.' She looks at Miriam. 'It's all about *learning to fail*.'

In my head, I chime an imaginary gong. *Well done, Adele – you've managed to include one of this term's buzz phrases. Good job.*

'And it helps to *build resilience*.'

Strike two! But can she go for the Holy Trinity? I hold my breath and watch as Adele gears up for her finale.

'And it's a perfect activity for *promoting a growth mindset*. It's literally like being born again!'

And the crowd goes wild! Adele for Teacher of the Year!

Across the room, Cassie catches my eye and raises her eyebrows.

'Are you hearing this bullshit?' whispers Peter. 'The scariest part is that I can't figure out if Adele is just winding her up or if she's being deadly serious.'

We stare at the Drama teacher. Her eyes are flashing with something that looks a lot like fanaticism. That, or she's been overdoing it on the energy drinks.

'I think she's serious,' I whisper back. 'I might just go and sit in the staff toilets for the rest of break time.'

But before I can move, Miriam claps her hands together and looks around at those of us who are unfortunate enough to be nearby.

'I've just had the most marvellous idea for our next Inset day!' she exclaims. She turns to Adele. 'Do you think you could run a drama workshop for us all? Something that incorporates this kind of thing?'

Adele's face lights up. 'Absolutely, Miriam!' She thinks for a second. 'I'll call it "Facing Your Fears" and we'll have lots of fantastic group activities that push everyone out of their comfort zones. We can start with the birthing mime and progress from there – I have plenty of ideas!'

'Wonderful!' Miriam looks at her watch. 'I'm free next period if you've got the time to run through a few thoughts about how we could structure the day?'

They stand up and leave, snippets of phrases such as *enlightenment* and *healing hands of self-reflection* floating back to the rest of us who are sitting in shock.

'She isn't serious, is she?' Beside me, Isobel has gone a funny colour. 'We're not actually going to have to re-enact our own birth in front of everyone?'

'I volunteer you to go first,' calls Cassie. 'You're the youngest. Sacrifices must be made.'

Nobody else speaks, each of us too caught up in our own horror to have the energy to console Isobel.

Eventually, Peter clears his throat.

'Does anyone know when the next Inset day actually is?' he enquires.

The Art teacher consults his diary. 'It's the first day back of the new school year,' he informs the room. 'The second of September.'

'That's something to look forward to then,' mutters Cassie. 'I think I might go somewhere very exotic and disease-ridden this summer. Maybe I'll contract something and need to take the first week back off work.'

Peter suddenly springs to his feet and grabs this week's copy of the *Times Educational Supplement* from the coffee table. 'I'll be having *that*, thank you very much,' he says, flicking the pages until he finds the vacancies section.

'Where's your team spirit?' I ask him, pulling a face. 'And anyway, there won't be many jobs in there at the moment.'

'That's where you're wrong,' he crows, peering at me over the top of the page. 'There's a job going here at St Hilda's and it's got my name written all over it.'

'Seriously?' I'm suddenly interested. 'Is it full time? I didn't think there'd be any jobs until after Easter.'

'Not only is it full time but it also offers a free lunch every single day. We don't get that here.'

St Hilda's. The school on the other side of town where the aspirational send their offspring and teachers go to die. There are never any vacancies at St Hilda's – nobody ever resigns or moves on. They just keel over at their desks, happy that they kept working in their idyllic, joy-filled school until their very last breath.

I wrench it out of his hands and scan the sheet. The St Hilda's school logo leaps off the page and I quickly read the job specification. Then I lower the paper and glare at my colleague.

'Peter. The only job going at St Hilda's is to work as an apprentice in the school canteen. And the reason that they're offering a free lunch is because they're paying below the minimum wage.'

'But I bet nobody would ask me to perform my own birth using interpretive dance,' he snaps. 'So it would be well worth the drop in salary.'

'To be fair, mate, she said we'd be using mime, not interpretive dance,' calls Danny. 'I think the two art forms are incredibly different.'

Beside me, Peter bristles and I have to work hard not to laugh out loud. It is an ill-hidden secret that Danny has an almighty crush on the terrifying Adele.

'Do you think they might have two apprenticeships going?' I ask Peter.

'No!' he snatches the paper back out of my hands and holds it to his chest, looking possessive. 'I saw it first. It's mine!'

'Oh bloody hell,' I groan, taking another swig of coffee. 'I'm doomed. I'm going to end up doing supply teaching and drinking whisky for breakfast.'

'What are you on about?' Peter pulls a packet of chocolate digestives out of his briefcase and offers one to Isobel and then one to me. 'Why on earth would you ever want to be a supply teacher?'

'I need the money,' I confess. 'Dylan's starting university this year and I'm not sure how much longer I can do the whole three-day-week thing. If I even *have* a job here by September.'

Peter grimaces. 'That's not good, Hannah. You know that supply teaching is the worst job going. You'll end up babysitting Year Seven in Physics and having to pretend that you know something about quantum mechanics or some such nonsense.'

'I heard that!' shouts Danny. 'And only an English teacher would have the audacity to describe quantum mechanics as nonsense.'

'Well, it is,' retaliates Peter. 'All that gubbins about a cat in a box and is it alive or dead and it could be either until you look at it. It's just an illogical riddle.'

'You're talking about Schrödinger's Cat and you're completely missing the point, as per usual.' Danny's face is starting to go red. 'For your information—'

'Did anyone do anything nice at the weekend?' I ask, looking around the room. 'Anything not related to school or physics or cats? Anyone?'

Isobel stretches her arms in the air and yawns.

'I made my boyfriend go to the cinema with me,' she tells us. 'Not that he was very happy about it.'

'Is he not a film fan?' I ask. 'I'd have thought a night out with you at the cinema would be a great way to spend a Saturday evening!'

'It's not that,' she says. 'He usually loves watching films. It was my choice of film that got him upset.'

'Oh my god!' squeals Cassie. 'I bet I know what you watched!'

Isobel looks at her and grins. 'You should do. You're the one who told me to take him in the first place!'

'So what did you see? Was it something gory?' I smile. 'Nick refuses to watch any horror film with me.'

Isobel laughs. 'No, it was nothing like that. We went to see that *Fifty Shades* film. You know, the one with Jamie Dornan in it!'

'Oh.' I gulp, and next to me, I feel Peter sink a little lower in his seat. Nobody else says a word and it feels like the responsibility is purely on me to keep the social awkwardness at bay. 'And was it a *nice* film?'

I sound like my mother. Although in all fairness, my mother would probably be dealing with this better than I am.

Cassie splutters into her mug of tea. 'It's not supposed to be *nice*, Hannah. It's about BDSM.'

I stare at her, mentally running the acronym.

'What does the D stand for?' I ask. 'I think I can work out the others but I don't know that one. Is it "dictatorship"?'

'You're pretty close.' She grins at me. 'It's "discipline", Hannah. Have you even read the books?'

I shake my head. 'No. Why would I?'

'I've read them,' pipes up the Design and Technology teacher. 'And I've seen the films. They're okay but not as good as the books.'

'Me too,' adds Mrs Knight, who must be sixty-five years old if she's a day. She's been at the school teaching Home Economics since the very beginning of time and is as much a part of the establishment as the walls and the desks. None of us know her first name and even the Head refers to her by her full title. 'I wasn't quite sure what all the fuss was about, to be honest. It seemed quite tame to me.'

My mouth drops open and all eyes turn to stare at her as we contemplate what she's just said.

'There are some pretty racy scenes in there, Mrs Knight,' ventures Isobel. 'Didn't you find any of them even a little bit shocking?'

Mrs Knight smiles kindly at her. 'Not at all, dear. I was a teenager in the Swinging Sixties, you know.' Her eyes glaze over as she takes a trip down memory lane. 'My goodness me, I don't think the likes of Christian Grey would have been able to keep up with us, back in the day!'

For the second time in fifteen minutes, the silence in the

staffroom is absolutely deafening. And then Mrs Knight blinks away whatever flashback she is happily reliving and looks at me.

'You really should read the books, Hannah dear. You're an English teacher now, for heaven's sake. Aren't you curious about how literature is evolving in the twenty-first century?'

So now it's my failure to read the *Fifty Shades of Grey* trilogy that is making me a crappy teacher? Excellent.

'I'll lend you my copies,' offers Isobel. 'It won't take you long to read them.'

'Thanks,' I say weakly, ignoring the snorts of muffled laughter coming from Peter and Cassie. 'I'm sure they'll be very informative.'

'Well, I've heard that they're really badly constructed,' says Danny. 'The author made an absolute fortune on the back of some poorly written fan fiction.'

'You seem to know an awful lot about it,' teases Peter. 'Are you a secret fan of erotic fiction, Danny?'

Danny flushes bright red. 'No! Not that it's any of your business what I read. And erotica can be a very well-respected genre, actually.'

'All I know is that they're easy to read and the author probably never has to work another day in her life,' says Cassie. 'I'd have written it if I had the slightest bit of writing ability. She's one of the highest-earning authors ever. I bet she doesn't give a monkey's flea-ridden backside what any critic says about it. It's her who got the last laugh.'

'And she isn't pretending that it's a literary masterpiece,' adds Isobel. 'It just is what it is.'

'Maybe I should try writing my own version,' chuckles Mrs Knight. 'I remember on one occasion, ooh – it must have been forty-seven years ago now, when I met a very charming young man who could do this amazing thing with his—'

The bell rings, thankfully saving us all from discovering exactly what the charming young man had done that was memorable enough to be remembered almost half a century later.

I leap out of my chair, brushing biscuit crumbs from my skirt.

'I'll pop the books in your pigeon hole tomorrow,' promises Isobel.

'Maybe you'll be inspired to do some writing of your own,' says Peter, heaving himself up. 'I bet E.L. James isn't contemplating becoming a kitchen hand in a school canteen.'

'So you know who wrote them, then!' shouts Danny, triumphantly. 'And you were having a go at *me*!'

'Daniel, my son.' Peter puts his hand on Danny's shoulder and propels him out of the room. 'Who do you think she modelled the love interest on?'

I can still hear the sound of Danny retching as they walk down the corridor.

Chapter 10

The day starts badly.

'Mum!' I haven't even opened my eyes before an anguished howl pierces the silence of the sleeping house. 'Muuuuum!'

'If he's been sick, it's definitely your turn,' I mutter, rolling over in bed and prodding Nick in the ribs.

'But he's calling for you, babe,' murmurs Nick. 'He wants his mummy.'

I scowl. I have told the kids more times than I can count that if they need us, they have *two* fit and able-bodied parents and that their father is just as capable of fighting off night-time monsters, or fetching glasses of water, or moving the bloody hamster to the landing where its unrelenting nocturnal exercise regime won't keep them awake, or cleaning up vomit from the middle of the duvet cover as I am. But it doesn't seem to matter how many times I lecture them. It is still *my* name that gets screeched whenever they are in need.

'Mum!' The shouts are getting louder, so whatever is ailing our child clearly isn't hindering his ability to walk. I stay buried beneath the cover and pretend that I'm still asleep.

'You have to wake up.' Benji is standing right next to my side of the bed now. I can feel his presence looming ominously above me. I keep my eyes scrunched shut while stretching out my foot and jabbing Nick on the leg.

'It's World Book Day, Mum! And we forgot!'

Bloody hell. How could I possibly have forgotten about bastarding World Book Day? For the past week, Facebook has been filled with photographs of children posing in elaborate costumes, each one more impressive than the last.

I sit bolt upright in bed and stare at Benji, trying to conceal my panic.

'It's fine,' I tell him, my voice high-pitched. 'We'll just find your costume from last year.'

Benji frowns. 'I can't be Where's Wally again – nearly everyone was in that costume and it'll look like we just haven't bothered.'

'We haven't,' mumbles Nick, from beneath the duvet. He is no use whatsoever.

'We can sort something else out then,' I say, clambering out of bed. 'Let's go and have a look in the dressing-up box.'

I pull on my dressing gown and smile reassuringly at my son.

'We'll find something brilliant!' I tell him. 'Nick! Get up and put the kettle on and then make sure that the other two are awake.'

Nick groans something incoherent and I speed out of the room, sweeping Benji along in my wake. The morning has hardly begun and I am already busy, busy, busy, doing something that wasn't even part of my already overscheduled day.

'Let's just drag the box out and then we can look at our options,' I say once we're in Benji's room. I kneel down next to the bed and pull out the plastic container, unperturbed by the thick layer of dust on the top. 'It's like a treasure trove. I bet there's some fabulous costumes in here!'

I lift off the lid and gaze inside. There are no fabulous costumes in here. The dressing-up box has been desecrated.

'Amazing!' crows Benji, swooping in over my shoulder. 'I've been looking for that Nintendo DS game for ages! And look, there's my Nerf gun. I thought Dylan had stolen that!'

He starts rummaging through the contents, flinging items onto the floor. I watch as a mountain of plastic crap and old comics and the occasional item of clothing piles up next to me.

'Where are all the lovely costumes?' I ask him, my voice sounding strained even to my ears. 'Why is this box full of rubbish?'

'This isn't rubbish!' says Benji indignantly. 'This is my stuff. It's treasures, like you said.'

I hold up an empty crisp packet and a broken matchbox car with three wheels. 'This is *not* treasure.'

Benji snatches them both off me and clutches them to his chest. 'They're mine! You gave me this car when I went to hospital. It's precious.'

'It's broken,' I point out.

'It's *memories*,' he volleys back and he has me there, because I am always going on about how they should all keep memory boxes that they can look at when they're old and withered and their youth is in the long-forgotten, mythical past.

'And the crisp packet?'

Benji's face spreads into a beam.

'That's from the day that Logan came over and you let us have a picnic in the garden but you said we could only eat healthy food because you'd just got that blender thingy and you wouldn't stop whizzing up yucky vegetables and pretending that they were delicious smoothies. And then Logan got stung by a bee and you remembered that you had loads of yummy food hidden in the cupboard that you always say is for grown-ups and you gave us loads of coke and chocolate and crisps to make him stop crying.' He holds the packet aloft. 'He told me later that it didn't even hurt that much, but he didn't want to say that in case you took away the treats and tried to make us drink spinach smoothies again.'

'Guess what you and Logan are having for tea the next time he comes over?' I tell him, shaking my head. 'Totally scrumptious kale and beetroot milkshake. With pasta made out of courgettes. Sound good?'

Benji grimaces and sticks his tongue out. 'I'm going to ask if I can live at Logan's house,' he informs me. 'They eat normal food over there.'

I ignore him and push my arm into the box, feeling around for anything that might be vaguely fancy-dress related. The sound of feet pounding along the landing momentarily distracts me, followed by a slamming bathroom door that makes the house rock on its foundations.

'Dylan!' hollers Scarlet from outside the door. 'Get out now! I told you I was first today!'

Dylan starts singing loudly from the sanctuary of the bathroom.

'Let it go! Let it go!' he wails, clearly standing just on the other side of the locked door. 'Don't hold it back anymoooooore!'

'Don't let it go!' yells Benji, quick to get in on the action. 'We don't want wee all over the carpet!'

He cracks up and Scarlet's head pokes around his bedroom door.

'You're hilarious,' she tells him. 'Mum. Tell Dylan to let me in.'

'Wait your turn,' I say, before twisting to direct my voice towards the wall separating Benji's room from the bathroom. 'Dylan! Hurry up. Your sister is waiting.'

'I remember this!' Scarlet crouches down next to me and pulls something out of the box, her anger forgotten. 'I wore this for Halloween one year.'

Thank every deity that is worshipped by man. She's only gone and found a costume. Maybe this day actually has a fighting chance.

'It's perfect,' I say, taking it from her. 'Benji! We've got your Book Day outfit sorted. I can assure you, nobody else is going to be wearing something like this!'

Scarlet turns to look at me. 'Are you being serious? You're actually going to make him go to school wearing *that*?'

'Why not?' I shoot her a look before giving Benji a big smile. 'It was good enough for you and I think he'll look great! Come on, let's put it on.'

I reach out my hand and tug Benji towards me. He seems reluctant, but when I glance at the alarm clock on his bedside table, I can see that his reluctance will have to do one. We have forty-five minutes to get everyone up, washed, dressed, breakfasted and out of the door, complete with homework and packed lunches.

'Step in through the top,' I coax him, holding the neck of the costume open. 'There we go! Both feet in.'

I yank the material up his legs, feeling surprised when the ends fall just below his knees.

'How old were you when Granny made this?' I ask Scarlet.

'Six,' she tells me. 'I was six years old, Mum. And I'm a girl.'

'I don't think World Book Day is about reinforcing gender stereotypes, darling, do you?' I say brightly. 'And besides, it's ridiculous to assume that this outfit is just for girls.'

Scarlet shrugs. 'I'm just saying. You're the one always going on about how we need to help him get prepared for secondary school. I'm merely suggesting that making him a laughing stock isn't exactly going to help his street cred.'

'Who's a laughing stock?' asks Dylan, emerging from the bathroom. His eyes alight on his little brother. 'Oh, right! That'd be Benji, then!'

'Nobody is going to be laughing at you,' I say, pulling the rest of the costume over Benji's resisting arms and twisting him round so that I can do up the tie at the back. 'You'll look amazing.'

'What are you doing, Mum?' Dylan leans against the door-frame and crosses his arms. 'Is this some cruel and unusual punishment that you've dreamt up? Because I'm fairly sure that Benji would rather have a smack than be forced to wear this monstrosity.'

Sometimes I really, really dislike teenagers.

'It's not a monstrosity,' I say, ramming the headpiece down over Benji's alarmed face. 'And if you've got any better suggestions for bloody World Book Day then by all means, voice them now. I am all ears.'

I rock back on my haunches and look at my youngest son.

'Take a look in the mirror,' suggests Scarlet, her voice shaking. 'The big one by your door, so that you can get the whole *fabulous* effect.'

I stand up and Benji steps cautiously across the floor. It's possible that the eyeholes are a teensy bit small. Hopefully they'll reduce his visibility when he sees his reflection.

There is silence as he moves in front of the glass and then a slight whimpering sound comes from inside the woollen head.

'What book character am I supposed to be?' he whispers.

Dylan and Scarlet look like they're about to explode. I am ready for this question.

'You're the lamb!' I say, moving to stand behind him and putting my hands on his shoulders. 'The gorgeous, sweet lamb!'

Benji erupts. 'I am not going to school dressed like a lamb!' he screeches, wrenching off the white, fleecy head. 'That's not even a real book character!'

'It is!' I tell him. 'There are loads of stories with lambs in.'

'Like what?' he howls, while Dylan and Scarlet rather unhelpfully start spluttering with laughter. 'Tell me one story that has a lamb in it. I bet you can't. I need a different outfit!'

'"Mary had a Little Lamb",' I say. 'Actually, it was quite a kick-ass lamb because it followed her to school one day, which was incredibly independent and anti-establishment.'

I need to talk my way through this situation; a costume change is definitely not on the cards. One, because we are running out of time; and two, because there *is* no other costume.

'Everyone will laugh at me.' Benji's shoulders droop and he hangs his head low. 'Nobody else will be wearing something like this. Logan's going as Mr Twit and Jasper McKenzie is going as Spider-Man and a load of people are dressing up as Gangsta Granny.'

I kneel down in front of him. 'It'll be okay,' I say. 'Nobody will laugh at you, Benji.' I pause, narrowing my eyes at my oldest children who finally stop sniggering. 'And it's good to be different from everyone else, you know? Nobody wants to be a sheep.'

The words are out before I can stop them. Over by the door, Dylan loses it entirely and yelps with mirth while Scarlet sits on the floor with her hand shoved over her mouth, desperately trying to hold back the brewing hysterics.

'But you've *made* me a sheep!' wails Benji. 'And I'm not going to school dressed like this.'

'Everything all right in here?' asks Nick, popping his head around the door. 'Have you got a costume sorted yet, mate?'

Benji pauses, midway through scrambling out of the lamb outfit.

'No! Mum thought I could go as a lamb but I can't, can I, Dad? Tell her that I can't!'

Nick grins. 'Not if you don't want to,' he tells Benji. Then he turns to me. 'What are the other options, Hannah?'

I sink down onto the bed and subject my husband to a serious dose of stink-eye.

'Well sadly, I lack the ability to whip a World Book Day costume out of my backside, ample as it may be. So I'm afraid that our son is limited to attending school as a lamb, or,' I take a deep breath and force myself to keep my voice steady, 'as a regular schoolboy who forgot to remind his parents that an outfit was required.'

'There was a letter,' Benji reminds me. 'I gave it to you last week.'

So there was. I remember skimming the contents and telling myself that it was ages away: World Book Day is in March and we were still in February. My bad.

Nick glances at his watch. If he goes to work now then he'll be sleeping with his precious Betty for the rest of the week.

'I've got the perfect thing for you,' he tells Benji. He looks across at me. 'You guys go and get breakfast started and we'll be down in a minute.'

I have no idea how he thinks he's going to conjure a costume in the next sixty seconds but I'm just grateful that he has a plan. Benji can go to school dressed as Hannibal Lecter for all I care, just as long as we don't have to stand in the playground being subjected to sympathetic glances from the perfect mothers, all muttering behind my back about how there's always one child who gets left out and how honestly, it's tantamount to neglect not to ensure that your child is dressed up; even though most of their kids will be dressed up in random princess and superhero costumes that aren't even from books and it isn't called World Fucking Disney Franchise Film Day, is it?

I stand up and point at Dylan and Scarlet.

'You. Make me a cup of tea. You. Put some bread in the toaster.'

'Sir! Yes, Sir!' Dylan salutes and snaps his heels together before marching dramatically out of the room. Scarlet follows at a more sedate speed and I am vaguely interested to see that she doesn't even go near the bathroom, despite the door now being wide open. Obviously her moment of need has passed. That, or she didn't need to go in there in the first place and, like her brother, was just engaged in some bizarre sibling ritual about who can do something first.

I walk downstairs and start gathering apples and packets of raisins for their packed lunches. I'm expecting Nick to take a while, despite his confidence, but true to his word, he and Benji walk into the kitchen just a couple of minutes after us.

'Ta-da!' Nick throws his arms out and gestures at our son. 'What do you think?'

'He's wearing his dressing gown,' states Scarlet. 'Who's he supposed to be?'

'Look closer,' Nick tells her and we all crane to stare at Benji, who is looking bemused but pleased.

And then I see the book, peeping out of his dressing gown pocket.

'You're a genius,' I tell Nick. 'That is actually brilliant!'

Nick puffs out his chest. 'I have my moments,' he agrees. 'And I have to admit, this is pretty great.'

'Nobody will be dressed like you,' I tell Benji. 'It's really clever!'

'Nice one!' says Dylan, putting his hand up so that Benji can give him a high-five. 'Good choice of book, little bro.'

'Dad chose it,' Benji tells us. 'I haven't read it yet but he says I can next year.'

'He's wearing his dressing gown,' repeats Scarlet. 'How does that make him a character for World Book Day? Who is he even supposed to be?'

'Arthur Dent,' chant Nick and Dylan in unison.

'He's from *The Hitchhiker's Guide to the Galaxy*,' I tell her. 'Look, Benji's got the book in his pocket!'

'So why is he wearing a dressing gown,' she asks, confused. 'Nobody goes hitchhiking in a dressing gown.'

'He isn't expecting to have to go anywhere,' Dylan explains patiently. 'But Earth gets demolished to make way for a hyper-space bypass and Arthur Dent ends up escaping by hitching a ride on an alien spaceship. Which is why he's in his dressing gown.'

'It sounds stupid,' mutters Scarlet. 'You should just draw a scar on his head and let him go as Harry Potter. Nobody's even going to know who he is.'

'I'll know,' Benji tells her. 'And I can show them the book.'

The smoke alarm goes off; the toast is ready. Nick takes a slurp of his tea and then pulls me in for a hug.

'I'll see you later,' he tells me. 'Have a good day.'

'You too,' I say, reaching up to give him a kiss. 'Thanks for helping this morning.'

I'm feeling less manic than I was ten minutes ago. There's a vague chance we're actually going to get out of the door on time. The day can yet be saved.

'No worries.' He shoulders his bag and opens the front door. 'You need to relax, Hannah. We're all quite capable of sorting ourselves out, you know. You don't need to organise everything on your own.'

I nod at him and give him a wave. I know that he's right; it's a conversation we have a lot. I've always been someone who likes to know what's going on and I hate leaving things to the last minute, but since becoming a parent, it sometimes feels like I'm responsible for everything in the universe, every second of the day. As Nick constantly reminds me, the world will not stop rotating if I take my foot off the accelerator now and again. I don't have to breathe for anyone but me.

I turn back to face the kids. In the few seconds that I've been saying goodbye to Nick, Benji has managed to knock over an almost-full bottle of milk. Dogger is enthusiastically lapping it up as if she's a cat and I don't know if milk is okay for dogs and I haven't got time to Google it. And Scarlet is screeching at Dylan and telling him that it wouldn't kill him to put the peanut butter away when he's finished with it and that every time he leaves the lid off the margarine he is contributing to the marginalisation of women everywhere and is he okay with that? Is he? And Dylan is asking if what she actually means is the *margarine-alisation* of women and that surely any attempt to *butter her up* is patronising and anti-feminist.

I know that I'm lucky to have times at home with the kids and not have to work all week, but it's mornings like this that make me long for a high-powered job with a six o'clock commuter train into London. I picture myself tucked into a window seat, clutching a cup of takeaway coffee and watching the world flit by outside the glass.

And then I sigh loudly and take a step towards the chaos.

Chapter 11

It's been another joy-filled half-week of living the teaching dream. Now it's Thursday again and I'm facing the prospect of two days off work: two days that I should be grateful to receive but that actually only serve to pile guilt onto my laden shoulders.

I start every Thursday with great intentions. I plan to clean the house and organise the food cupboards and get all the shopping done and sort the laundry and make sure that all my planning and marking is up to date for the following week. Usually, by the end of Thursday, I have achieved one fifth of those tasks and spent a lot of time shouting at the inane and illiterate status updates on Facebook.

Today, though, once Nick has left for work and the kids are all safely deposited at school, I settle down in the kitchen and open the notebook that Scarlet gave me for my birthday. Things cannot continue as they are. I need a plan.

I am immediately thwarted by the fact that Scarlet has already commandeered my notebook. Her messy writing is scrawled across the first page and I peer to take a closer look.

Reasons My Name Should be Spelt Scarlett With Two Ts.
- *Scarlett with two ts is more exotic and much more glamorous.*
- *Scarlett Johansson is a very successful actress and makes loads of money.*
- *It looks better with two ts.*
- *Scarlet with one t is a colour, not a name.*
- *If you actually love me then you should want me to be happy and I will be happy all of the time if you let me be Scarlett with two ts.*

I do what any decent parent would do and rip out the page before writing my own title at the top of the new, blank piece of paper.

Potential Ways to Make Money and Also Find My True Calling

Then I spend two minutes rummaging in the bottom of my school bag for a ruler, because really, how can I hope to take myself seriously if my plan looks shoddy?

I don't find a ruler but I do find the raunchy books that Isobel, true to her word, had left in my pigeon hole and which I had instantly rammed into my bag before anyone could see them and start up the whole awkward conversation again.

I stack the books neatly on the table and go on a hunt, eventually unearthing a ruler from the cutlery drawer. Then I carefully underline the title before sitting back in my seat and chewing on the end of my pen. *Ways to make money.*

There must be loads of them for someone like me. I have tons of skills.

A few minutes tick by while I try to let my mind roam around my options. The only problem is that my mind doesn't appear to want to dream up new and innovative ways to earn some extra cash or think about where my passions might lie. Instead, it's wondering if Scarlet remembered to take her water bottle to school this morning because I've been noticing that she often forgets, and dehydration is no joke. And it's contemplating whether it can be bothered to cook chilli tonight or if it can get away with serving up pizza and chips for the second time this week. And then it decides that actually it isn't at work today so how on earth can it justify anything other than a nutritious and delicious meal for the rest of the family who have all been out at school and who deserve hearty fare? And then it starts whimpering and saying that this is *exactly* the problem and it isn't as if it spends all day painting its nails when it isn't at school and that it's sick to death of feeling obliged to cook and clean and shop and do the laundry when it is working just as hard as everyone else but nobody seems to understand that.

I just need to write something down. Anything, just to get me started.

Determinedly, I write the number one at the side of the page, enclosing it in a small circle. It doesn't look quite special enough though, so I take my pencil case out of my bag and find my neon highlighters, carefully shading in the circle in pink before adding small lines in yellow that look like the sun's rays.

When I'm finally happy with the presentation, I glance at the clock. It's now twenty to ten. I have spent thirteen minutes doing absolutely faff all.

I steel my resolve and write down the first thing that pops into my head.

Dog Walker.

I embellish the page with tiny doodles of puppies, twisting the idea around in my head. I walk Dogger every day. Surely it wouldn't be too much hassle to take another couple of dogs with us? And I remember that Cassie was talking recently about a friend of hers who does it and according to Cassie, he makes *loads* of money.

But then again, Dogger is quite a daft dog and I have to watch her at all times when she's off the lead. I'm not sure that I could pay attention to more than one animal at a time. And then there's the poo. I love Dogger and so I'm prepared to deal with the necessary disgusting elements of dog ownership but there's no way on this planet that I could cope with picking up after someone else's pet. Urgh – the thought alone makes me feel sick.

I strike a neat line through the words.

It's okay, I tell myself. I'm not going to find the perfect solution first time. This is what brainstorming is all about. I just need to keep going.

What are you good at, Hannah? I ask myself. *What skills do you have?* I think for moment. Since leaving university I have effectively had two roles. I am a mother and I am a teacher, so it makes sense that I should utilise those strengths and work out how I can make use of them. I am used to looking after other people's children and I understand the needs of young people.

The answer is staring me in the face. I write down *Child Minder* before frantically crossing it out again.

Not a chance. Just because I spend my days teaching other people's kids does not mean that I necessarily like them. And teenagers might be tricky but little kids are a different thing altogether. They're needy and demanding and random. There is absolutely no way that I could remain sane and be a child minder, not without the aid of copious amounts of red wine; and I suspect that being responsible for minors while under the influence is probably frowned upon.

I stand up and walk across to the window. It's finally stopped raining and the first few spring flowers are attempting to brave the elements. I feel an urge to pull on my wellies and go for a walk; anything to get away from my growing sense of unease.

Whistling to Dogger, I attach her lead and grab my coat.

It's cold outside, the weak early-spring sun doing little to warm the air, but I walk briskly while Dogger plods along beside me. The grass verges are springing to life, delicate primroses pushing up between clumps of daffodils. Part of me is aware that I should love this sense of freedom, knowing that I have free rein to go wherever I want until three o'clock.

But I can't shake the feeling that I'm playing truant. Nick is at work and the kids are at school and I am just here, wasting time worrying about money. I might as well be at work.

I should be at work.

I reach the local shop and pause for a minute, staring at the window. There are always several postcards taped to the glass, some of them advertising situations vacant and others requesting any work that might be available. I scan through the jobs.

Person wanted to muck out stables.

I could do that! I mean, I'm not really a massive fan of horses, ever since a traumatic school trip to Dartmoor when the pony I was given to ride turned out to be the size of a Shire horse with the personality of a sloth. Everyone else disappeared onto the moor while I sat helpless and terrified, too scared to do anything to encourage my steed to stop eating grass and actually walk, other than to whisper expletives beneath my breath. I read the rest of the postcard.

Person wanted to muck out stables in return for riding lessons.

Oh. Perhaps not, then.

I move onto the next one.

Book Keeper required. Must have relevant qualifications and excellent references.

My attempts to stick to a weekly food budget probably won't impress.

Sighing, I turn back down the lane and head for home, ignoring Dogger's plaintive looks as we pass the stile for the field. There's nothing for it. Unless I'm prepared to take up Scarlet's suggestion of applying for a job in Nando's then I'm going to have to suck it up and talk to Miriam about getting put on the list for supply cover. It'll be grim and depressing and there's absolutely no future or career advancement in it but at least it'll bring in the extra money that we need. I am just going to have to put my big girl knickers on and remind myself that it's no big deal if I have to spend the next twenty years in a job that I dislike. People do it all the time.

I slam through the garden gate and trudge down the path towards the front door, angry with myself for being so pathetic. Who exactly do I think I am? I have a lovely home. I have a job that isn't demeaning or degrading (although Adele somehow terrified me into agreeing to showcase a talent for the end of term Christmas show last year and my rendition of 'Respect' got me booed off stage by Year Nine, even though I'd spent weeks watching YouTube videos of Aretha and thought my vocals were a fairly passable interpretation of the original – that was pretty degrading).

You're forty-three years old, Hannah, I curse myself as I walk into the hall and hang up my coat. *This mid-life angst and diva-esque soul searching is neither appropriate nor attractive. You've had your time and now you need to put everyone else first.* I plod into the kitchen and put the kettle on, slapping away the little voice that is whispering in my ear, asking me if I even know when *my time* supposedly was and whether, in the past eighteen years, I have ever once stopped putting other people before me.

Kettle boiled and tea made, I make my way back to the kitchen table. I will make a new list outlining how much money we need for the next year, and then I will work out exactly how many supply days I'll need to do.

As I reach for my pen, something else catches my eye.

The stack of books that Isobel lent to me.

I reach out for the top one, glancing furtively around the kitchen as if someone might be judging me. The cover looks innocent enough. I flick it open and pick up my tea. Mrs Knight was probably right. It's my duty as an English teacher to stay abreast of the latest developments in fiction, so to speak. And after Isobel went to all the effort of bringing them in for me, it'd be rude to immediately hand them back. I'll read the first chapter, just to get a feel for the genre.

The rumbling of my stomach eventually becomes loud enough for me to hear, immersed as I am in the world of Mr Grey. I blink and swim back to reality, struggling for a second to place myself in my normal kitchen after the things I've just read. The clock on the wall tells me that I've been reading for hours and that I'm going to have to get a move on if I'm going to collect the kids from school.

I stand up and stretch my arms over my head. I need to eat and I need to put in a load of laundry unless I want to spend the whole of tomorrow up to my eyebrows in dirty pants. But I'm three quarters of the way through now and as I'm always telling my pupils, once you get on a reading roll it's a crime to stop. And I've always hated hypocrisy.

I walk over to the cupboard where I keep the stuff for the kids' packed lunches, pushing aside the improbably sized packets of raisins and dried fruit in the shape of a pencil and bars made out of birdseed. Right at the back I find what I'm looking for, and I head back to the table with a KitKat in one hand and a Wagon Wheel in the other. Then I grab my phone and send a text to Logan's mum.

Hi! Any chance you can drop B off as you drive past? Something's come up here, lol! Thanks x

I press send, sniggering to myself. Logan's mum is lovely and worthy and very, very proper. She'd be horrified if she knew that I was eschewing pick-up duties to read *Fifty Shades of Grey*.

My next two texts are to Dylan and Scarlet.

Get the bus x

Then, before I can change my mind, I take my chocolate and Mr Grey over to the comfy chair next to the window, where I can read in peace and keep an eye out for the kids.

Chapter 12

I spend all of the next day reading the second book in the trilogy, stopping on several occasions to shout at the main female character and telling her to grow some self-respect. By the time it's Friday night, I am a bundle of mixed emotions. It's awful. The entire premise is absolutely terrible. But I can kind of see the appeal.

Nick brings home a bottle of Prosecco and we drink a toast to Fizzy Friday and the end of the week.

'Here's to a slightly less stressful seven days,' he says, holding his glass in the air. 'Maybe we'll win the lottery tomorrow night and all our worries will be behind us!'

'We'd have to buy a ticket to do that,' I point out, snuggling up next to him on the sofa and tucking my feet under his legs. 'And anyway, I reckon winning a huge amount of money would cause more issues than it would solve.'

I take a huge gulp of my drink.

'Do you really?' Nick looks at me in surprise.

'Of course I don't! I'd bloody love to win more money than I could count!'

Nick laughs. 'Why do people always say that, though? That money brings its own problems?'

'I bet nobody poor ever says it,' I mutter darkly.

Nick nods in agreement. 'Too right! Now, where have those annoying kids hidden the remote?'

'It was in the fridge yesterday,' I remind him. After a good twenty minutes searching, Nick had found it balanced on top of the cheese. Benji eventually confessed that it might possibly have been him who put it there when he was looking for the milk; and by the way, did we know that there was no milk left?

'I've told them that they're banned from watching TV if they can't treat our belongings with respect,' Nick complains, sitting up and ramming his hand down the side of the sofa. 'But do they pay the slightest bit of attention?'

'Those noise-cancelling headphones don't exactly help,' I say. 'I had to scream Scarlet's name three times earlier and I was standing right next to her.'

'She probably heard you the first time.' Nick turns his attention towards the cushions that line the back of the sofa.

Time suddenly warps; I can see exactly what is about to happen in slow motion but am powerless to stop it.

'Nooooo!' I shout, but I am too late. Nick pulls the middle cushion forward and his hands grip around the book.

I turn fifty shades of puce.

'What's this?' He picks it up, turns it over and examines the cover, his eyes widening when he sees the title. 'Oh my god, Hannah!'

'I can explain,' I say, trying to pull the evidence away from him. He stares at me, his face contorted with concern.

'What do you know about this?' he asks, narrowing his eyes.

I remind myself that this is the twenty-first century and I do not have anything to feel ashamed about. I don't care who knows that I read these books. It doesn't make me a bad person. Nobody has the right to judge me for it. I'm not going to be made to feel ashamed just because I read something that is a little to the left of centre. Or is it to the right of centre?

I take a deep breath.

'If you'll just listen, then I can—'

But Nick doesn't let me continue. He stands up and starts pacing the floor. 'I can't believe you didn't tell me,' he mutters. 'It's not right, Hannah.'

I have to admit, I'm slightly shocked at his reaction. Nick has never been someone who I would describe as prudish. Maybe he's been having a mid-life crisis too? Oh god, what if my loving, caring, gorgeous husband has been feeling insecure and now thinks that I'm turning to Christian Grey to get my kicks?

I feel absolutely terrible.

'It's not a big deal.' The words rush out of my mouth in my eagerness to reassure him. 'Honestly.'

'It's porn, Hannah! Porn! And you think that's okay?' He stares at me in disbelief.

I stand up and meet his gaze. 'It's not porn, it's erotic fiction,' I state, more confidently than I feel. 'And you need to stop overreacting.'

'She's only sixteen, for god's sake,' Nick howls. 'Is nothing sacred anymore?'

I pause, thinking back to the books. Then I shake my head. 'Nope. She's definitely in her twenties. The plot holes feel criminal, but it's all legal, Nick.'

Nick looks at me like I'm speaking an alien language. '*Scarlet* is only sixteen,' he says. 'I'm talking about the fact that you seem to think it's fine for our daughter to read this stuff!'

'What?' I shake my head. 'I wouldn't let Scarlet read these books, and I can't imagine her wanting to. She still pretends to throw up when you give me a goodbye kiss! What are you going on about?'

Nick sinks back onto the sofa and holds the offending book in the air. 'So if Scarlet didn't hide this behind the cushion then who did?' he asks.

Oh. Right. I can see where this is heading now. I wonder if I can get away with changing my story and blaming it all on my only daughter. Would that make me the worst mother in the universe? But what am I even thinking? I am a grown-ass woman. I am allowed to read whatever I like without having to explain myself to anyone.

'I hid it.' I jut my chin in the air and defiantly await Nick's reaction. If he tries to make me feel bad then I'm going to have a meltdown. 'I've been reading the books and I hid that one there because I didn't want the kids to find it. The only mistake that I've made is not choosing a better hiding place.'

Nick leans back on the sofa and puts the book down. 'Babe.' His voice is low. 'How come I never knew you were into this stuff?'

I sit down next to him and fix him with a steely glare. 'I

am not *into* this stuff. It was research. I *am* an English teacher, you know.'

Nick sniggers. 'Whatever you say, Hannah. I wasn't aware that this was part of the GCSE curriculum. Or has Miriam got you teaching sex education now?'

I shudder and pick up my wine glass. 'Well if I was, I would definitely not be using this story as a helpful example. Woman meets man. Man is very, very rich. Woman wouldn't have looked twice at man if he were working a dead-end job for minimum wage. Man stalks woman and manipulates her into becoming his girlfriend. They have some kinky sex, which mostly involves woman being weak and powerless. The end. Repeat for the sequel.'

I take a huge slug of drink, emptying my glass.

Nick laughs. 'So there's nothing sexy about the story at all?' he asks. 'Only, I seem to remember hearing that these books made an indecent amount of money and got a whole load of people reading. They can't be that bad!'

'I didn't say that they aren't *sexy*.' I curl up on the sofa and think for a moment. 'It's just all so fake. None of the sex scenes are even recognisable. Nobody would accept any of it if Christian Grey wasn't drop-dead gorgeous and totally minted.'

'Well, if people are prepared to pay for this stuff then I guess that's up to them,' Nick says. 'And you can't have thought they were *so* awful; not if you read more than one of them.'

'It was research,' I repeat. 'That's all. I was interested to see what everyone was going on about.'

Nick puts his hand on my knee and gives it a squeeze.

'Well, I think it's great that you're broadening your horizons. We're never too old to switch things up a bit.'

I raise one eyebrow. 'I'm not sure that I know what you're talking about, Mr Thompson,' I say. 'But we still don't appear to have found the remote, so Netflix is not an option this evening.'

Nick stands up and reaches a hand down to me, pulling me off the sofa. 'I think I like having a wife who reads porn,' he mulls. 'It's quite exciting.'

I elbow him sharply in the ribs. 'If you call it porn one more time, I'm going to re-enact some of the scenes from that stupid book,' I tell him. 'One of the chapters with the pain but minus *any kind of pleasure*. Do you understand?'

'Yes, Ma'am!' Nick salutes and marches across the room. 'I actually think you're perfectly suited to life as a dominatrix, Hannah. You're bossy and controlling and you can't stand anyone doing anything that you haven't sanctioned. I think you've found your calling in life!'

He darts up the stairs before I can find a suitable item to whip him with.

Chapter 13

The pub is crowded when I arrive, but Cassie has bagged us a table in the corner. I go straight to the bar and order two glasses of Prosecco and a packet of peanuts before heading across to where she's sitting.

'Sorry I'm late,' I say, handing her a glass. 'I would have been here sooner, only Dylan decided to have a crisis about going to university and then Scarlet didn't want to be outdone so she sat on my bed while I was attempting to get ready and told me all about how stressed she is about her exams and did I know that there are literally only two months to go and why haven't we got her a tutor for Maths, even though she's never once mentioned needing extra help. Then she asked me how illegal it is to forge a bank note and looked highly shady when I asked why she wanted to know.'

I take a deep breath and sit down opposite Cassie. 'And then just when I thought it was safe to leave, Benji fell off his skateboard and landed on Dogger and Nick was incapable of providing hugs because the stupid toilet was leaking and apparently, unless I want to return home to a house filled with piss then he needed to sort it out immediately. So I left them all to it.'

I knock back half my drink. 'Does that make me a bad mother?'

Cassie laughs. 'God, no. It makes you someone who needs more than one glass of Prosecco though.'

I grin at her and feel myself starting to relax. 'So what's new? What did I miss at work on Thursday and Friday?'

'Not a lot.' Cassie rips open the peanuts and offers me the packet. 'Nothing as exciting as Mrs Knight's sex revelations!'

'Bloody hell, that was excruciating, wasn't it?' I pour myself a handful of peanuts. 'I really thought she was about to give us an X-rated description of her glory days.'

'At least she has an X-rated version,' moans Cassie, casting her eyes around the pub.

I sit back in my chair and wait for her to finish her recon; since her divorce, Cassie is constantly on the lookout for eligible men. Sadly for her, they are thin on the ground in this neck of the woods.

I glance around at the assembled males. There's Mark Rotherham who works in the butcher's – I've always thought that he would make quite a good catch apart from the minor issue that he's covered in blood for the majority of the working day. That's a tiny bit off-putting. Over at the pool table is Gary Peters. He's a personal trainer and incredibly fit and handsome. He also left our school about five years ago, which puts him firmly in the 'ewww' category. And then there's Timmo, who's definitely in the correct age group, and lives just down the road from me. With his mother. That's barrier number one, for sure. Barrier number two is the fact that he still refers to himself as Timmo. I can't look at him without picturing an enthusiastic Labrador puppy with a wagging tail.

'We need to get out more,' Cassie tells me. 'But anyway, I'm not interested in men tonight.' She brandishes her empty glass at me. 'I appear to be in need of more sustenance. Shall we just get a bottle?'

I think for a second. It's Sunday tomorrow and I need to be up at some ungodly hour to take Benji to his swimming lesson. I suppose that I can do that just as well with a hang-over. I nod.

The evening snowballs. The bubbly flows as fast as the conversation; we discuss every topic from Trump's latest cock-up to impending menopause and how we are supposed to know whether we're menopausal or actually dying, because the symptoms seem frighteningly similar. We debate the possible ways that we can avoid the Inset day and the birth reenactment, ending up in a particularly macabre conversation about all the things that we would rather do than act out our own birth.

'Have you met my mother?' Cassie splutters, brandishing her glass in the air. 'She's absolutely terrifying. It's impossible to imagine her even contemplating any kind of act that resulted in conception, never mind being forced to spend time thinking about her vagina.'

'Maybe we could change career completely?' I suggest, squinting to see her in the dim light of the pub. 'We're not too old. We could start all over again as something completely new.'

Yes. This is a brilliant and cunning plan. Cassie always has the best ideas – I'll lure her into a conversation about different jobs and then steal her best ones for myself.

Cassie's eyes light up. 'Totally! We could be astronauts! Or brain surgeons! Or dustbin men – I've always wanted to drive a bin lorry.'

'I think they're called Refuse Collectors now,' I inform her. 'And that would be a horrible job. What if you found body parts in a bin bag, like they're always doing on crime programmes?'

Cassie nods seriously. 'That is a very good point. Not bin men then.' She scans her eyes around the room. 'Maybe we could be high-end escorts? You know, the kind that get paid to go for posh meals and wear nice dresses with rich businessmen?'

I stare at her. 'You mean *women of the night*?'

'That sounds like a cheesy Mills and Boon title. But on that subject,' she leans across the table, 'tell me what you thought about the books, Hannah! I know you read them!'

I attempt a confused look for all of three seconds before caving in.

'Oh. My. God.' I pick up the bottle but it's empty. 'Where do I start?'

'I knew it!' shrieks Cassie. 'Are you going to be one of those middle-aged housewives who give their husband a heart attack by producing a set of handcuffs and a blindfold on a Saturday night after *Britain's Got Talent*?'

I snort. 'Not bloody likely. It's not exactly sexy, is it?'

Cassie stares at me. 'You're telling me that the highest-grossing book of all time, written purely about sex, isn't *sexy*? What's wrong with you, girl?'

I look across at the bar and use international sign language to signal my need for more Prosecco. Thankfully the bartender (who I taught in my Biology class six years ago) understands my request and does not interpret it as me making an obscene gesture towards him, which has happened on a previous occasion. He brings us our drinks and I wait until he leaves before replying. I am, as always, a consummate professional and do not wish to shock the younger generation.

Then I put my hands on the table and stare Cassie down. 'There's nothing wrong with me, thank you very much. It's just not very real. It's like reading the Disney version of what a relationship should be like. And I don't find that particularly sexy.'

My best friend gawps at me for a second and then bursts out laughing. 'The

Disney version? What are you on about?'

'It's fake and glossy and complete fantasy,' I tell her. 'Nobody actually behaves like that in real life. I'm surprised that nobody's thought to make a musical version. Christian Grey breaking into song about how messed up he is and how he can only find happiness through hurting women before breaking into a snazzy dance number with all his former submissives.'

'I can see it now.' Cassie holds up her hands and spreads them apart, as if weaving a magical tale.

'I'm a rich man and I like things pretty dark,' she sings loudly, to the tune of Adele's 'Rolling in the Deep'.

'Come close to me, my love and let me make my mark,' I contribute, raising my voice to match hers.

'I'll show you my playroom and the things I keep inside,' she warbles.

'If you have the slightest sense you'll run away and hide!' I finish, slamming my fist triumphantly on the table before we both collapse in a fit of cackling laughter.

It's possible that we have drunk slightly more than is good for us.

'She did make a ton of money,' says Cassie eventually, once we've calmed down. 'And she did actually write three books. That's quite an achievement.'

'But she must have written them in two minutes,' I protest. 'Honestly, Cassie! I could do a better job with my hands tied behind my back.'

'And wearing a blindfold?'

We start sniggering again, like the mature women that we are.

'I'm serious,' I tell her, pouring us each another drink. I haven't had a night out like this in months. I know that I'm going to regret it in the morning, but right now in the warm pub, I'm in a happy, Prosecco-filled bubble. 'Anyone could have written those books.'

'So do it.' Cassie peers at me over the top of her glass. 'You're an English teacher now. You have *all the words* right here.' She wiggles her fingers in the air. 'All the words at your disposal, Hannah. You could totally write your own erotica!'

'I do know a lot of the words,' I agree, nodding slowly. 'How hard can it be?'

'I think it has to be pretty hard,' snorts Cassie. 'Flaccid or limp or drooping isn't really going to cut it.'

I spit a mouthful of drink across the table. 'Cassie! You're shameless!'

My inebriated friend gives me a wicked grin. 'And that's what you're going to have to be, if you're going to write this stuff,' she informs me. 'One hundred per cent brazen and utterly raunch-tastic. You need to write the most erotic-est, sexiest book out there and then whack it online so that all the mummies can download it onto their Kindles and read it in private. That's a thing, isn't it? Mummy porn?'

She's right. I could do this. I can write about hunky men and their craven ways. I can be sexy and erotic. This could be my reinvention. *Hannah Thompson – Licence to Thrill*.

'But I haven't tried to write anything since before Dylan was born.' I think back to the last thing that I remember writing. 'Although actually, it was pretty good, if I say so myself.'

Cassie looks interested. 'What was it? I didn't know you'd ever written anything, you dark horse.'

I smile to myself, lost in the beauty of the words. 'It was a poem.' I sit up, trying to get the words straight in my mind. 'Something beautiful about daffodils and clouds and wandering along all by myself.'

There is a pause and then Cassie smirks at me.

'I'm pretty sure you didn't write that, Hannah. Even I've heard that poem and I teach Chemistry.'

Oh. Bugger. I think she might be right.

I sink back down and frown. 'What if I can't do it? What if I write it and it's rubbish?'

Cassie shrugs. 'What if it is? Are you not even going to try, just in case you can't do it?'

Her words remind me of something I said to Dylan only last week when he was worrying about his A Levels. Thinking of Dylan brings up an even greater concern.

'What if anyone found out that I was writing stuff like that, though?' I glance around the room, imagining the stares and the judgement. 'What if I write something rude and my kids get to hear about it? It would traumatise them for life!'

Cassie is unimpressed, I can tell. She puts down her glass and looks at me with disappointment in her eyes.

'Number one: who cares what anyone thinks? Number two: erotic fiction isn't rude, Hannah. It's a long-established and well-respected genre of literature.' She fixes me with a piercing gaze. 'Do you think that *sex* is rude and something that shouldn't be talked about?'

I shake my head. 'No! Absolutely not.'

Although there's a time and a place, obviously.

'Number three: your kids will never need to know anything about it, will they? This is something that *you're* doing, not them. And number four: you never know, you might even make a few quid off the back of it. Sex sells, Hannah. It's the oldest trade in the world.'

She makes some very reasonable points. And it isn't as if I've got a whole lot of other options right now. I can't exactly choose to be fussy.

'Are you up for it, Hannah?' Cassie's voice breaks through my thoughts.

I pause, possibility buzzing through my veins, although that might just be the fizz. I haven't felt this excited in ages. The idea of spending my non-teaching days at home, being a writer, is intoxicating, exhilarating and glamorous. It is exactly what I need to get me out of my mid-life slump.

I raise my glass in the air, ignoring the sensation of cold liquid splashing down my arm. 'I am absolutely up for it!' I proclaim. 'I will write some smutty, cheesy, glossy fake sex and you,' I point at Cassie, my arm wobbling with the effort of holding itself up, 'you will be the first person to read it!'

Cassie bangs her glass on the table. 'Cheers to that!' she shouts. 'Cheers. To. That!'

It's gone midnight when I finally stagger into the house. I am being as quiet as a very, incredibly quiet mouse who has lost her squeak, so I am surprised when Nick emerges from the living room, yawning and rubbing his eyes.

'Did I wake you up?' I whisper.

He winces and puts his finger to his lips. 'Stop yelling, Hannah – you'll wake the kids! And no – I was waiting up for you.' He walks down the hallway and helps me take off my coat, which is super helpful of him as for some reason I have forgotten whether I should be pulling the zipper up or down. 'You know that I can't go to bed when you're not home.'

'You are a very lovely man,' I slur, kicking off my heels. 'I don't think I appreciate you enough, you know?'

'I do know,' agrees Nick, putting his arm around me and leading me towards the stairs. 'But don't worry about it, babe.'

I stop and clutch the banister, turning to look at him.

'I've got something to tell you. Something important.'

'Can it wait until morning?' he asks. 'When you might actually be able to speak coherently?'

'No!' I grab his arm. 'S'important, Nick! I need to tell you now!'

Nick sighs. 'Just for the record, I am going to take anything that comes out of your mouth with a supreme dose of salt.'

I scowl at him. 'S'got nothing to do with salt.'

I slump down onto the stairs and after a second, Nick joins me.

'Come on then. What's so important that we have to talk about it *right* now?'

I pause for dramatic effect, then emit a loud, Prosecco-fuelled burp that reverberates around the upstairs landing.

'I am going to write a book!' I announce, watching Nick's face for his reaction. 'A real, actual book!'

He is not as excited as I thought he'd be.

'That's great,' he tells me, standing up and pulling me gently by the elbow. 'Now let's get you into bed and you can sleep it off. I'll take Benji to his swimming lesson tomorrow – I don't think you're going to be in a fit state to drive.'

'Did you hear me?' I protest. 'I'm going to be a writer, Nick! A lovely, lovely writer! I am going to waft around the house all day, getting inspired. And then I will pour out my musings onto the page and it will all be marvellous.'

'So what are you going to write?' he asks, propelling me into the bedroom. 'And where are your pyjamas?'

I smile at him, trying to look alluring and mysterious. 'Sex,' I say and finally I have his attention.

'Are you sure?' Nick looks conflicted. 'I really think you should just get some sleep, Hannah. I haven't seen you this pissed in ages.'

I bat away his comments. 'No – I'm going to *write* about sex. You know. Like the *Fifty Shades* books!'

'Porn!' Nick's face breaks into a wide beam. '*You're* going to write porn?'

'It. Is. Not. Porn,' I say, flopping face first onto the bed. 'It's erotica. And it's not rude or dirty or embarrassing in any way, for your information.'

'I didn't say it was,' says Nick. 'And don't go to sleep yet. You need to drink some water first.'

'You are quite nice to me,' I mutter. 'I like you.'

'I like you too, you old lush.' Nick pulls me up to a sitting position and holds the glass in front of me. 'What's going to happen in this not-rude sex book, then?'

I take a big gulp of water and hand him back the glass before starting to take off my tights. 'Not sure. I need to think about a plot. I'll start tomorrow. When my brain is working properly.'

'You'd better let me read it.' Nick pulls back the duvet cover. 'And if you want a research partner then I'm your man.'

I try to answer him but the buttons on my shirt are being particularly challenging. I decide that pyjamas are overrated and that going to bed in tonight's clothes is cost-effective and will save on laundry, or something to that effect. And then my head is on the pillow and the light is out and I sink into a very deep sleep that mostly consists of strange, vivid dreams about walking round the supermarket with Christian Grey and him acting like a toddler, insisting on filling the trolley with unsuitable sugary cereals and fizzy drinks and packets of Wotsits.

Chapter 14

By the time I get up on Sunday morning, Nick has taken Benji to his swimming lesson, done the shopping and put a roast dinner in the oven. I stagger into the kitchen, wondering if I can get away without anybody noticing how hungover I am.

My powers of delusion never cease to amaze me.

'Daddy took me swimming and then bought me hot chocolate!' Benji hurtles across the room and throws himself at me. 'And I managed to swim nearly a whole length underwater!'

I glance towards the oven where Nick is basting the lamb.

'Thank you,' I mouth at him. He blows me a kiss in return.

'You look like a celebrity, Mummy.' Benji gazes up at me and I feel a warm glow of happiness. It's true what they say. Mothers really are the centre of their little boys' universes.

'Which celebrity do I look like?' I ask, bending down and dropping a kiss on top of his damp head. I'm hanging out for Angelina Jolie, but I'll take Posh Spice at a push.

Benji's forehead wrinkles up in thought. 'I don't know. But you look like those photographs in the paper when a famous person comes out of a hospital with a bandage wrapped round their head.'

Scarlet walks in, just in time to hear this proclamation. She takes one look at me and bursts out laughing. 'He means plastic surgery!' She gives me an appraising look. 'Your face does look a bit puffy, Mum. And what's with the sunglasses?'

I pat my hands against my skin, hoping that my cool palms might help reduce the apparent swelling. Clearly the alcohol has migrated to my cheeks. I am a Prosecco hamster, storing it in my pouches for emergency purposes.

'I'm just feeling a little bit fragile this morning,' I explain, ignoring the snort that comes from over by the oven. 'And the sun is very low in the sky at this time of year, which can make it quite harsh on the eyes.'

'I heard you trying to get your key in the front door last night.' Scarlet's voice is sly. 'It took you long enough. Just how drunk were you?'

'I was not drunk,' I snap. 'I was merry. Which, as a forty-three-year-old woman, is something that I am absolutely entitled to be, now and again.'

Scarlet sits down at the kitchen table and starts painting her nails in a lurid yellow colour that makes me feel sick.

'We've been learning about the impact of alcohol in Biology,' she informs me. 'Sir showed us a video about a woman who drinks *way* less than you, Mum, and her body was a right mess. Would you consider having a liver function test, just to see if you've done any damage?'

I stare at her in horror.

'Are you saying that you think I'm an alcoholic?' I ask. 'Because I can assure you, I most definitely am not.'

I've been on the DrinkAware app several times over the last few months. It has reassured me that as long as I do not *regularly* exceed the recommended number of alcoholic units every week, then I am just fine and dandy, thank you very much. It does not actually give a definition of exactly how much *regularly* means; for that, I am thankful.

Scarlet grins up at me and I know that she knows she's hit a nerve. 'I don't think you're an *actual* alcoholic,' she says, slowly. 'But I wouldn't want to drink as much as you and Dad do.'

Nick makes a warning noise in the back of his throat. *Remember the rules, Hannah.* Do not engage. Do not negotiate. And above all, do not try to justify yourself to your offspring.

'Well, *I* wouldn't want you to drink as much as we do either,' I tell her. 'Because *you* are still a *child*.'

I turn, feeling like my response was sensible and calm and measured. I have nipped this attempt at insubordination in the bud. I am a parenting guru, even when my head is banging and my legs feel like they've been replaced with two strands of spaghetti.

'And also,' I whirl back to face her, 'just for your information, we never used to drink. In fact, we barely touched alcohol until you and your brother became teenagers. Think about *that* the next time that you're concerned about my liver.'

'Oh, that's nice,' snaps Scarlet. 'So if you die from cirrhosis then it's all my fault, then?'

'Not just your fault,' points out Benji. 'It'll be Dylan's fault too.'

'Nobody is dying,' soothes Nick, draining the carrots into a colander. 'Benji, lay the table. Scarlet, fill the water jug.' He turns to me. 'Why don't you just sit down, Hannah?'

'You're wrong, you know,' mutters Scarlet, stomping across to the cupboard. 'We're all dying. It's crazy really that we call it living. We're just counting down the days until we're dead.'

My daughter is a proper little ray of sunshine sometimes.

I am saved from having to comment by the sight of Dylan strolling through the door, making our happy family complete. As always, Dylan is not alone. A noisy aura surrounds him: he is incapable of going anywhere without his very own soundtrack. Normally I am open to all new music but today, in my current tender state, it's just too much.

'For goodness' sake, Dylan.' I cringe as he walks towards me, his phone blasting out what sounds like Bedlam and Hades rolled into one. 'Turn that racket off. What even is it? It sounds terrible!'

Dylan plonks himself down into the seat opposite and looks at me, his mouth curving up at the sides as he registers my sunglasses.

'Asshole.'

And that is absolutely it. My last nerve has been trampled on one time too many. I'll show these ungrateful, disrespectful teenagers that I am not here to be abused and bad-mouthed and generally treated like something that they've trodden in.

'I have had enough!' I roar, making my head throb. Over by the sink, Scarlet fumbles with the water jug. We all freeze for a long second while it starts its descent towards our unforgiving floor tiles before she miraculously manages to catch it.

'I will *not* be spoken to like this in my own home. Or in anyone else's home, for that matter.' I stand up and place my hands on the table, leaning forward to get right into Dylan's face. 'I don't understand what I've done to deserve such treatment and I don't know what makes you suddenly think that it's okay to behave like a thuggish yob when you've always been so bloody lovely. I can only imagine that your hormones have gone psychotic and that this is some kind of weird transition for leaving home and that you think by calling me rude names it'll make it easier for you to make the break, but it's all so pointless and unfair and I didn't sign up to be called "asshole" in my kitchen when I am quietly sitting *minding my own business*!'

I pause to catch my breath, the sound of my loud panting competing with the cacophony pouring out of the speaker that Dylan has put down on the table. Nick and Scarlet and Benji have all frozen in position, stilled by my outburst, while Dylan gawps at me with his mouth open.

And I am glad that they are shocked into silence. I have shown them that I am not to be messed with.

Call me names at your peril. I am woman. My bite is infinitely worse than my bark. Go ahead, punks. Disrespect me one more time. Make my freaking day.

'Permission to speak?' ventures Dylan after a few moments have passed.

I nod. 'Granted.'

Never let it be said that I am not gracious in victory.

'The song is called "Asshole", Mother.' He jerks his chin towards the speaker. 'The song. You asked me what it was and I told you. "Asshole", by Eminem.'

Oh. Bugger.

I think I might have overreacted just a tiny bit.

Nick comes to the rescue. 'Let's all sit down and enjoy this delicious meal that I have spent all sodding morning preparing,' he says. 'Dylan – if we have to listen to music then perhaps you can find something more acceptable to your mother's delicate disposition?'

Dylan grimaces and turns his phone off. 'I'd rather listen to silence than any of the banal crap that you guys think is music.'

I close my eyes. 'Silence will be just lovely.'

Everyone sits down and Nick passes out the food. For a few minutes, the only sounds are of cutlery clattering against the edges of plates, and contented groans. I start to relax, feeling the gravy-soaked meat hitting my stomach, providing a very welcome protective layer. This is exactly what I needed. Maybe after lunch I'll go and curl up on the sofa and have a little snooze before attacking the illiterate ramblings of my Year Nine English class.

'Watch it! If you break that then you're paying for it!' Dylan's shouts interrupt my thoughts. I look up to see that Benji is dangling the gravy boat perilously close to Dylan's speaker and phone. We got him the speaker for Christmas and, if I remember correctly, it was fairly expensive.

'You shouldn't have either of those on the table,' Nick tells him. 'They're your property so they're your responsibility.'

'Yeah, well, you wanted me to play some chilled tunes a minute ago,' Dylan reminds his dad. 'Make your mind up.'

I see Nick's jaw tighten and I steel myself to leap in and de-escalate the situation. Thankfully, Benji gets there first.

'Why does your speaker have "Anker" written on the side?' he asks, carefully putting the gravy boat back on the table. 'It's a weird name.'

Dylan reaches for the offending items and twists in his chair to place them out of harm's way. 'It's just the name of the brand,' he says. 'And it's no weirder than other names.' He looks at his little brother. 'If you think about it, Benji is a bit of a weird name. You would suit Anker far better.'

Benji sits up straight, his face reddening. 'My name isn't weird!' he squawks. 'It's not, is it, Mum?'

'It's a brilliant name,' I tell him. 'Dad and I chose it for you because we knew that you were going to be a brilliant boy.'

'And Anker isn't a good name, is it?' Benji has decided to take this conversation to heart and I glare at my oldest son, trying to let him know that I am *not happy* about having to placate his brother.

'It'd make a fab name for Dylan, though,' mumbles Scarlet through a mouthful of potato. 'Especially if it had a w in front of it. Maybe you could change his name by deed poll at the same time that you actually get round to spelling my name correctly with *two ts*.'

At the far end of the table, Nick makes a choking noise and I have to work hard to keep the corners of my mouth from tugging into a grin. Dylan, thinking that I haven't noticed, flicks two fingers up at his sister.

'Can we all please eat this meal?' Nick begs, recovering from his coughing fit. 'Just twenty minutes pretending that we are all capable of spending quality family time together and then you can all go and plug yourselves into whatever devices are currently floating your boat.'

I load my fork with some carrots and peas and take a big mouthful.

'*Wanker*!'

I spit my peas across the table where they join the food that has been unceremoniously ejected from the mouths of Nick, Dylan and Scarlet.

'I worked it out!' Benji is exuberant. 'If you have Anker and you put a w in front then you make—'

'No!' For the first time all mealtime, four voices are united in utter harmony. 'Do *not* say it again, for the love of god!'

Later, when the clearing up has been done and the children have all migrated to different parts of the house, Nick and I snuggle up on the sofa.

'So, how much do you remember about the conversation we had last night?' Nick starts, giving me a grin. 'You were pretty out of it, Hannah.'

I grimace. 'I know. I'm blaming Cassie – she's a bad influence.'

'You said some fairly interesting stuff.' Nick stretches out his legs. 'You know, about writing some steamy fiction?'

I lean my head back and close my eyes. I haven't forgotten; of course I haven't. It was the first thing that I thought about this morning and it's been a presence in the back of my mind all day. I know that I drank far too much last night and that Cassie and I were talking complete and utter crap by the end of the evening, but this idea just won't leave me alone.

'Do you think I could do it, then?' I relax into the cushions, drowsy and full of roast dinner. 'Do you think I could write a book?'

Nick's leg pushes against mine. 'I have absolutely no doubt,' he tells me. His voice is sincere and when I crank open my eyes, he is looking at me with a serious expression on his face. 'The Hannah that I met was convinced that she could rule the world, if she chose to. You haven't changed that much. If you want to do this then you should give it a go. What have you got to lose?'

'My dignity? My reputation?'

Nick snorts. 'You'd better start writing then.'

I sit up, suddenly wide awake. 'But I haven't got a clue where to start. I don't know the first thing about erotic fiction. I don't think reading *Fifty Shades* necessarily qualifies me for writing my own book.'

'So do what you're good at,' Nick tells me. For a moment my brain whirs as I wonder where he's going with this. 'You never do anything without finding out every single last thing about it. You won't let us plan a holiday without weeks of exhausting conversation about locations and travel distances and fuel prices and accommodation details. And you're the only person in the known universe who actually understands electricity tariffs.'

I am not sure how my obsession with not getting ripped

off by utility companies will equip me to write about sex, but Nick hasn't finished.

'Research, Hannah!' he says. 'Do your research! Find out everything that there is to know about writing in this genre and then do it yourself.'

Just occasionally, every now and again and usually in the vicinity of a blue moon, my husband has some very intelligent ideas.

Chapter 15

I wait until Benji is tucked up in bed and Dylan is out with Zoe, who appears to have become his new girlfriend without me really noticing it happening. Scarlet is in her room, supposedly revising for her exams while simultaneously tapping out Snapchat messages to her friends and watching a programme on Netflix about teenagers who live in a small town that just happens to be plagued with a serial killer. I tried asking her if it was suitable because it didn't sound very nice, but she laughed at me and said that it was preparing her for real life. And then she said that I might not have noticed, but she is actually sixteen years old now and the days of her reading *Milly Molly Mandy* before bedtime are long gone.

I left her in peace when she started talking about how *Milly Molly Mandy Turns Psycho* could be a winning film title.

I check that Nick is still in the shower and then grab my laptop and head into the kitchen. I don't want him to know what I'm doing, even though he's been nothing but supportive. If he knows about it then we'll have to talk about it and I don't want to scare the idea away.

Plus, this is embarrassing. Not that it should be, because

sex isn't embarrassing, obviously. It's normal and natural and the survival of the human species depends upon it, so actually it would be weirder if I *weren't* learning about erotica, when you think about it. It's all just biology in the end. I'm good at biology.

Closing the door, I sit down at the table and open up the laptop lid. Then I navigate to the appropriate website and click through to the e-book section. I scroll down the list and decide that 'Literature and Fiction' will be a good start. Then, for the first time in my entire life, I take a deep breath and click on 'Erotica' before quickly scrunching my eyes shut.

I'm briefly reminded of the time that I watched *Silence of the Lambs* when I was around Scarlet's age. My best friend somehow got a copy on video and we waited until her mum was out to huddle together on her sofa and watch it in full VCR glory. The illicit thrill had been completely ruined by the terror that I would instantly turn into a psychopath, as threatened by the morality brigade. I spent weeks afterwards interrogating myself and probing the innermost parts of my mind to check for murderous musings, but the most sinister thoughts that I could muster were for my GCSE Maths teacher, and I just wanted her to get a job somewhere else, not actually die.

I am not entirely sure what I'm anticipating. Part of my brain is almost expecting a siren to go off, alerting one and all to the fact that I have just entered a forbidden part of the Internet. But there are no alarms, and when I steel myself and glance tentatively at the screen in front of me, it is definitely less terrifying than I had imagined it would be.

The page is filled with images of book covers, the majority of which are in black and white and feature scantily clad men and women. These are not the kind of men and women that I would expect see in the aisles of my local supermarket. These fine specimens of humankind presumably bring traffic to a standstill every time they step out of their front door. I peer closer at one man who is wearing a pair of tightly fitting jeans and nothing else, which is slightly impractical as he is sitting astride a rather large motorbike. His tattoos are prominent, but what grabs my attention is the pair of absolutely massive man-breasts that he is sporting. They're bigger than mine, although he doesn't seem to be fighting the same battle with gravity that I am facing. I suspect Photoshop has been involved in the production of this particular image.

I scan through the titles, cringing at the tackiness of it all. But I'm not here to judge, I'm here to learn, and I don't have much time. I click onto one book with the word 'Playboy' in the title, which sounds fairly promising, and then double-check that I have selected 'Hannah's e-reader' for delivery. Nick and I share an account with the kids and I do *not* want this book ending up on any of their devices. I then choose another book, which, confusingly, seems to be about a vampire, and then a third, with a title that makes me cringe so much that I am struggling to believe that anyone would actually purchase it. But Nick was right – I like to be thorough in my research. I need to read around the whole area if I'm going to get a good understanding of the task ahead.

Once I've downloaded all three books, I select the first book about the playboy. It seems like it might be the least intimidating. I start skimming through the pages as fast as possible, scanning the words and logging the pertinent details in my head as I read.

1. First, we are introduced to an incredibly wealthy and improbably gorgeous young man who has everything that a person could ever want, including sex whenever he feels like it, which is basically all the time. Literally. All. The. Time.
2. Enter a feisty, intelligent young woman who has been living a successful and fulfilled life until she meets aforementioned wealthy and gorgeous young man. He manages to suck her brain out through her ears within two minutes of catching her eye across a crowded room. This is presumably why vampires are popular in this genre – the brain-sucking must be more literal and less figurative in those books.
3. The wealthy and gorgeous young man suddenly realises that he has been living a lie and that there is more to life than he previously understood. Even though he has everything that money can buy, the only thing that he really wants is to have All Of The Sex, All Of The Time with the now-brainless young woman.
4. The gorgeous man proceeds to act in a distinctly creepy and stalkerish manner. We discover that the brainless woman has not been given advice from her mother on how to deal with unwanted attention.
5. The brainless woman rides a rollercoaster of feelings over the course of the next twenty-four hours, ranging from

mild perturbation that the gorgeous man would even want to talk to her, to concern that her new beau appears to be a bit of a freak with a fetish that makes her squirm with discomfort. She then swings wildly towards a desire to please him and make up for the deficiencies in his emotional life, before protesting that she is a strong, independent woman who will never submit. This is followed by her complete and utter submission. She ends up sweet and slightly confused, with no understanding of the fact that she has just been royally screwed.

I sit back in my chair and slurp my now-cold cup of tea. This stuff is unbelievable, and I mean that literally. I know I'm not an expert but it feels completely formulaic, like there's a rulebook on how to create erotic fiction.

Because it *is* fiction, isn't it? Of course it is. I sip my drink and wonder about the person who wrote this particular epic. Does he or she really think that this is what regular people do when they're alone? How very sad for them.

Suddenly, the quiz that I took in Elise's magazine pops into my mind. Maybe there *are* real people out there who could answer A for each question. People who happily strut their stuff with confidence and don't spend the entire time debating whether to lie on their back and make their stomach look flatter but risk losing each breast under an armpit, or whether to get more adventurous and let it all hang out; and I do mean that quite literally.

Is it possible that this is what all the regular people are doing? What if everyone else in the world is getting it on with the help of props and food items and Nick and I failed to get the memo? How are we supposed to know? The last thing I expected to feel when I read this stuff was threatened and inadequate, for god's sake.

I didn't pay any attention to the names of the authors when I chose the books. I flip open my laptop lid and wake up the screen. Then I navigate back to the first page and run my eyes down the list.

Candy Love.

Kitty Strange.

These are clearly not real people. Candy Love sounds like the name of a girl band. Kitty Strange is a serial killer. These authors are as fictitious as their plotlines.

I breathe out loudly and remind myself that I am reading this for research. And so what if the rest of the adult population *is* more exciting in the bedroom than we are? So what, Candy Love? I am a strong, independent and empowered woman and I am absolutely not going to allow one stupid and, frankly, badly written book to challenge my self-esteem. No way.

But while I'm sitting here, I might skim quickly through one of the other titles, just to get a good understanding of the market. It can't hurt to be thorough. If I happen to pick up a few top tips in the process then I'm sure they'll come in very handy when I start writing. Or next time I find myself needing to spice things up a bit.

Chapter 16

I decide to start my next lesson with Year Nine, Class C with a quick dictation exercise to focus on spellings and speed writing. Once everyone has settled down and found a pen (I long for the day that the whole class will arrive with a well-stocked pencil case, but I fear that I might as well long for the moon), I grab a textbook filled with short writing extracts and start to read.

'In the summer of 1015, a Viking fleet set sail for England. The invasion force was led by a man who came from a long line of Scandinavian rulers and his name was King Cnut.'

'You're reading too fast, miss,' complains Wayne. 'I can't write that quickly.'

'You can't write at all!' quips Brody, gaining a snigger from the rest of the class.

'That's enough.' I glare at anyone who dares to make eye contact with me. 'I will repeat the second sentence one more time. "The invasion force was led by a man who came from a long line of Scandinavian rulers and his name was King Cnut."'

'How do you spell that, miss?' asks Elise. At the same time,

I see Vincent trying to reach across the gap between the desks and jab Wayne with a pair of compasses.

'Vincent!' I stride across the floor. 'Hand that to me immediately. And the King's name is spelt C – U – N—'

My brain finally catches up with my mouth, leaving the final letter hanging on my lips.

'I mean, it's spelt C – N—'

But it is far, far too late. Of course it is. This class of thirteen and fourteen year-olds who never listen to a damn word that I say are *all* listening the one single time that I spectacularly mess up.

'Oh my god!' screeches Elise. 'Miss! You did not just say that!'

'Miss made me write a rude word in my book!' yells Brody.

'The *worst* word,' adds Wayne, with relish. 'I've written it too!'

'And me!' shouts Vincent and then the room is filled with the sound of kids proclaiming that they have written the foulest of foul words in their English books.

And that I made them do it.

There is only one way to handle this situation.

'Okay, calm down.' I cross my arms and let my gaze roam across the class. 'Everyone settle down. There's no need for all this fuss. I'm sure that *nobody* was daft enough to write the wrong word, just because I mixed up my letters.'

'I was daft enough!' screeches Vincent. 'Look!'

He holds up his book and even from here I can see *the word*, firmly printed on his page. It appears to be the only word that Vincent has actually spelt correctly.

'So was I,' Brody tells me. I frown as another book is held up and then another and another until almost the entire class is brandishing their English books in the air and I am confronted with a sea of expletives.

I remember the story of King Cnut proving that he couldn't turn back the tide and feel his pain.

Slowly, I walk alongside the desks, staring at each book. The writing is mostly illegible, a scrawled mess of ink and blotches and crossings out. The Danish king's misspelt name stands out in stark contrast. In Wayne's book, it appears to be the only word that he has actually written today, which is an improvement on yesterday's effort. Not that I can reward him for writing *the word* in capital letters across his entire page.

Miriam will annihilate me if she catches wind of this incident. In fact, she'll probably get my teaching certificate revoked and I'll never work again.

I say nothing, but my brain is working overtime as I head back down the other side of the classroom. By the time I reach my desk I am ready to conduct some damage limitation.

'Who wants to watch a film for the rest of the lesson?' I ask. 'I've got *The Lion King* on DVD.'

Twenty-five hands shoot into the air. The twenty-sixth remains firmly planted on the desk in front of her.

'We're supposed to be studying Shakespeare,' she states. 'Some of us do actually want to get an education, you know.'

There's always bloody one. I resist the urge to ask Elise exactly who she thinks she is, coming in here with her fancy-pants talk of aspiration and self-improvement, and smile sweetly at her.

'And an education you will absolutely be getting,' I tell her, swiping the disc from my drawer and ramming it into the computer. 'It's a well-known fact that *The Lion King* has a similar plot to Hamlet. A king murdered by his own brother. A young prince who is exiled and who receives a visit from his father from beyond the grave.'

I press play and start walking around the room, gathering up all the books.

'Did you bring popcorn, miss?' enquires Brody, putting his feet up on the desk. 'Because popcorn might help me to forget that terrible word you made us write.'

'There will be no popcorn,' I snarl. 'And if you carry on like that then I might well be asking you to write a summary of all the similarities between the relationship of Hamlet with his brother, Claudius and of Mufasa with *his* brother, Scar.'

Brody shudders. 'I think we'll cope without the popcorn.'

I nod approvingly and then spend the next fifty minutes going through each of the books, liberally applying corrector fluid to *the word* and writing it correctly over the top. When I get to Wayne's book I realise that I'm running low on supply so I rip out the offending page, glancing up to make sure that I'm not being watched. Fortunately for me, Year Nine, Class C are entranced by the film, most of them singing along to 'I Just Can't Wait to Be King' with a surprising lack of self-consciousness. I do feel a slight pang of guilt when I spot Elise with her head down, feverishly making notes on a scrap of paper, but then I remember the disparaging look she has in her eyes whenever I speak to her and I get over it.

By the time the bell rings, order has been restored. The

class gets to their feet and Vincent sticks his foot out, tripping Wayne up as he walks down the aisle. Wayne starts shrieking at him, telling anyone who will listen that he's going to punch Vincent in the face at lunchtime and then Brody wades in to break it up (or cause more trouble) and I end up threatening a week's worth of detentions if they don't all leave my sight this instant.

They tumble out of the room, bags hanging from shoulders and voices raised in the excitement of a potential fight. And I know that I should probably keep Wayne and Vincent behind and warn them of the consequences of any further altercations but I'm just so pleased that the earlier incident appears to have been forgotten and they're both as bad as each other, really. Besides, I've seen these boys in action and honestly, it's like watching kittens playing rough-house. If it was one of the girls threatening to get physical then I'd be worried, but Vincent and Wayne aren't capable of walking the walk.

Plus there's always the hope that they'll either knock some sense into each other or get excluded.

It is the first proper sunny day of the year. From down below, the sound of approximately eight hundred and ninety-six teenagers enjoying the freedom of lunchtime wafts in through the open windows. Here in the staffroom, the entirety of the teaching staff is huddled on chairs and perched on tables while Miriam lectures us on the upcoming lesson observations.

'They're nothing to worry about!' she trills, shuffling through a file of papers. 'Don't think of it as being judged –

we're observing you purely in the capacity of offering professional support.'

'Last time they did observations they started poor old Kurt on incompetence proceedings,' Peter mutters to me.

We both look across the room at where Kurt Jenkins, one of the Maths teachers, is staring in confusion at a box of teabags as if he's unsure about what to do with them.

'To be fair, he is a teeny little bit incompetent,' I whisper back. 'I can't remember the last time that anyone in his class actually passed Maths. Lovely man though. Very avid cyclist, apparently.'

Kurt shakes his head at the box and puts it down, reaching instead for the coffee.

'So we'll be seeing each of you over the next month,' continues Miriam. 'Apologies if you end up having to wait for a few weeks, but we've decided that in the spirit of true professional development, it would be beneficial to sit in on a whole lesson and there's a lot of you to get through.'

She looks at the Head, who is slumped in a corner of the room playing Candy Crush on his phone. He used to be fairly dynamic before Miriam was appointed as his deputy. I think she's worn him down with her relentless enthusiasm. It won't surprise any of us if he's gone by the end of the year.

There's a pause while her words sink in.

And then there is uproar.

'You're observing us for an entire hour?' howls Danny. 'That's totally unfair!'

Adele stands up and starts pacing around the crowded room. 'I can't keep Year Nine together for six minutes, never mind sixty,' she says. 'You can't watch me teaching them – you just can't.'

I am going to lose my job. Miriam has probably orchestrated this entire situation just so that she can get rid of me. Everyone else is just collateral damage – it's me that she's after.

Cassie grins at me from across the table. 'I'd have thought you would have had them under control by now, Adele?' she calls out. 'What happened to calming the savage beast through the medium of interpretive dance and mindfulness techniques?'

'Year Nine would make a savage beast look like a pussy cat,' snaps back Adele. 'I'm considering banning the entire year group from the Drama department – you should see what they did to my props cupboard last week.'

Isobel stands up and I look at her in surprise. Since she started here in September she's barely spoken when the whole staff is gathered together. She taps on the table to get everyone's attention.

'Just so you all know, I am the new union representative now that Kurt is – well, ermm, you know.' She falters and looks anxiously at Kurt, who has finally managed to make his drink and is leaning against the fridge looking relaxed.

'Now that Kurt is pursuing pastures new,' he calls, helping her out.

There's a smattering of applause and Kurt smiles at us all. 'From September, I will be the new manager at Pizza Parade,' he says. 'I'm ready to move on now really, but I don't want to let the kids down, so I'll be here until the end of term.'

There are murmurs of 'good of you,' and 'so dedicated'. I join in while making a mental note to talk to Nick about whether we can afford that Maths tutor for Scarlet, just for a few weeks until the exams are done.

'Anyway.' Isobel clears her throat. 'I'm the union rep and so if any of you feel that this observation violates your teacher rights in any way, you know where I am.'

She sits down and there is silence. Beside me, Peter's shoulders shake and I can tell that he's struggling not to lose it. The very idea of anyone giving the slightest consideration to our rights is cause for amusement.

'That's very sweet of you, Isobel.' Miriam does not sound like she thinks there is anything remotely sweet about Isobel's announcement. 'However, I think everyone will agree that observations and appraisals are a positive and beneficial part of the school year, yes?'

She looks around the room. Nobody speaks. Miriam is undeterred.

'In fact, only the other day I was reading about a school who schedule weekly peer-to-peer observations.' She turns to the Head. 'I was going to talk to you about it, actually. It's a really innovative process, using peer coaching to identify areas of strength and weakness. For example, Danny from Physics would watch Peter from English and give him feedback about his teaching strategies and methods, providing him with a list of areas for improvement. And then Peter would return the favour the following week. What do you think?'

Nobody gets to find out what the Head thinks about this

terrible plan, because before any of us can even blink, Peter is out of his seat.

'There's no need for any silly union talk,' he tells Isobel, who sinks back into her chair looking embarrassed. 'We're teachers. Having our rights violated is part of the job! Not even Amnesty International is interested in us!'

His empty laugh echoes around the room.

'So you're coming in to watch us for an hour, you say?' He bares his teeth at Miriam in an approximation of a smile. 'Where do we sign up?'

The meeting ends, finally, and people start to drift out of the room.

'Tell me that Brandon Hopkins threw a desk at my head and put me in a coma,' groans Peter, his head slumped into his hands. 'Please tell me that I'm currently lying in Intensive Care, hooked up to a life support machine, and I'm having the weirdest and worst dream ever imaginable?'

'Sorry.' I pat his hand. 'It is a sad fact of reality that you just supported Miriam in a staff meeting *and* volunteered to go first in the lesson observations.'

'It was worth it though.' Peter shudders. 'The very thought of that twerpish boy giving *me* feedback on *my* lessons when he's been in teaching for all of two minutes is enough to make me consider early retirement.'

'I still think it's a violation of the educational code of conduct,' complains Isobel. 'They can't just demand to come into our classrooms and stay for as long as they like. It's distracting and off-putting.'

'They can,' I tell her. 'They can do whatever they want. Didn't you read your contract?'

Isobel flushes and shakes her head. 'They said on my teaching course that we'd only ever be watched for twenty minutes at a time. I can cope for twenty minutes, but an hour? I've never had a lesson that's good for the whole time.'

'None of us have,' says Peter, reassuringly. 'It isn't possible.'

'He's right,' adds Danny, coming across to our side of the room. 'They've done studies on it and the evidence was totally conclusive. Nobody can be expected to teach a lesson to a room full of teenagers and not have at least three disasters. That's the average rate, by the way. One disaster every twenty minutes.'

I think about the English lesson that I've just taught to Year Nine, Class C.

'I'd say that's quite a conservative estimate, to be honest,' I tell Danny. 'Are you sure the research didn't say that the average was twenty disasters every three minutes?'

There's a pause while we all consider the implications of being observed for an entire hour. Over by the fridge, Kurt unwraps a bar of chocolate and takes a loud bite.

'There may well be vacancies going at Pizza Parade,' he says. 'But I won't have room for you all. I can only employ the most skilled.' He scrunches up the wrapper. 'And it's minimum wage, obviously.'

The bell rings and I pick up my bag. On the outside I hope I am still managing to fake the look of a calm, professional teacher, but inside, my stomach is churning and my brain is whirring. I have got to do something about this situation. If

Miriam observes me teaching a whole lesson then I'll probably be fired instantly. And I can't afford to work for Kurt at Pizza Parade – not that I could even be assured of a position by the sound of it. I'm not exactly an expert at making dough.

The time has come to stick my courage to whatever place it is that you're supposed to stick it to. I will stick it to anyone who doubts me. I will stick it to The Man. I will write my book and somehow figure out how to get it published.

And then I will start practising my dough-kneading techniques.

Chapter 17

I am woken by a terrible screeching noise. Swinging my legs out of bed, I hit the ground running and race out of the room only a step behind Nick.

We sprint across the landing and barge into Benji's room, where I scan the surroundings to see exactly what or who is causing our youngest child to scream like he's being tortured.

'What's wrong?' pants Nick, running over to Benji who is yelling his head off in the middle of his bed, entangled in his duvet. 'What's the matter?'

Benji pauses and looks up at us with a stricken expression on his face. 'It's Fluffy Rocket,' he gulps. 'Look!'

My stomach lurches as I turn. Bloody hell – this is not the start to the brilliant first day of writing that I was anticipating. We only bought the stupid hamster because I read in some middle-class, wannabe-liberal newspaper that keeping small pets is an excellent way to introduce your child to the circle of life, to show them that death is natural and can be a calm, painless experience.

What the article did not make clear is that small pets have

not been given the memo explaining their role in this whole thing. Our goldfish jumped out of its tank and was found on the living room carpet, gasping pathetically for breath. Our gerbil swelled up to three times its usual size and then sat in its cage looking at us pathetically over the Easter weekend, until I could bear it no longer and rushed it to the emergency vet. When the invoice arrived in the post, it showed that we owed one pound for the euthanasia of a small animal and forty-nine pounds and ninety-nine pence for an appointment on a bank holiday, which made Nick mutter dark comments such as 'never again' and 'bucket of water'. We have had furry pets and wet pets and stick-type pets that never seemed to be alive in the first place and what every single one of them has had in common is that they have died horribly, and I have had to deal with them.

So as I turn towards the cage, I am steeling myself for the sight of Fluffy Rocket lying on his back with his little hamster legs in the air. I am preparing myself to murmur calming and reassuring words to Benji about lives well lived and hamster heaven, while reminding myself that I must absolutely not, under any circumstances, agree to him getting another pet.

'He's escaped!' howls Benji, pointing towards the table in the corner of the room. 'Fluffy Rocket has run away!'

I see now what I failed to notice when I carried out my initial risk assessment. The door to the hamster cage is wide open and Fluffy Rocket is nowhere to be seen.

I instantly drop to my knees and start crawling across the floor, gingerly lifting up stray socks and discarded school uniform. 'Here, Fluffy Rocket,' I call gently. 'Where are you, boy?'

Nick crouches down next to me and starts peering under Benji's bed. 'It's a hamster, not a dog. It's not exactly got good recall, Hannah.'

'But it's not deaf, either, is it?' I snap back. 'And you don't know what's going through its little hamster mind. It's all alone in a strange environment and it's probably terrified. It might recognise its name and follow my voice to safety.'

'I don't want Fluffy Rocket to be terrified,' sobs Benji. 'Or lonely.'

Nick sits next to Benji on the bed. 'I don't think hamsters get lonely,' he tells him. 'They're solitary creatures. They don't really like company.'

'But he likes me,' wails Benji. 'And now he's gone forever!'

'We'll find him,' I say, dropping onto my elbows, commando-style, to look under the wardrobe. 'He can't have gone too far.'

'Do you think that you might have left the cage door open last night?' Nick's voice is gentle and non-accusatory, but his words unleash a fresh peal of sobbing from Benji.

'Nooooo! I always close the door.'

I look up. 'He's right,' I say. 'I remember checking last night and it was definitely shut.'

I check the cage every night, as part of my tucking-in routine. I haven't trusted that bloody hamster since the day we got him. I had a hunch that he was bad news.

'So the hamster let himself out, then?' Nick looks dubious, but I ignore him. He knows nothing about the twisted minds of small rodents. They'll do whatever it takes to make your life a misery. Fluffy Rocket has probably been planning this little escapade for weeks, biding his time and just waiting for the most opportune moment.

'What's going on?' Dylan appears in the doorway, followed seconds later by Scarlet. Their arrival prompts another bout of pitiful wailing and soon all four of us are crawling around the floor in our pyjamas, taking directions from the dictator perched on his bed, as he loudly informs us of all the places that we haven't yet looked.

'I've found something!' Dylan's announcement makes the rest of us pause. 'And it looks like hamster poo.'

I hurry across to where Dylan is kneeling by the bedroom door, and stare at the object in question.

'That is definitely hamster poo,' I confirm.

'That's gross.' Scarlet jumps onto the bed next to Benji. 'I'm not walking around here if I'm going to be treading in rodent faeces.'

'There's another one here, just outside the door.' I walk with my head down, eyes scanning the carpet for clues. 'And another.'

Nick and the boys join me and then there's a thud as Scarlet launches herself off the bed and out of the room, making little squawking noises as she attempts to avoid the horrors of Benji's bedroom floor. Slowly, we proceed along the landing, following the barely perceptible line of evidence that Fluffy Rocket has so helpfully left for us.

'It's like Hansel and Gretel,' says Benji excitedly. 'Only instead of a gingerbread house, we're going to find my hamster!'

'Lucky us, to have a shit trail instead of a breadcrumb trail,' points out Dylan. 'I'm not sure that even the Brothers Grimm would have gone that far.'

I am too engrossed in my search to admonish him for having a potty mouth but I mentally log the moment, to address at a later date.

The poo leads us towards the bathroom and for a brief moment I am optimistic. There is nowhere to hide in the bathroom. I walk through the door, fully expecting to find Fluffy Rocket sitting in the middle of the linoleum, waving a white flag.

I am clearly deluded; the freaking hamster is obviously cleverer than the lot of us. The trail leads towards a teeny, tiny gap between the bath and the wall and then disappears. I glance at Nick, who grimaces at me and shrugs slightly before looking at his watch and raising his eyebrows. I know what that means. It is going to be left to me to deal with a missing-presumed-dead hamster and a ten-year-old who is going to be devastated.

I turn to face the kids, speedily working out how I'm going to play this. My choices, as far as I can see them, are tragedy, comedy, history or farce.

'So.' I turn to Benji and give him a big grin. 'It looks like Fluffy Rocket has been kidnapped! We're just going to have to wait for the ransom note and then see if you have enough pocket money to get him back! And in the meantime, we've all got to get dressed and have some breakfast and go to school. Okay?'

As soon as the words are out of my mouth, I realise that

I've got it wrong. Comedy was clearly a mistake. I should have gone with tragedy and given everyone the day off. Even Scarlet looks appalled at my lack of compassion.

'But I can't go to school and just leave him!' Benji's face is anguished. 'How am I supposed to concentrate on work when Fluffy Rocket is missing? And we've got a SPaG test today and I'm too upset to remember the difference between subordinating conjunctions and coordinating conjunctions.'

'God. Like primary school tests even matter.' Scarlet's voice is dripping with disdain. 'Nobody cares what results you get, Benji. They're not important.'

'They *are* important!' screams Benji, already over the edge. 'Miss Brown said that *every* test we do is important. They're just as important as your GCSEs and Dylan's A Levels.' He turns to me. 'Aren't they, Mum?'

I am absolutely not in the mood to get into this conversation for the millionth time.

'Nobody is getting any decent results if you don't all get ready for school. Now hurry up or there'll be no time for breakfast.' I turn to look at Nick. 'Have you got time for a coffee before you go?'

Nick nods. 'I'll just get some clothes on and then I'll be straight down.' He walks out of the room and I follow him, pausing as I reach our bedroom door. Today is the day I will begin my book. Today I will be a writer. And writers do not need to worry themselves with petty, trivial things like getting dressed. No – instead, I will fling on my dressing gown and drive the kids to school in my pyjamas and nobody will bat an eyelid because that is just how us creative, bohemian types like to roll.

It turns out that it is exceptionally hard to write a book. I had absolutely no idea. I thought that I had everything ready – I've done some research and my laptop was on charge all night so that I can avoid the trauma of running out of battery just as I'm getting into my stride. I have got dressed and made myself a cup of tea and I'm sitting at the kitchen table, prepared to create something brilliant.

But things keep on not being right.

First of all, it's the temperature of the room. I don't normally have the heating on when it's just me here on my own, but my feet are really cold and they're distracting me. I type the words *Chapter One* onto my screen, but I can't stop thinking about my freezing cold toes. So I get up and then spend five minutes deliberating over whether a real writer would wear anything as uncool as a pair of slippers, before deciding that a real writer wouldn't actually *care* if they were being cool or uncool because they can write their own definition of cool, and my definition absolutely includes having warm feet.

And then, just as I'm figuring out my first sentence, the postman rings the doorbell and I have to sign for a parcel and somehow, while I'm signing my name, the conversation slips into how I'm actually writing a book and how it's incredibly difficult but also amazingly rewarding, and the postman is genuinely interested because it turns out that *he* is writing a book too and he wants to know what my book is about, but I suddenly remember that I'm supposed to be incognito and I don't really want to tell the very jolly postman that I am writing erotic fiction, so I quickly make up a whole new book and spend ten minutes outlining the plot for a children's book about a dog and a hamster and their hilarious antics, and by the time he leaves, the jolly postman is looking a bit confused.

And after that, I think that I should probably figure out an author signature that looks professional and confident and avant-garde and a bit maverick, while in no way looking like my own actual signature so that I can maintain my anonymity.

And then it's time for some lunch, and the house is in quite a state and I don't think I can write while the floor is so dirty, so I do some vacuuming and then dig out the mop that hasn't been used in at least eighteen months and give the tiles a good once-over.

And then I have to collect the kids and explain to Benji that no, Fluffy Rocket has not reappeared, while simultaneously hoping that I didn't inadvertently hoover the damn thing up when I was cleaning the house.

So by the end of my first day as a real writer, I have a word count of twenty-three, a house that is sparkling and a newfound respect for E.L. James.

Chapter 18

Despite the continuing upset over the missing hamster, I am feeling buoyant as I enter the kitchen. The sun is shining and there is a real hint of spring in the air. The house is cleaner than it has ever been and I am ready to embark on my writing, just as soon as I've had some coffee and deposited my offspring at school with a cheery goodbye and a positive attitude. This is a new beginning for us all and I intend to put my money where my mouth is, starting right now with the kids' packed lunches. No more dry cheese sandwiches and a boring apple, chucked into a plastic Tupperware that is probably leaching nasty hormones and chemicals into my darling children's food.

Today I am a new person.

I am not merely surviving – I am *living*.

I stand in the middle of the kitchen and think hard, remembering an article I saw online recently about the gentrification of the packed lunch. It involved using Mason jars and quinoa and spinach leaves and it all looked rather lovely and exactly the kind of thing that an aspiring author would send her children to school with. I imagine the scene in the hall at

Benji's school, as the lunchtime supervisors coo and gasp at his nutritional-yet-delicious lunch. The Headteacher might even feature it in this week's newsletter. Despite the fact that I have had three children go through primary school, I have never managed to reach the heady heights of being selected for the *What's in Your Lunchbox?* column.

I am thoroughly committed to my reinvention and that can include becoming an efficient, twenty-first-century mummy if I want it to.

I march purposefully across the room and fling open a cupboard door, revealing a selection of glass jars. They're not exactly Mason jars, but they're a decent size and when I give them a quick sniff, you can barely smell the pickled onions and cabbage that used to be inside. I remove three of them and then spend several minutes trying to find matching lids, which is a bit of a pain but I get there in the end.

Then I line the jars up on the counter and open the fridge, trying to remember exactly what the article suggested using. I haven't got any spinach but there's a bag of salad at the back of the fridge and when I open it up, it's only a tiny bit limp looking. I grab a couple of handfuls and ram it into the jars before chucking in a few cherry tomatoes and standing back to admire the results. The jars are looking quite colourful but I don't think that three tomatoes and a bit of lettuce are going to sustain my growing children. I need some protein.

I head back to the cupboards and eventually manage to hunt down a packet of quinoa. Dusting it off, I check the small print and see that it went out of date more than five years ago. I have a healthy disregard for sell-by dates but even so, I think the quinoa may have seen better days. I throw it in the bin and go back to the fridge. For some reason we are out of cheese apart from a couple of Babybels, and their red wax packaging will completely ruin my aesthetic so they aren't an option. Pushing the yoghurts to one side, I strike gold. Rammed at the very back of the shelf is a packet of the insanely cheap, nasty-looking little cocktail sausages that I buy whenever I need to get Dogger to take her worming tablet. It always works a treat – one cocktail sausage to lull her into a false sense of security, followed by the tablet and then another sausage to make her forget the entire incident.

I open the packet and insert a few sausages into each jar, hesitating briefly before telling myself that I'm being ridiculous. They aren't *actually* food for dogs and I'm not really about to worm the kids.

I screw the lids onto the jars and put the kettle on, a sense of maternal bliss spreading through me. I'm particularly excited to see Scarlet's reaction to my hipster-worthy lunch effort. She'll probably want to Instagram it to show all her friends.

I'm just reaching for a couple of mugs when I see it. It takes a few, long seconds for my brain to process what I'm actually looking at and when it does, I really, really wish that it hadn't.

'Nick!' My voice comes out in a throaty whisper that can't possibly be heard outside the kitchen. There is no way that I want to alert the kids to this new turn of events. 'Nick!'

'Is the coffee ready?' My husband walks into the room,

doing up his tie. 'I've got a meeting with the new contractors and I can't be late.'

'Look at this.' I stand back and point to the kitchen counter. 'Can you see it?'

Together we stare at the surface and the speckled bits of green dust that are scattered across it.

'Isn't that–?' begins Nick.

'Rat poison,' I finish.

We look up at the wooden box that runs diagonally along the length of our kitchen wall, housing the water pipes that lead from underneath our upstairs bathroom to the drain outside. The same wooden box that had a rat problem when we first moved here two years ago. The same wooden box that now contains an industrial quantity of rat poison and rat traps that are large enough to break the back of the largest rodent.

In our darkest hours of rat-gate we always knew that they were scampering about, because a) they made a terrible noise, equivalent to that of a huge man in hob-nailed boots stamping around inside the walls, and b) they would dislodge the dust and the green poison inside the box would fall out through the joints, forcing me into a clinical level of cleanliness with our kitchen counters. Which means one of two things is now happening. The rats are back, or Fluffy Rocket's Most Excellent Adventure has gone horribly, horribly wrong.

I think that I might be sick.

Nick throws himself into action. 'Get my screwdriver!' he whispers loudly, pulling off his suit jacket. 'And don't let the kids come in here.'

I sprint into the hall and grab his toolkit from the shelf. At the same time, footsteps come pounding down the stairs.

'Do *not* come down!' I hiss at Dylan. 'Take your brother and sister and lock yourselves in your room! Don't look back, Dylan – whatever you do, do *not* look back!'

Dylan flings himself round the banister. 'Are we being home invaded?' he yells. 'Where's Dad?'

I realise that I am not calming the situation and make a monumental effort to slow my breathing.

'It's fine,' I say, backing away from him towards the kitchen. 'It's the H – A –M – S – T – E – R.'

Dylan looks at me like I've completely lost the plot, but he does what I ask and I hear him calling to Scarlet and Benji, telling them to come and listen to his latest remix in his room.

In the kitchen, Nick is tapping gently at the box. He turns when I walk in, his face pale. 'I think I heard something,' he tells me. 'Pass me that screwdriver.'

He works in silence, while my heart beats a tattoo against my chest. Visions of mangled hamster dance in my head and I grip the worktop, trying to be brave and cursing the day I brought the poor, doomed, stupid animal into our house. The circle of life should not have to involve this kind of thing.

Nick removes all the screws and gently lifts the wooden access panel out. I hold my breath as he peers inside, steeling myself for scenes akin to something from *The Silence of the Hamsters.*

'I can see something!' he calls. 'I can see Fluffy Rocket.'

'Is he dead?' I swallow hard. 'Is he in one piece?'

'He's alive.'

Two small words that change everything. I close my eyes and smile, saying a silent thank you to whoever it is that spared the life of my child's beloved pet.

'But he's caught in a rat trap. Oh shit, Hannah – it's snapped completely closed.'

I stop humming 'Hakuna Matata' and come crashing back down to reality.

This cannot be happening.

'Can you bring the trap out?' I ask. 'Then we can figure out what to do?'

Nick shakes his head. 'There's another trap in the way. If I move this one then I risk setting that one off and I could break my finger. I can't see clearly into the gap.' He moves back and looks at me. 'You're going to have to help me.'

My legs start twitching. I do not *want* to help. I do not want to go anywhere near a rat trap, and I do not want to see the state that the miserable hamster is in.

But I am a mother, and like all the other emergency services, it is my job to run in when anyone sane would run out.

Courageously, I nod at Nick. 'Tell me what you need me to do.'

Which is how I end up crouching on the kitchen counter wearing the thickest gardening gloves that I could find, directing Nick towards the snapped trap and hoping that this isn't one of those occasions where I mix up my left and right.

'Move your hand a few centimetres forward,' I say. 'Careful! Not *there*, for the love of god!'

'Bloody hell, Hannah,' growls Nick, sweat beading on his forehead. 'Can you be a bit less dramatic please?'

'Sorry,' I huff. 'Just trying to stop you losing a finger. Now move to the left, just a tiny bit. Now slightly down ... and you're there!'

Nick grips the trap and pulls on the metal spring. 'It's really hard to move it,' he grunts. 'I can barely make it budge.'

'He just twitched!' I call. 'Do it for the hamster, Nick! Come on!'

And with the Herculean strength that mothers exhibit when moving huge buses off their small children, Nick eases the wire up a tiny bit and I reach in and grab Fluffy Rocket.

Nick drops the trap. I stand very still, not daring to look at what I've picked up.

'Can you see any injuries?' I whisper.

Nick peers closer. 'He looks fine.' I can hear confusion in his voice. 'There's not a mark on him apart from here.'

I take a breath and look down at my gloved hand. The cause of all this distress is looking slightly dazed, but not anywhere near as squashed or splatted or squished as I had imagined. In fact, he resembles the same hamster that he's always been apart from a bald patch, right on his bottom.

'I think he got trapped by the fluff on his arse,' murmurs Nick, his voice filled with awe. 'Talk about a lucky escape.'

I cup him between my gloved hands, trying to be as gentle as possible.

'Can you get me a shoebox?' I ask. 'I need to get him to the vet. He might have eaten some of that rat poison.'

Nick scrabbles around in the cupboard underneath the sink, the dumping ground for everything that I can't bear to get rid of, and passes me a box. I lower Fluffy Rocket inside.

'I don't think there's a lot the vet can do for him if he has,' Nick tells me. 'Is it really worth the bother?'

At that moment, Benji comes hurtling into the kitchen with Dylan and Scarlet hot on his heels.

'Have you found Fluffy Rocket?' he yells. 'Did you save his life?'

Nick catches my eye and nods. We both know that it's worth the hassle, if not the eye-watering bill that we're about to get landed with.

After Nick has dashed off to work, I leave Dylan in charge of the shoebox while Scarlet pours cereal into three bowls. I sprint upstairs to throw on some clothes. I may be a fledgling writer but even us arty types draw the line at visiting the vets in our tartan flannel pyjamas. Then I run back downstairs, thanking the heavens that at least I managed to get lunch sorted.

'Here you are!' I say, passing a jar to each child. 'Put these in your bags.'

There is silence as my delightful offspring examine the offerings that I have placed before them.

'What's this?' Benji is the first to break. 'Where are my sandwiches?'

'This is instead of sandwiches,' I say brightly. 'Aren't you lucky? Everyone else has boring old sandwiches and you get to take in this delicious salad!'

'I want the same as everyone else,' Benji mutters, mutinously. 'They'll all laugh when they see this.'

'I can't take this to school.' Scarlet stares at me with a look on her face that would suggest I have committed some kind of culinary crime. 'Do you seriously think I'm going to carry a jam jar around all day?'

'It's a pickled onion jar, *for your information*.' This is not how I imagined my thoughtful lunches would be received. 'And I'm sure it's no heavier than your lunchbox.'

'Is that Dogger's sausages in there?' Dylan is peering closely into his jar, his face suspicious. 'Have you given us dog food for lunch?'

I sigh loudly. 'They are not dog sausages. They are human sausages that I happen to buy for Dogger.'

'I don't want to eat human sausages!' wails Benji, looking stricken. 'That's horrible, Mum.'

I look at the clock, wondering if the vet might be persuaded to write me a prescription for a tranquiliser. Just something to take the edge off.

'There'll be a riot if I take this into the school canteen,' states Scarlet. 'Honestly, you've got no idea, Mum. You sit up there in the staffroom where it's all nice and cosy but it's like a warzone down in the hall. I've seen the damage that Ashley Dunsford can inflict with a Tupperware. Believe me, you do not want someone like him getting his hands on anything made of glass. It'll be carnage.' She pauses and gives me a strange look. 'Also, is it true that if someone dies in the middle of an exam then everyone else gets an immediate A grade?'

I've had enough.

'Take the jar or go hungry.' I pick up the shoebox. 'I'm getting in the car and I will be leaving in two minutes. And I am deadly serious when I say that if you're not all sitting in your seats then I will leave you behind.'

The drive to school is subdued. None of us are much in the mood for talking. I drop the older two at the main entrance and then head across to Benji's school next door.

'I'm taking Fluffy Rocket to the vet now,' I tell him. 'Just to get him checked out.'

'Thank you, Mummy.' Benji strokes the top of the shoebox before leaning across and giving me a hug. I haven't been 'Mummy' for a while now and even though I know it's because he's upset, part of me rejoices in hearing my old name.

I tell our tale of woe to the vet's receptionist, who listens with her jaw gaping open, especially when I spin out the part where we found the hamster stuck in the rat trap. She whisks us straight through to the vet's room where I repeat the whole sorry saga.

'... trapped only by the fluff on his backside,' I finish. 'So I thought it'd be good to get him checked out, given the fact that there is an awful lot of poison in the walls.'

The vet reaches into the box and picks up Fluffy Rocket, who promptly bites him on the finger. I hear the vet mutter something that sounds distinctively like *little shit*, but I must be mistaken because surely that's against the veterinary code of conduct or something? I'm not allowed to say that about my Year Nine class so I'm pretty sure that the vet isn't allowed to say it about a poor, defenceless hamster who has just gone through a near-death experience.

'I suppose he might not have touched the poison,' I say hopefully. 'He would appear to be quite an intelligent hamster.'

The vet puts Fluffy Rocket back in the box and looks at me pityingly.

'Not a chance, I'm afraid. Rat poison has an attractor in it. It's designed to be as appealing as possible to all rodents, and in this case that unfortunately includes runaway hamsters. Your pet will definitely have ingested the poison. There's nothing that can really be done at this point.'

'Is there an antidote?' I enquire, feeling like I'm on a particularly unusual episode of Casualty. 'Is there anything we can do, doctor?'

The vet scratches his head and stares down into the box where Fluffy Rocket is frantically stuffing bedding into his voluminous cheeks.

'Well,' he draws out, sounding reluctant. 'We could give him twice-daily injections of Vitamin K in an effort to combat the effects of the poison and thicken his blood. But that would mean you bringing him here every morning and evening and it would be incredibly costly and also quite painful for the little chap.'

We both pause and watch Fluffy Rocket, who is now regurgitating his bedding.

'Would it definitely help him?' I ask.

The vet shakes his head. 'It would be a long shot,' he tells me. 'If you want my advice, it would be to go home and put him back in his cage. Then put the cage somewhere that your son can't see it. Internal bleeding can be a messy business.'

'Will it be quick?' I cross my fingers, praying for some good news.

The vet squeezes his lips together. 'Look, I'll be honest with you. You need to be prepared for a particularly long and horrific death. If you like, I could just do the kind thing and euthanise him now.'

The fucking circle of life.

For one moment I am tempted. But then I look down and see that the hamster is staring up at me, like I am its only hope in the entire word. And I think about my little boy and him calling me 'Mummy' and I know that I have to at least try.

'No thank you.' I pick up the shoebox and clutch it to my chest. 'I shall take him home and we will see out his last days with dignity.'

Then I drive home, playing the vet's words over and over on repeat. Internal bleeding and Vitamin K and nasty injections. And a thought pops into my head, so the instant I get through the front door I deposit Fluffy Rocket back in his cage and pull out my phone, calling upon the wisdom of the World Wide Web to check out my theory. Then I race back to the car and speed to the supermarket, where I buy three overpriced packets of posh, organic cabbage, which, according to Dr Google, is a rich source of Vitamin K.

And so it is that instead of spending my day writing chapter one of my brilliant erotic novel, I spend it forcing a hamster to eat five times its own body weight in kale.

Chapter 19

I. Am. Writing.

I am actually, honest-to-god, writing, and it feels brilliant. The words are flying out of my fingertips and onto the screen in front of me and it's like being the queen of the world. I have never felt more powerful in my entire life.

Downstairs, Benji is engrossed on his iPad and Scarlet is pretending to revise while watching Netflix. Dylan is out at his girlfriend's house and I'm not collecting him for hours yet. Nick keeps popping in to our bedroom to replenish the cups of tea that I have no time or inclination to drink, because this story is telling itself and it's all I can do to keep up with it.

I lean back, stretching out the kinks in my back. I know that sitting on my bed isn't great for my posture, but it's peaceful up here and I need to be somewhere that I won't be disturbed if Bella Rose and Daxx are going to tell their tale.

It took me a while to come up with my main characters' names. In fact, I'd go so far as to say that it has got to be one of the most stressful parts of writing; possibly even harder than choosing the names for our own kids. For starters, every name I thought about seemed to belong to some pupil I've taught over the years, or a colleague who I've worked with, and that would just be inappropriate. And secondly, the names have to be right. All my research suggests that the heroes and heroines of erotic fiction have names that befit their sexy status. There are no characters called Vera or Bob in this game.

I read the paragraph that I've just written.

Bella Rose peeped up through her improbably long eyelashes, wondering just who this incredibly gorgeous man, with his come-hither eyes, thought he was. She'd seen him around before but he'd never so much as glanced in her direction. Not that she cared. With looks like those, he was probably a complete prick …

Hmmm. I'm not entirely sure that I'm striking the right mood here. Pressing the delete button, I erase the first sentence and rewrite it, this time making Bella Rose *peep up through her implausibly and remarkably long eyelashes* at the *exquisite and pulchritudinous man before her*. It'll do for now.

Maybe it's time to take a break.

'How goes the work?' asks Nick as I walk into the kitchen. He closes his laptop and takes a slurp of tea. 'Do you fancy getting takeaway tonight?'

I look at the clock and see that I've been writing for hours.

'Definitely. I can collect something when I'm out getting Dylan.' I sink into a chair and give him a grin. 'And the work is going okay. I think.'

'So tell me what you've written so far. What's it actually about?'

I lean forward, keen to share my vision for Bella Rose and Daxx's story.

'Right. Well, there's a guy called Daxx – that's with two x's – and he owns a ranch. And he's also totally sex-on-legs, obviously. And then there's a woman called Bella Rose who has to sell her horse because she's down on her luck and is all alone in the world, and so she sells it to Daxx who instantly falls in love with her, although he has to fight his feelings because he has taken a vow to never love anyone ever again after his first and only true love fell to her death in the mountains, and—'

Nick puts his hand up, stopping me. 'Can I ask a quick question?'

I nod, although I was in full flow there and I do think it's a little bit rude to interrupt someone when the creative juices are flowing, so to speak.

'Where exactly is this story set?'

'Wyoming,' I explain. 'It just makes sense because there are loads of ranches in Wyoming.'

Nick looks puzzled. 'But you've never been to Wyoming, Hannah. And as far as I'm aware, you've never even ridden a horse.'

'I have, actually,' I remind him. 'I've told you about my horrendous experience pony trekking on Dartmoor when I was a teenager. And anyway, what's your point?'

'I just thought that writers were supposed to write about what they know.' Nick's mouth starts twitching at the corners. 'I had no idea that you were so knowledgeable about the ins and outs of cowboys and studs.'

'Ha bloody ha.' I am not impressed. 'I am writing *erotic fiction*, Nick.'

'I am aware of that.' He holds up his hands as if he's placating me. 'I'm just wondering why it has to be set in a place that you've never even been?'

I wonder if all writers have to cope with the small-worldliness of their spouses?

'Look,' I tell him, trying to keep my voice calm. 'George R.R. Martin has never been to Westeros, has he? And J.K. Rowling hasn't visited Hogwarts. If they'd only written about what they *knew* then the world would never have experienced the delights of Harry Potter and *A Game of Thrones*.'

'Now that sounds like a book worth reading.' Nick snorts. I shoot him my death-glare.

'As I was saying,' I continue. 'I am writing erotic fiction. My research has led me to understand that there are certain rules that you have to follow if you want to appeal to your readers.'

'Like what?'

'Like setting the story in a sexy environment.' I lean back in my chair and wave my hand around the room. 'Readers want to hear about ranch hands or billionaires in penthouses or vampires in mansions. They don't want to read about their own lives. They want escapism. They *want* Wyoming.'

'What if your readers live in Wyoming?' Nick asks. 'Don't they want to read about rural England? Maybe our lives sound exotic to them.'

Now it's my turn to laugh. 'Yeah, right. I've not exactly seen a ton of erotic fiction set in the Shires.'

Nick pulls a face. 'That's a bit of a shame. Maybe there's a gap in the market for some Hobbit porn?'

And then we both start sniggering because the whole thing is so ridiculous. It feels so damn good to have something in my life that isn't connected to school or parenting.

It is now day six since Hamstergate and miraculously, incredibly, improbably, Fluffy Rocket is still alive and kicking. I have bought our local supermarket out of kale and I swear that the poor animal goes a bit pale when I advance upon it each morning, brandishing a fresh packet, but I'm invested in its survival now and I'm buggered if it's going to die on my watch. Nick found a padlock and now even the most cunning of criminals would struggle to escape from the confines of the cage.

The bell rings for the end of morning break and I reluctantly pull myself up from my chair.

'Are you teaching next lesson?' asks Cassie, glancing up from the pages of her magazine. 'Bad luck.'

'I've got Year Nine, Class C,' I tell her, picking up my bag. 'I wouldn't exactly call it teaching. More like crowd-control-slash-babysitting-slash-why-do-I-bother?'

Cassie laughs. 'The pay cheque, my darling. That is why we bother.'

I walk down the corridor, studiously ignoring the pupils with missing ties and skirts that are the length of a handkerchief and hair that would make a unicorn look a bit shabby. I am not paid enough to notice these things. When I enter my room, the majority of the class is already there, draping themselves over the desks and hanging off the backs of chairs. They do not look like they are ready to engage in learning, which comes as no surprise but is a perpetual source of disappointment.

'Okay, let's make a start.' I dump my bag on the floor and walk across to the whiteboard. 'Who can remember where we left off last lesson?'

'Oh my god!' howls Wayne from over by the window. 'You will not believe what car Mr Jenkins is driving!'

There is a mass surge as everyone piles across the room, pressing their eager little noses up against the glass. I shake my head but from the jeers and general noises of contempt, it's obviously a car worth commenting on, so I stroll across the room and peer over their shoulders.

'Yo! It's like, a *granny* car, dog!' sneers Brody. 'I ain't be seen dead driving that lame-ass piece of crap.'

I clear my throat loudly. 'Language, Brody. It's *would not* be seen dead, not *ain't*.'

'I'm just keepin' it real, miss,' Brody tells me. 'And that is one ugly piece of metal right there, ya feel me?'

I am not entirely sure what has got into him. Year Nine, Class C might not be the brightest sandwiches in the lunchbox but I've never heard Brody talk like this before. I'm mildly embarrassed on his behalf, to be perfectly honest.

'You got the swagga, homie!' calls Vincent. I may choose to ignore the occasional bit of swearing in my classroom but I absolutely draw the line at prejudice.

'That's quite enough!' I snap. 'I will not tolerate homophobic slurs in this room. Vincent – apologise to Brody this instant.'

Vincent looks at me with a vacant expression on his face. 'You what, miss?'

'She thinks you called Brody gay,' explains Elise, turning away from the window. 'That's what homophobic means, you dumbass.'

'You calling me gay, boi?' explodes Brody. He pushes himself away from the glass and rounds on Vincent, grabbing a ruler that he brandishes before him like a sword. 'Yo – you better be followin' that up with some serious attitude, my dawg. 'Cos I's gonna whip your lily-white ass all the way to the playground and back if you be throwin' shade in my direction.'

I have thankfully never had the misfortune to witness either boy's backside, but judging on the evidence in front of me, I would think it fair to assume that they are both as lily-white as each other.

'I didn't call you anything,' shouts back Vincent. 'Back off, Brody!'

'You are all so incredibly stupid,' sighs Elise, and the rest of the class murmur in agreement. She turns to me. 'Miss, Vincent called Brody a "homie".'

I glare at Vincent and nod. 'Exactly. And we do not use a person's sexual preference as an insult in this school. Nor their gender, while I'm on the subject. Brody is free to identify as whatever sexuality and gender he, she or they prefer. Apologise right now.'

'"Homie" means homeboy,' continues Elise, rolling her eyes in a way that would normally cause me to give her a detention, but that today I'm prepared to overlook because it would appear that I need her translating skills. 'Not homosexual.'

How on earth was I supposed to know that?

'It's gangster speak, miss,' adds Vincent helpfully. 'He's my homie, yeah bruv?'

Brody nods and lowers the ruler. 'You my bruvver from another muvver, Vincenzo. YknowI'msayin'?

'I have no idea *what* you're saying,' I say. 'Or why you have both decided to start spouting utter gibberish.' I spin on my heel and walk back towards my desk. 'And if you aren't all sitting in your seats with your books out in five seconds flat, then your lunchtime will be spent in my delightful presence. Do you all feel *that*?'

I just about resist the urge to throw in a *motherfuckaaaaa*, for shock value, as I have no doubt that Miriam would walk in just as I embarked on the third syllable.

'You're in a good mood.' Nick hangs up his coat and walks into the kitchen where I'm making pasta sauce and gently humming some Rage Against the Machine while I chop tomatoes. 'Had a good day?'

'It was okay.' I tip the tomatoes into a pan and turn on the heat. 'It's over, which is possibly the best part of it. And tomorrow I can write all day and I've had a brilliant idea for a scene where Bella Rose goes out in a thunderstorm and her horse gets spooked and Daxx has to save her and it's raining and they kiss and—'

'Isn't that a bit clichéd?' interrupts Nick, pulling a bottle out of the fridge. 'Wine Wednesday, by the way?'

I nod to both questions. 'Yes to wine. And of course it's clichéd. That's exactly what the erotic-fiction fan wants. Duh.'

Nick shrugs. 'If you say so. I wouldn't have a clue.'

He pours us both a glass and I join him at the table. 'That's why I've done all the research,' I tell him. 'I know what I need to write to make this work.'

I take a sip of wine and let myself relax. It might only be Wednesday, but my weeks are starting to have real shape and I love knowing that the next two days are going to be spent writing. Hamsters allowing, of course.

'Oh. My. Actual. God!' Scarlet's shriek can probably be heard down the street. 'What even is this?'

I don't move. The last few months have exceeded even my wildest expectations of what it means to have a drama-queen, angst-ridden, hormonal tornado of a teenage daughter in the house. The cause of this distress could be any number of things, ranging from forgotten homework to an Instagram post that doesn't have enough likes to someone forgetting to flush the toilet. It is simply impossible to react to her every single time.

'I think I'm going to be sick.'

That gets my attention, if only because I have no intention of spending my precious Thursday steam-cleaning the living room carpet.

'What's the matter?' I yell, rolling my eyes at Nick, who sensibly takes a hearty slug of wine. 'Do you need me?'

Footsteps pound across the floor and then Scarlet appears in the doorway, brandishing her e-reader.

'Which one of you did this?' she demands, furiously. 'Are you trying to traumatise me or something?'

'Perhaps you could do us the courtesy of speaking at a

reasonable volume and with a bit more respect,' Nick tells her. 'What is it that we're supposed to have done?'

'*You're* going to talk to *me* about courtesy and respect?' Scarlet's voice rises a few more octaves, her indignation giving her the ability to commune with dolphins. 'That's rich, when *you're* the one looking at *porn*!'

Oh holy mother of the sweet baby Jesus. This cannot be happening.

'Why are you yelling about porn?' Dylan appears, as if by magic. Typical. I can waste ten minutes screaming upstairs at the top of my lungs to tell him that supper is going cold. It would seem that I have been shouting the wrong word to be assured of his attention.

Scarlet glowers at him. 'There are some very dodgy books on my e-reader and I didn't order them. In fact, I think I'm going to need to wash my eyes out with soap. Some things just can't be unseen.'

'I deleted them off my device,' I mutter, making frantic eye contact with Nick. 'I don't understand why they're still on there.'

Scarlet spins round, her mouth twisted in conflict. She's clearly undecided about whether she should find this funny or appalling.

'It was *you*? You've been reading porn? Oh my god, Mother. That is just so, so, *ewww*. It's just, *argghhh* – I don't even know what to say.'

I have never once seen our daughter lost for words.

Please find it funny. Please. Let's all behave like grown-up about this.

Scarlet looks down at her e-reader for a moment and then stares back at us. 'I'm sorry for accusing you, Dad. I wasn't thinking straight. I guess *Too Hard to Handle Billionaire* isn't really your gig.'

The silence that follows is possibly the most uncomfortable twenty seconds of my life so far. But then hysterical laughing erupts from my two oldest children, swiftly followed by my husband: there is more indignity to come.

It's fine. I'm sure that nobody ever died from complete and utter public humiliation.

'What are the others called?' gasps Dylan, clutching the back of a chair to keep himself upright, such is his mirth.

'Okay, okay.' Scarlet grabs his arm and shoots me what I can only describe as an evil grin. 'Get ready for this!'

'Is that the title of the book?' yelps Dylan and they both dissolve into gleeful howls.

I rest my elbows on the table and place my head in my hands. There is nothing to be done but to sit this out. I'm sure there is some quote about it not being how you survive the storm but how you dance in the rain. It's quite hard to see how this applies to your teenage children discovering raunchy trash-sex books in your e-book account though.

'No, no – it gets better!' splutters Scarlet.

'That's what she said,' adds Dylan and now they are crying; actual tears of joy are flowing down the innocent, childish faces that I have warped with my research.

My children are making sex jokes at my expense.

I want to give them both a good smack.

Nick pushes his wine across the table towards me and

when I look down, I see that mine is already empty. This is how alcoholism starts, I know that. Drinking without even knowing that you're doing it.

Very, very consciously and making sure that I am aware of every last drop, I drain his glass.

Chapter 20

I glance again at the word count at the bottom of my screen. It hasn't changed since the last time I looked, which was approximately three minutes ago. I am still only eight hundred words into my literary masterpiece and I've been writing for days. At this rate, the only chance I've got of being published is posthumously, which is a very depressing thought indeed.

The doorbell rings, jolting me out of my self-pity. Walking down the hall, I see the outline of my mother in the glass. I'm not expecting to see her today, and for a second my heart speeds up, anticipating a crisis of some kind.

'I've brought buns.' My mother breezes past me the second the door is opened. 'Get the kettle on, Hannah.'

I do as I'm told and then, once the tea is made, grab some plates and sit down on the battered, old, squishy sofa that is tucked into the corner of the kitchen. 'Is everything okay, Mum?'

My mother kicks off her shoes and curls up next to me.

'That's what I was going to ask *you*. Scarlet sent me a text this morning. She thinks you're having a mid-life crisis, so I thought I'd better pop over and check that you weren't buying a motorbike or planning on getting a tattoo.'

I grimace and reach for a sticky bun. 'Honestly, that child. She thought I was pregnant a few weeks ago and now it's a mid-life crisis, is it? She needs to make her mind up.'

Mum pats me on the hand. 'It's all the hormones flying around. They can make a person feel like they're going mad.'

I nod in agreement. 'Scarlet's a walking bundle of hormones at the moment.'

Mum laughs. 'I meant *you*, Hannah! It's your hormones that are having a wild old time right now.'

I take a large bite of bun to stop myself from saying something rude to my mother. She doesn't know what she's on about. There's nothing wrong with my hormones and I can't possibly be having a mid-life crisis because I'm only forty-three years old. I haven't even reached my peak yet.

'Are you and Scarlet having a bit of trouble at the moment?' Mum isn't going to let this go. 'I've always thought that Mother Nature was being particularly thoughtless to combine peri-menopausal women with teenage daughters. It's a recipe for disaster, it really is.'

'I am not peri-menopausal, Mother.'

Am I? Last time I went online and looked up the symptoms of menopause it all sounded so horrific that I think I mentally blocked it out. Maybe I need to check it out again.

'It's nothing to feel embarrassed or ashamed about,' she continues. 'It's different now – everyone talks about these things.' She picks up her tea and takes a delicate sip. 'Not like it was for me. It was a lonely business. I had you blossoming into a glorious young woman while I felt as if time was slipping through my fingers. I sometimes used to look at the two of us in the mirror and think that you were like a beautiful butterfly, all fresh and bright and colourful while I felt like a crinkly, dried up, dull old moth.' She laughs and puts down her cup. 'I expect you feel like that when you look at Scarlet, don't you?'

'Absolutely,' I say, gritting my teeth. Absolutely *not*. That heartwarming analogy had not entered my head. But guess what I'm going to think the next time I have the misfortune to be standing next to Scarlet in a changing room? Thanks a lot, Mum.

'So what have you done to upset that daughter of yours, then? I don't suppose it takes a lot at the moment, does it?'

She smiles at me, and I remember that she came all the way over here just to check that I'm okay. And she may be quite blunt and outspoken, but she'll also do whatever it takes to support me. And she's the only woman I know who has never, ever been shocked by anything that I have told her.

That does *not* mean that I'm happy to share everything with her, however.

'Oh, the usual.' I pull a face. 'Do you want some more hot water in your drink?'

Mum gives me a look, like she's trying not to laugh. 'My drink is fine, Hannah. And I think you're already *in* hot water, from the sounds of it!'

I narrow my eyes at her. 'What do you mean?'

'Oh, nothing! How's your bun?'

'Delicious.' I glare at her, feeling suspicious. 'Just spit it out, Mother. Why are you really here?'

Mum puts down her plate and pats her hair into position before turning to face me. 'I told you. Scarlet sent me a text. I thought I'd just pop in and see how everything is going.' She pauses for a beat. 'See if you had any good book recommendations?'

I close my eyes so that I can't see her pathetic attempt to keep a straight face. There's absolutely no point in lying to her – she obviously already knows, and even if she didn't, her maternal instincts include a sniffer-dog ability to smell a secret from one hundred yards away. I make a decision.

'Scarlet found some erotic fiction on our e-book account,' I say. 'I was doing some research and I thought that I'd deleted it but it turns out that I only removed it from my e-reader and not the actual account so it popped up on Scarlet's screen.' I open my eyes. 'There's a possibility that she's going to require some form of counselling.'

Mum waves away this last comment with a flick of her hand. 'What were you researching for?' she asks. 'Surely not for school?'

I shake my head. 'I'm trying to write a book.' I say the words slowly, gauging her response. 'You know – a bit like those *Fifty Shades* books that everyone talks about?'

Her face lights up. 'I've always thought that you should write a book! How fantastic!' She thinks for a second, mulling over what I've said. 'I suggested reading those books for our book club a few months ago. But Pam said that it would be inappropriate, for some reason.' She narrows her eyes. 'I'm not sure what is *inappropriate* about a load of women in their sixties reading about sex, though. It's not like it's a new invention.'

I think about Mrs Knight from school and make a mental note to never let her meet my mother. The two of them together could be dangerous.

Mum looks at me. 'How exciting, Hannah! How much have you written so far?'

I take a big slurp of tea.

'It's really, really difficult!' I blurt. 'I thought it'd be easy but it's actually impossible. I keep thinking in my head about what I want the story to look like but every time I write something, it doesn't go in the direction that I thought it would.'

Mum smiles. 'But you've made a start and that's more than most people do. Ooh – I can't wait to tell my book club about it!'

I reach across the table and clutch her arm. 'No! You can't say a word! I'm serious, Mum. I don't want anybody to know about this, particularly not the kids.'

'So what did you tell Scarlet, then? When she found the *research*?' Mum raises her eyebrows at me in a way that is supposed to suggest that she isn't buying the research story for one minute, which is offensive but I haven't got time to address it right now.

I let go of her arm and put my hand in front of my eyes, in a pathetic attempt to block out the memory of the conversation that followed Scarlet's discovery.

'I might have suggested that I was just a bit curious,' I

mumble. 'And then I might have said that it was different in our day and that sex education mostly consisted of an elderly teacher trying to put a condom on a banana while we all died a thousand mortified deaths. And that I was just trying to educate myself.'

Mum stares at me. 'Would it not have been less embarrassing to tell her the actual truth? That you're going to write porn?'

I shake my head fiercely. 'No way! Can you imagine their reaction if I told them that I was doing something like that?' I stand up and start pacing the floor. 'And it's erotica, by the way, not porn. It's perfectly healthy and acceptable and nothing to be ashamed about.'

'Well, that's rather my point,' Mum chuckles. 'Why lie about it? And it's no wonder that poor Scarlet sent me that text. She obviously thinks that her mother has turned into some kind of sex fiend!'

'You're really not helping, Mother.' I sink back down next to her on the sofa. 'And do you honestly think I should have told them what I'm really doing?'

Mum stops laughing and puts her hand on my knee. 'Actually no, I don't. And of course I won't breathe a word to anyone – I can see why you'd want to keep your porn career separate to your everyday life.'

I don't bother to correct her. At least she's on my side.

'So what are you going to call yourself?' Mum continues. 'You can't use your real name, not if you want to be incognito.'

Now this is the kind of conversation I can get behind. Even though I know it's utterly ridiculous when I haven't even finished the second chapter yet, this is fast becoming my favourite game. Trying to choose a pseudonym and planning my launch party. In fact, I'd go so far as to say that these two things are the best parts of writing.

'I'm not sure,' I tell her. 'But you're right – I can't have Hannah Thompson as my author name. Even if I wasn't trying to be anonymous, it doesn't exactly scream erotica at you, does it?'

Mum nods thoughtfully. 'Why don't you choose the name of a writer who's already successful?' she suggests. 'That way, people will buy your books thinking that they've been written by someone good.'

I give her the look that I usually reserve for my Year Nine class.

'I'm pretty sure that's not allowed, Mum. And if, somehow, I actually manage to write a book that's good enough to publish then I want a name that means something to *me* on the front cover.'

Mum thinks for a moment. 'Oh, I've got it! What about using your great-great-granny's name? That will be meaningful and I'm fairly sure it's quite unique.'

I like the idea of using a name that's linked to me. This could actually be a good idea.

'What was her name?' I ask.

Mum grins at me. 'Edna Tickle,' she says, working hard to keep her expression deadpan and failing miserably. 'I think it's perfect!'

'Is that the time?' I stand up and stare pointedly at the clock. 'I'm sure you're busy, Mum. I don't want to keep you.'

'I'll keep giving it some thought.' Mum pulls on her shoes before straightening up and miming pulling a zip closed across her lips. 'And mum's the word, Hannah. Don't you worry!'

I stand on the front step and keep waving until she's out of sight, just to make sure that she's really gone. Then I close the door and trudge back into the kitchen where my laptop is waiting.

When it comes to my mother, I would always be wise to worry.

Chapter 21

I wake up feeling determined. Today, nothing is going to get in my way. I take the kids to school then hurry home, lock the front door behind me and put my phone on silent. I'm going to take the advice that I dish out to my pupils and not overthink my writing. I am going to let the words flow and I'm going to splurge them onto the page without too much thought about whether they're actually any good or not.

And so I write. And actually, once I relax and let my mind wander to Wyoming and the situation that Bella Rose and Daxx find themselves in, the scene plays out in my head like a film reel and my fingers fly across the keyboard, trying to keep up.

> *The horse galloped along the vast plains* [note: do they have plains in Wyoming? Ask Google later] *but Bella Rose barely noticed the incredible scenery as it flashed by. Instead, her mind was churning with the feelings that Daxx had aroused in her.* [Note: good use of word 'aroused'. Subtly suggests something sensual without being too obvious.] *He may be the most gorgeous man that she had*

ever had the good fortune to rest her eyes upon, but he was also the most stubborn, pig-headed son-of-a-gun that she had ever met. [Note: add more colloquialisms like that – makes it more authentic and clearly set in Wyoming not the Shires. They do not say 'son-of-a-gun' in the Shires.]

I write all morning, stopping only for a brief sandwich at lunchtime, and then I keep writing all afternoon. And by the time it's three o'clock, I have written two thousand words. Two thousand! And if that doesn't call for Fizzy Friday then I do not know what does.

I nip into the supermarket before collecting the kids and purchase a bottle of their cheapest Prosecco. Then I drive home, letting my offspring's inane ramblings wash over me, a feeling of warmth and happiness creating a barrier between their end-of-week outpourings and my sense of achievement at actually having created something tangible.

Which is why I am not really aware of the building tension until we get into the house and Dylan erupts.

'He's a dick, Scarlet. I don't understand why you'd even speak to him, never mind hang around with him.'

'Who's a dick?' I ask. 'Benji, don't forget to empty your lunchbox. And that'll be twenty pence in the swear jar, Dylan.'

'You don't even know him.' Scarlet is very quiet. Far too quiet actually; and it is this that gets my attention. When I turn to look at her, I see the same thing that people who have witnessed tsunamis have experienced. A terrible calm before all hell lets loose.

'Why don't we get a snack and you can tell me about your days?' I start to herd them into the kitchen where I am hoping the presence of chocolate biscuits will defuse the situation.

You would think that I had been parenting for the last eighteen minutes, not the last eighteen years, with ignorance like that.

'I don't *want* to know him.' Dylan slams his bag onto the floor and stalks across the room towards the fridge. 'And neither should you, if you've got any sense. Ashley Dunsford is seriously bad news.'

Ashley Dunsford. He isn't in any of my English classes but I've heard all about him. He moved here at the start of the school year and is single-handedly responsible for the fact that pupils now have random bag searches to check for illicit items. I had no idea that Scarlet had anything to do with him, other than issuing dire warnings about his ability to start a riot with Tupperware.

Scarlet assumes the position: hands on hips and feet slightly apart. Then she fixes her brother with a hard stare and lets it all pour out.

'Who do you think you are?' As an opener, it's hardly unique. 'It's none of your business who I hang around with.'

I pass the biscuits to Benji and nod my head towards the sofa where Dogger is curled up, fast asleep. He takes the hint and sits down next to her, out of the firing line.

'Excuse me for looking out for you,' snarls Dylan, his head buried deep inside the fridge. 'I won't bother in future. You can get yourself out of trouble next time.'

'Will somebody please tell me what is going on?' I put the

kettle on: this sounds like a situation where I'm going to need some kind of fortitude and I'm not prepared to waste my celebratory Prosecco on teenagers. Then I turn to face Scarlet. 'What trouble did you need to get out of?'

Scarlet scowls at Dylan's back. 'It was nothing. He's just trying to stir stuff up.'

'Ha!' Dylan finally emerges from inside the fridge, for some reason holding a packet of cheese and a red pepper. 'Yeah, okay. If by *nothing*, you mean that you've got mixed up with a drug-dealing scumbag like Ashley, then I guess you're right. It's nothing.'

Every parent has certain key words and phrases that are guaranteed to trigger a reaction. I think it is a fair assumption to make that for most of us, the word 'drugs' is pretty high on the list, alongside 'pregnancy', 'tattoos', 'Snapchat' and 'I need some money'.

I point at Scarlet. 'You. Sit down.' Then I turn to Dylan. 'And you. Right now. Next to her.'

I walk across to where Benji is sitting, jaw gaping open, biscuit held out in front of him. 'Have you got any homework?' I ask. He shakes his head, his eyes wide.

'Is Scarlet on drugs?' he whispers loudly. 'Because that's definitely very bad. We've been learning about drugs in school. We saw a picture, Mum. They make the inside of your nose fall apart.'

He cranes round me and stares at Scarlet. 'Do you want to look like Voldemort?' he asks her. ''Cos that's what's going to happen if you take drugs. Your nose is going to collapse.'

'For fuck's sake,' mutters Scarlet. I shoot her an evil glare before turning back to Benji.

'She's not on drugs.' I give him a quick smile. 'But she does now owe the swear jar fifty pence, doesn't she?'

Benji grins at me, the worry dropping from his face.

'I need to talk to your brother and sister and I think that it would be okay for you to take one more biscuit and have some iPad time,' I tell him. 'Just because it's Friday. And take Dogger with you.'

I don't need the dog getting any ideas about delinquent behaviour either.

I wait for him to skip out of the room and then I sit down opposite my two oldest children and wait. One of them will crack before too long; they always do.

'Dylan is being a prick.' Scarlet obviously feels that attack is the best form of defence in this instance. 'He doesn't know what he's talking about.'

Dylan rolls his eyes. 'Everyone knows that he's a drug dealer.'

'Whoop-de-doo. Big freaking deal.' My daughter and I obviously have different ideas about what constitutes a big deal.

I take a deep breath. 'Scarlet. I am going to ask you some questions and the answers will be either yes or no. Do not attempt to go off-topic or muddy the waters by slinging insults at your brother. I will accept one-word, one-syllable answers only, otherwise you are grounded for the next month, regardless of whatever you have or have not done. Is that understood?'

Scarlet nods sullenly. I never used to speak to my children like I was an off-duty prosecutor, but experience has taught me that unless I wish to drown in excuses and explanations then it is wise to limit their opportunity to talk.

'Are we talking about Ashley Dunsford from school?' I say gently, despite knowing the answer. Best to start your suspect off with a simple question. It helps to create trust and build a sense of security.

Scarlet nods, which I accept. For now.

'And is he a friend of yours?' I smile encouragingly at my daughter, putting her at ease.

'Well, I wouldn't say he's a friend as much as—'

'Ah, ah, ah.' I wag my finger at her. 'Yes or no?'

She glowers across the table. 'Yes.'

I would actually make a great interrogator. There would be no need for any unpleasantness either; it would all be very civilised and clean.

'And does Ashley partake in illegal substances?' I enquire, dropping my voice an octave. I read somewhere that children are so accustomed to the high-pitched sounds of the female voice that they respond to a lower-pitched voice with more respect and authority.

'What?' Scarlet looks at me in confusion. 'What's wrong with your throat?'

'Is he on drugs?' I ask, in my normal voice this time.

Scarlet shrugs. 'You'd have to ask him that, Mum. It's not like he's shooting up in our Maths lesson or anything.'

'That's not an answer, young lady.' I lean forward so that she can't avoid my stare. 'Does he take drugs?'

'Fine. Yes. Sometimes, I guess.' Scarlet stares back at me with defiance. 'But you can't be mad at me because I happen to know someone who does something that you don't like.'

'It's not about whether I like it or not,' I tell her. 'It's about whether you're friends with people who are safe.'

And for your information, young lady, I do not like it. Not one little bit.

'He's not going to ram a needle into my arm while I'm trying to figure out quadratic equations,' snorts my daughter. Even Dylan cracks a smile. 'Not without me noticing, anyway.'

'What drugs does he take, exactly?' I pale, imagining scenes from *Trainspotting* in the Year Eleven toilets. 'I need to speak to the Head about this.'

'No!' Scarlet looks panic-stricken. 'Honestly, Mum. If you grass him up then don't be surprised if you start getting bits of my body delivered to you in the post. There's a code of conduct, you know.'

I stare at her for a moment, feeling my stomach drop. And then Dylan bursts out laughing.

'She's winding you up, Mum. Our school might be crap but it isn't run by the Mafia.'

I push my chair back and stand up, feeling both angry and foolish; a dangerous combination. 'That's it. If you aren't prepared to have a serious conversation about something that is clearly a serious subject then I'm going straight to the Head and you can tell him all about it yourself.'

Scarlet holds up her hands. 'Ok, I'm sorry. Sit down and I'll tell you what happened today.'

I stare at her suspiciously, but I don't really have any choice. 'Does he really take drugs or was that your idea of a joke too?'

She nods. 'He smokes a bit of weed now and then. And he might sell it to his mates, which is what Mr Moral Police over here was going on about.' She jerks her head at Dylan. 'But you don't need to worry, Mum. I'm not interested in that stuff.'

I have no idea if she's telling me the truth. I only have her word to go on. It hits me, not for the first time, that parenting teenagers involves an awful lot of blind faith.

I stare at my beautiful girl and contemplate how the last sixteen years can possibly have flown by so quickly. I wonder if Nick and I have equipped her with the necessary skills to navigate this complex, murky world that, despite all our best efforts, is totally bewildering to anybody under the age of thirty-five.

Scarlet stands up and walks behind my chair, bending down to rest her chin on my head.

'I'm serious,' she says and there's no joking in her voice now. 'I like talking to Ashley because he's a laugh but I'm not mixed up in the crowd that he hangs out with. They're not particularly nice to girls, if you know what I mean?'

I twist my head and look at her, hoping that my voice sounds calm and unthreatening. 'In what way?'

Scarlet moves back to her seat. 'Oh, you know. They think that every girl is put on this earth to give them something to look at.' She pauses for a second and picks up her mug. 'It's kind of hard to work out whether it's worse if they think you're pretty or totally ugly – you get the same amount of attention, just a different flavour of abuse.'

'Do they say things to you?' I ask, glancing at Dylan. His jaw is set and he looks angry.

Scarlet laughs. 'I'm female. Of course they do!'

'And do they say things about you being nice to look at, or—' I stop. These are not questions that I want to ask my daughter. It won't somehow be less awful if the boys think she's attractive.

Scarlet shrugs. 'It depends on what's going on. Like, when Martin wanted to go out with me then he wouldn't stop talking about how sexy I am and then, when he finally got the message that I wasn't interested, they all started slagging me off whenever they saw me, asking me if I was a lesbian or frigid.' She rolls her eyes. 'As if those are the only possible reasons that a person might have for not wanting to go out with pervy Martin.'

I am speechless.

Dylan is not.

'Which one is Martin?' His voice is low. 'Is he the one who sent the revenge porn of that girl in the year below you?'

Scarlet nods. 'That's the one. He's a charmer, can't you tell? He's good-looking but he's a bit of a nob.'

I shake my head, trying to activate my brain. 'Did he get punished for doing that?' I don't remember any incident involving a Year Ten girl.

'Who was going to punish him, Mum?' Scarlet picks at her nail varnish. 'The girl was too embarrassed to report him and her friends probably all fancy him. And all the boys who saw it probably got off on it, so they weren't exactly going to complain, were they?'

This is hideous.

'We need to do something.' I slam my hands on the table.

'I can't just sit here and listen to you telling me that this kind of thing is happening in the place where you're supposed to be safe, for god's sake.'

'What can you possibly do?' Scarlet sounds curious. 'Boys want girls to act like they've just stepped off the set of a porn flick – it's how it is. You can't change how they think.'

'Not all boys, thanks very much.' Dylan glares at her. 'Don't lump us all in with the likes of pervy Martin.'

In the midst of everything, I feel a sense of relief about Dylan's response. He's right. Not all boys. Not my boys.

Scarlet nods. 'Okay. *Some* boys want girls to act like porn stars and *some* girls are prepared to play along, especially if the boy is gorgeous. But you don't need to worry, Mum. I'm not that stupid.'

I want to tell her that stupid will usually dress itself up as all kinds of other things. Stupid is a superb chameleon, disguising itself as love or bravery or a desire for recognition or acceptance. Nobody embarks on a situation thinking that they're being stupid.

But I don't, because the one skill that my daughter needs above all others is self-confidence and a belief that she can make decisions that won't hurt her. I give her a hug, crack open the bar of emergency chocolate that I keep hidden at the back of the fridge and sit with my girl at the kitchen table while she talks about everything and nothing. The dramas and the angst and the friendship issues and the worries that are all so incredibly easy to dismiss as teenage hormones, but which are the foundations of her world right now.

Chapter 22

Cassie phones me during the afternoon and begs me to meet her for a drink.

'I thought you had a hot date?' I ask, gesturing silently at Benji to stop chasing Dogger around the kitchen table. It's been raining solidly for the last week and both Benji and the dog have got a serious dose of cabin fever. The weekend feels like it's going on forever, despite the fact that it's only two o'clock on Saturday.

'He stood me up.' Cassie sounds indignant. 'Can you believe the cheek of the guy. He didn't even bother to lie about it – just sent me a message to say that he'd been reviewing my online profile and had second thoughts about our matchability.'

I stifle a laugh. Cassie created her online dating profile one night when we'd both had too much to drink and I have to admit, if I were looking for an Internet date then Cassie's profile would terrify me. It mostly consists of a list of non-negotiables that include things like 'no excessive facial hair' and 'no wearing socks with sandals' and 'no eating avocado on toast'. I suggested, once we'd sobered up and reviewed her account, that she might want to edit it a little bit, but Cassie was adamant that it stayed as it was. She said it would weed out the hipsters and therefore was entirely what she wanted.

Sadly for Cassie, there seem to be an awful lot of bearded men wearing socks and sandals in our locality who appear to enjoy a cheeky avocado toast as a late-night snack.

'So I'm your second choice then?' I dodge to the side as Benji leaps over a chair, trying to encourage an aged and slightly overweight Dogger to follow him. Dogger, never one to forfeit a challenge, gives it a valiant attempt.

'Yep. Will you come?'

The chair crashes to the floor, narrowly avoiding squashing Dogger into a two-dimensional replica of herself.

'I'll be there.' I glare at Benji, who is standing in the middle of the kitchen, looking sheepish. 'In fact, I might head down there now and get the drinks in while I wait for you.'

In reality, I do not spend the rest of the day sitting peacefully in the pub. Instead, I race around the supermarket as if I am a crazed contestant on a quiz show, before dashing home and attempting to cook lasagne while simultaneously juggling laundry and supervising homework and asking Benji to clean out Fluffy Rocket's cage about fifty million times before he actually does it.

Throughout all this, Nick is lying underneath his bloody Land Rover, making muttering noises and occasionally swearing loudly. I hope the neighbours don't hear; I work very hard to pretend that we are a nice, normal family who don't do things like swear in front of their kids or open bottles of wine at four o'clock in the afternoon.

I have just put the lasagne in the oven and am contemplating whether I have time to shower and change into my slightly less unfashionable jeans when Scarlet comes into the kitchen.

'What do you think?'

I turn around and see her striking a pose. Her hair is glossy and her skin is clean and she looks healthy and fresh and gorgeous. And she is wearing a T-shirt that has the words *Feminist as F*ck* emblazoned across the front.

I am presented with a variety of options.

I am too tired to consider which of these options makes me the best parent.

'Very nice,' I say, wiping my hands on a tea towel.

Her face drops in disappointment and I feel a distinctly un-maternal flash of triumph.

'Have they got one in my size? We could wear them together and make double the statement?' I'm on a roll now.

Scarlet frowns at me and flops out of her vogue pose. 'Why would *you* want one?'

I smile kindly at her. 'I know that this may come as a shock to you, but your generation did not invent feminism. Neither did mine, actually. Women have been campaigning for equal rights for years and years, in many different ways. I'm just as feminist as you are.'

Take that, Millennium child.

'Yeah, right.' Scarlet puts her hands on her hips and stares me down. 'So what have you ever done, then?'

Where do I even start, young lady? I cast my mind back

over the last forty-three years, searching for the most pertinent examples from my lifelong membership of the feminist club.

'I have three children and I also go out to work,' I tell her. 'That isn't something that used to happen. Women were expected to stay at home and tend the fire and scrub the floors on their hands and knees.'

Scarlet shrugs. So much for the sisterhood.

'Big deal. You only work part time and you always tell Dad that it's his job to light the fire.' She pauses and then delivers the real blow. 'And I haven't ever seen you scrub the kitchen floor.'

We both glance down at the floor in question. There are dog paw prints everywhere and breadcrumbs lining the gaps between the tiles. I don't dare to look under the table where I know full well that the dust bunnies will be having a party. I don't know why I even bother trying to keep this house clean.

'Do you think I've got it easy, then?' I keep my voice level. 'Because I know that Dad works full time, but I'm not exactly sitting on my backside on my days off, you know.'

Oh dear me, no. I'm eating chocolate and trying to write the increasingly frustrating story of the gorgeous but slightly freaky Daxx and the vulnerable yet up-for-anything Bella Rose. It's harder than you might think to pull off those two characteristics and remain within the realms of realism.

'I didn't say you've got it easy.' Scarlet swings herself up onto the kitchen counter. 'But it's not exactly chaining yourself to the railings outside Buckingham Palace is it?'

'There are lots of ways to fight inequality, Scarlet.' I can hear my voice rising in pitch and make a concerted effort to keep my cool. 'But while we're on the subject, I'm not entirely sure that the slogan on your T-shirt is much of a rallying cry. It *is* possible to make your point without being offensive.'

Scarlet gives me a look. 'What's so offensive about it, then?'

I am absolutely not in the mood for this, but my daughter is clearly spoiling for a fight. I am going to take this opportunity to show her that, contrary to her own, firmly held opinion, the world was not created by people born in the twenty-first century.

'It says "Feminist as Fuck" on the front.'

I am calm. I am measured. I am merely stating the facts. Not even a sixteen-year-old girl can argue with that.

Scarlet's eyes light up.

'It doesn't, actually. It says "Feminist as F – asterisk – C – K".'

I have walked straight into her trap. The only way out is obscured by teenage logic and pig-headedness.

I sigh, showing her that I am incredibly bored by this whole transaction.

'Don't treat me like an idiot, Scarlet. We all know what the suggested implication is and removing one letter doesn't make any difference. Everyone who sees that T-shirt is going to know exactly what you're saying, which is why it's fine to wear in the house but not out in public.'

Scarlet scowls at me. 'I bought it to wear on non-uniform day next week.'

I scowl back. 'Over my dead body.'

My delightful daughter gives me a look that suggests that this is a price she may be willing to pay.

'It's hardly my fault if your brain sees a swear word, Mother.' She leaps down from the counter and walks across to the fridge. 'Maybe it means "Feminist as Fock". Or "Feminist as Fick".'

Dylan chooses this moment to walk into the room, catching the tail end of the conversation.

'It could mean Fack,' he suggests, grinning at his sister before turning to me. 'That's a song by Eminem in case you're wondering. Do *not* Google the lyrics, Mum. I'm serious.'

Scarlet screws up her face. 'That song is disgusting. It's offensive to women and it's totally against animal rights. Ashley played it in our Maths class the other day and I thought I was going to throw up.'

I wonder when they started to listen to music that needs a parental advisory alert, and how I'm supposed to police what they're listening to as well as everything else.

Dylan laughs. 'Good point. Being "Feminist as Fack" is the total opposite of equality. It's not going to work as a pro-feminism slogan, that's for sure.'

'Do you even know what a feminist is?' Scarlet asks him. 'Or are you just like the rest of them?'

Dylan shrugs. 'The dictionary definition of feminist is "hates all men", yeah?'

Scarlet's howl of fury makes my ears ring.

'I'm joking!' Dylan holds his hands up in self-defence as she starts towards him. 'Honestly Scarlet, you need to chill out.'

'You try chilling out when you're asked fifty times a day if you're a lesbian and called a feminazi when you walk into a classroom.' Her face is red and her eyes look suspiciously bright.

'She's right,' I tell Dylan. 'And you should know better.' An image of Daxx pops into my head. I wonder if somehow I've been allowing Dylan to get away with the same arrogant and shoddy behaviour that Daxx displays. The idea is mortifying.

'You can't go around treating women like they're your possessions,' I snap at Dylan now. 'And a feminist is not someone who hates men, for crying out loud. A feminist is someone who believes in equal opportunities for men *and* women. It's the opposite of hatred. True feminism is about love and respect for your fellow humans.'

'Preach it, Mum.' Scarlet gives me the first smile I've seen from her in days and I feel the fire of righteousness burn in the pit of my belly.

'If I thought that I had raised a son who, however misguidedly, propagates the myth that feminism is against men, then I would be very disappointed.' I stare pointedly at Dylan. When he was small, the very mention of me being disappointed was enough to reduce him to tears of dismay.

But now he just gives me an infuriating grin and turns away, pulling his hoodie over his head.

'I'm deadly serious,' I warn him. 'I thought you were smarter than – oh.'

Dylan turns back to look at me and my eyes fall to the slogan printed across the front of what is obviously a new

T-shirt. Today is clearly the day for statement-making in the Thompson house.

'Zoe got me a present,' he tells us. 'She said that I'm the only man she's ever met with the credentials to wear it.'

'You're a boy, not a man,' I mutter.

'Nice!' Scarlet takes a step forward and offers Dylan a high-five, her indignation forgotten. 'You might want to tell Zoe to buy from a better website next time though. There's only one m in feminist.'

'It's still a lovely thought,' I add quickly, desperate to prevent another outburst. 'And "This Is What A Femmininininist Looks Like" is a great message. I'm very proud of you, Dylan.'

'You thought I was a raving misogynist a minute ago,' he smirks at me. 'You were pretty quick to judge me there, Mum.'

I have had quite enough now.

'Go and tell your dad that he needs to finish cooking the supper,' I tell Scarlet. 'This femmininininist is going to the pub.'

I throw down my oven gloves and march towards the door, only pausing to fling my final shot. 'And if you want the kitchen floors scrubbing then the pair of you can do it yourselves.'

And then I exit, ignoring the confused look on Dylan's face and the smug look on Scarlet's. I never did finish the conversation about her wearing the T-shirt to school; that is Nick's problem now. He can deal with militant feminism and badly spelt feminism and under-cooked lasagne while I drink Prosecco with Cassie.

Chapter 23

I pull open the doors of the pub, searching the room for my friend. It's busy this evening, but I spot her at our usual table. Pushing my way through the assembled throng, I apologise as I step on feet and shoulder-barge past people clutching their wine glasses as if their lives depend on it. It obviously isn't just me that's had a stressful week.

Sitting down opposite Cassie, I allow myself a huge sigh.

'God, it's good to be out. Have you been waiting long?'

She shakes her head. 'Not long enough,' she tells me, her eyes flicking over my shoulder. 'I could have happily sat here for another two hours, enjoying the view.'

I twist my head, trying to act casually. I clearly need to work on my sleuth skills, though, because the moment that I turn to look, an incredibly gorgeous man at the table behind me gives me a cheery wave.

I spin back to Cassie, my cheeks burning. 'I think he's noticed you,' I tell her. 'I might have given you away.'

She smiles. 'I think I might have given myself away,' she says. 'When I wrote my phone number down on his hand before you arrived.'

My mouth drops open. 'You didn't? Cassie! What if he's an axe murderer or something?'

Cassie sips her wine and gives me an appraising look. 'How many axe murderers have you ever met, Hannah?'

I'm about to take her point but then she ruins it with her next comment. 'And anyway, have you actually looked at him? He's hot!'

I slam my glass down with more force than I intended. 'That's exactly the problem,' I say, as she looks at me in surprise. 'We're conditioned to accept bad behaviour from beautiful people.' I wave my hand in the air, gesturing behind me. 'If he was ugly as sin, with a massive nose and spots, you wouldn't think it was okay that he could be a potential axe murderer, would you?'

Cassie laughs. 'Better a good-looking axe murderer than an ugly one,' she says.

Behind us, there's the sound of someone clearing his throat. I turn to see the man in question looking slightly flustered.

'I'm sorry, ladies, but I couldn't help overhearing and I just thought I'd confirm that I am not, and have never been, an axe murderer. Or any other kind of murderer, for that matter. I'm an accountant, if that helps at all.'

'Whatever.' Cassie waves her hand in the air, dismissing both his reassurance and his presence. He's annoyed her by taking our conversation seriously and I know that in the rare event that he does try to contact her, she'll have blocked his number before you can say 'serial mood killer'.

She turns to me. 'What's got you all riled up, then? Bad week?'

I'm about to answer when a sudden noise behind us makes me turn. Over by the pool table a group of young men are jeering at one of their friends, who apparently has just suffered the indignity of being beaten by a female acquaintance.

'Thrashed by a girl!' mocks his mate. 'She owned you, you loser.'

'*That* is what's got me riled up,' I say, glaring at the men. 'When did everything become about gender?'

Cassie sits back in her seat and looks at me in disbelief. 'Are you serious, Hannah? It's always been about gender. And sex. Those two things are the root of absolutely everything.'

I shake my head. 'Not true. Some things have got nothing to do with that.'

Cassie grins and leans forward. 'Name one thing,' she says. 'Name one thing that doesn't somehow feature gender or sex.'

I think for a second, noticing again the good-looking man that Cassie propositioned. 'Murder.'

She snorts. 'Do you and Nick not watch Netflix? Every single murder is about sex. Someone isn't getting it or someone is getting it with the wrong person or someone can't get it and so kills everyone else in a bout of frustration.'

She sits back, pleased with herself. 'Try again.'

'Supermarkets.' I smirk at her. 'Try telling me that gender and sex is the foundation that our local supermarket is built upon.'

Cassie rolls her eyes. 'That's too easy. Okay, what ratio of men to women do you see on the checkouts?'

'There's probably more women than men, but that might

just be job preference,' I tell her. 'It doesn't mean that the supermarket is based on sex.'

'And how many women do you see patrolling around in charge with those dinky little headsets on? As many as the men?'

I shake my head reluctantly. 'Probably not.'

'And how many supermarket employees are currently shagging other supermarket employees, do you think? That's how the system works, you know. It's the only way to get to the top.'

I laugh. 'You are being very unfair. And for your information, I have never been asked to sleep my way to the top.'

Cassie smiles sweetly at me. 'And that is why you're a lowly English teacher who only works three days a week.'

I pull a face at her and take another gulp of wine. 'I'm sure it wasn't like it is now when we were younger. I didn't have to endure endless abuse from boys about whether I was up for it or not.'

Cassie is unimpressed with my argument. 'So you never got wolf-whistled or beeped by car horns when you were walking to school, then.'

'Of course I did. And I hated it. But Scarlet has been telling me all about what goes on at school and it just seems different. It's all more personal.'

'And that's why it seems worse to you now, Hannah. Because you're looking at it through the eyes of your daughter and it hurts much more than it did when it was happening to you.' Cassie grimaces. 'But you're right about one thing. It *is* different now. Kids can access whatever they like online and every teenager thinks they have to be a porn star if they're going to get any attention.' She slurps her wine. 'Bloody hell, it was all I could do to tame the hair on my head when I was sixteen years old. If someone had suggested that I had to do something with the rest of it then I think I'd have chucked myself under a bus.'

We sit in silence for a moment, contemplating a lost existence where Brazilians were people who lived in South America and a time where, if someone had offered us a vajazzle, we'd have been expecting some kind of Eighties ice-lolly; something akin to the Nobbly Bobbly or Sparkle, or maybe even the Screwball.

'So, how's the writing going?' asks Cassie after a while. 'Have you written anything juicy yet?'

I pick up my glass and twirl the stem between my fingers. 'I'm struggling a bit,' I confess. 'I don't know how E.L. James wrote one book, never mind a trilogy. Seriously, I'm never going to let anyone say a bad word about her again. The woman is clearly a genius.'

'So what's the problem?' Cassie waves her empty glass in the air. 'Have you got writer's block or something?'

I shake my head. 'It's not that. I can write the words but I just can't get into the headspace of my female character. She's a bit of an enigma, to be honest. Do you want another drink?'

'Are bears Catholic?' Cassie holds out her glass. 'But don't go thinking that this conversation is over. I need to hear details about your enigmatic main character!'

I queue up at the bar, thinking about what to tell Cassie. I haven't shared any of my writing with anyone so far, not even Nick. I'm trying to convince myself that this isn't because I'm embarrassed about it, but I'm failing. This is the perfect time to talk about the characters and the plot and get a bit of feedback from someone who, let's face it, almost undoubtedly has more knowledge about this kind of thing than I do.

'Okay, so the main female is called Bella Rose,' I say, launching right into it the instant that the drinks are on the table. 'And she's your typical erotic-fiction heroine. Shy, fragile and delicate.'

'Sounds okay so far.' Cassie gives me an encouraging look. 'What's the problem?'

'Well, Bella Rose is madly attracted to a stud owner called Daxx,' I explain. 'That's with two xs obviously, because he's from Wyoming.'

Cassie squints a bit at this, which is marginally off-putting, but I tell myself that it could just be the wine hitting her system.

'And this attraction is a problem because Daxx is aloof and arrogant.'

Cassie starts ripping pieces off the beermat. 'That sounds like the plot of every erotic story ever written,' she tells me. 'Still not seeing the enigma issue.'

'It *is* the plot of every erotic story,' I agree, feeling a happy glow spread through me. 'Do you really think my book sounds like all the others out there?'

Cassie screws her face up. 'Yeah,' she says slowly. 'Sorry, Hannah. I don't want to be rude.'

I laugh. 'Don't be daft! It's good that it's the same. That's what the readers want, isn't it? The same old story with slightly different characters. I must be doing something right if that's what you think!'

'I don't know if that's entirely accurate,' says Cassie. 'But what do I know? I teach Chemistry. So tell me why this Bella Rose character is causing you such grief.'

'It's because I just don't get it. Daxx is into some weird, erotic stuff and she's just supposed to flip from being sweet and cute and innocent one moment to porn-star princess in the next.' I take a sip of wine. 'It's not very likely, is it?'

Cassie sits up straight. 'What weird stuff is Daxx into?' she asks. 'Come on, Hannah. Give me details.'

'I mean, it's the logistics of it all that's bothering me as much as anything else,' I say, ignoring her last comment. I'm not going to be tricked into talking about sex in the middle of the pub. 'If I walked into some stables and there was a gorgeous guy mucking out the horses and he propositioned me to frolic in the hay, I might be a bit tempted, but I'd need to consider all the variables first. Like, has the aforementioned gorgeous man had a chance to have a thorough wash? And is the hay fresh or is there the possibility that some horse manure might get on my hair?'

I look at Cassie in frustration. 'And what about protection? Is one to assume that all gorgeous men muck out stables with contraception in their back pockets? Or does a little STD among friends not really count, as long as the man is hot?'

There is a brief moment of silence before Cassie starts laughing. Not a gentle, encouraging I-feel-your-pain kind of laughter either. No, this is a rip-roaring, throat-gurgling howl of laughter that echoes around the pub, causing most people to pause in their conversations and stare at our table where I am rapidly turning red.

'You're too funny, Hannah!' she splutters. 'The whole point of erotic fiction is that it isn't supposed to be real. It's fantasy. Escapism. Bodice-ripping action instead of some bloke bending over to take off his socks and giving you an unwelcome display of his arse!'

'Well, it seems stupid if you ask me.' I take another sip of wine and glare at her over the top of my glass. 'And fake. Women don't just relinquish their principles for the first gorgeous man they meet. Bella Rose is a fraud – if she was as naive as she makes out then she'd run a mile from someone like Daxx.'

Cassie gives me yet another uninterpretable look. 'But you're the one writing her,' she says slowly. 'Change the way she behaves if you don't like it. Give her some balls.'

I put my glass down, slightly misjudging the distance and crashing it onto the table. 'If only it were that easy,' I say sadly, shaking my head. 'You don't understand, Cassie. When you unleash these characters they take on lives of their own.' I gaze across the room, trying to focus on the clock above the bar. 'It's as if I, the author, have given birth to them and now I have to let them tell their own story.'

'Are you serious?' Cassie slams her hand down, getting my attention back on her. 'You'll be wafting around in a floaty kaftan next, wearing flowers in your hair and joining Adele and Miriam on their self-improvement Inset day. That is the biggest load of cock I have ever heard.'

'Do you think that Daxx would have a big one?' I ask,

prompted by her insult. This is another issue that has been bothering me.

'A big *what*, Hannah?' Cassie challenges. 'Come on, you can't expect anyone to take you seriously as an erotic writer if you can't even say the word.'

I can say the word. I can say all the words. I am absolutely not a prude. In fact, I've always taken great pride in teaching our kids the proper words for parts of the body. No ridiculous slang terms in our house, thank you very much. I have a degree in Biology. I call a spade a spade; or in this case, I call a vagina a vagina.

I eyeball Cassie. 'I've been wondering if Daxx would have a big penis.' I enunciate the final word so that it rings out clearly around the pub.

Cassie snorts into her drink, spluttering wine onto the table.

'Please tell me that isn't what you're writing in your book? For the love of all that is Mills and Boon, please don't do that to me.'

'I have no idea what you're on about.' I adopt a haughty tone. 'I am an English teacher now, Cassie. I have absolutely no problem with utilising the proper words for things.'

Cassie clasps her hand over her mouth and shakes her head.

'Mmmmm-mmmm-mmmm,' she mumbles. I think she's probably had quite enough to drink.

'You're going to have to be slightly more eloquent if you want me to understand you,' I say, stumbling a tiny bit over the word 'eloquent' because my tongue suddenly seems to have doubled in size. 'What words of wisdom are you trying to offer me on my writing career?'

Cassie moves her hand, her eyes glinting wickedly.

'I said, nobody wants to read about penises and vaginas and mammary glands, Hannah. Which presumably is what your book is filled with!'

I shake my head violently and then instantly regret it. Once the room has stopped spinning, I fix her with my most serious look. It's time to deal with this ridiculousness once and for all.

'What is the actual plural of "penis"?' I ask. 'Is it "penises"?'

'Or it could be "peni"?' offers Cassie. 'Like fungi.'

'I think it should be "pena",' I tell her. 'Although that does sound a bit like a type of pasta.'

'Ooh, ooh, I've got it,' cries Cassie. 'You know that "goose" becomes "geese"? What if one penis becomes many "poonis"?'

I start sniggering. 'I'd rather deal with a penis than a poonis. No matter how many of them there were.'

Cassie nods sagely. 'Sadly, I have never been in a situation where I have needed to refer to multiple members of male genitalia. But if I ever am, I will definitely be referring to the gaggle of poonis in the room.'

The sound of our cackling reverberates around the pub. Once we've calmed down, Cassie gestures to the man behind the bar to bring more wine but he shakes his head, signifying that our evening has come to an end.

We stagger out into the cold night air and start scanning the street for a taxi. We strike it lucky when Geoff pulls up alongside the kerb. We've known Geoff for years – he used to be the school caretaker until he decided that fixing toilet doors and unblocking drains on an hourly basis was not his life's passion and took up cab-driving instead.

Once inside, we huddle together on the back seat and try to get warm. Geoff is listening to Radio One and the sound of manic dance tunes makes my head spin, so I lean back against the seat and watch the streetlights flash by: my own private rave.

When we pull into Cassie's street she hands over her share of the fare before reaching for the door handle.

'Thanks for a fabulous evening,' she tells me. 'Glad I haven't got any irritating kids to wake me up bright and early tomorrow morning.'

'Nick can sort them out,' I mumble, half-asleep. But then something makes me sit up and grab her arm before she can leave.

'What word should I use?' I ask. 'If I can't use "penis"?'

'The clock's ticking, love,' calls Geoff from the front.

'One minute,' I tell him. 'This is very, very important.'

Cassie puts one leg out of the taxi. 'I don't know about you,' she says. 'And obviously, it's not me that's the writer here. But I've always found the term "ding-a-ling" has a certain something about it.'

She pushes herself out of the door and then turns back and bends down to look at me. 'That or "disco-stick". Or maybe "schlong".'

I blink, trying to work out if I've heard her correctly. 'You think I should write about Daxx's "disco-stick"? Are you serious? He's a stud owner in Wyoming, Cassie. I'm not even sure that they have disco there.'

Geoff clears his throat. 'Look, ladies, I've got work to do. If you don't want me to drive then you're going to need to get out of my cab.'

'I'm sorry,' I tell him. 'I'm just trying to figure out if my so-called best friend honestly thinks that "ding-a-ling" is a legitimate word to use for a man's penis.'

He looks at me in the rear-view mirror. 'Can't say I've ever met any self-respecting bloke who'd use that term, myself.'

'Exactly.' I thump the back of the seat and turn back to Cassie who is doubled over with laughter, her legs crossed in what I can only assume is an attempt to prevent her from wetting herself.

'Do you want my advice?' Geoff swivels round in his seat. 'Go with something realistic. Something like "Geoff Junior", for example.'

Oh god oh god oh god. He did not just say that.

'That's an excellent idea, Geoff,' says Cassie. 'There you are, Hannah. Problem sorted. Daxx can refer to his "Geoff Junior" when he's attempting to proposition Bella Rose.'

'I'm not sure that's particularly relevant,' I say weakly. 'But thanks for the suggestion.'

'Or there's always "Captain Geoff",' he continues. 'If the fella is feeling confident, that is.'

'I'm going to get out here,' I say, thrusting the money forward. 'Nick won't mind coming to collect me from yours, Cassie. Thanks anyway, Geoff.'

'As you like.' Geoff is unperturbed. 'I'll see you around, ladies.'

I clamber out and we watch as he pulls off down the road.

'There he goes, good old Captain Geoff,' calls Cassie, snapping her heels together and saluting.

'That was awful,' I tell her, pulling out my phone. 'And it was all your fault.'

Cassie puts on her I-have-no-idea-what-you're-on-about face. 'It wasn't me that brought up the whole subject,' she says. 'And for what it's worth, I still think that "ding-a-ling" is a contender.'

The phone connects and I hear Nick's voice at the other end.

'Is everything okay, Hannah? I expected you home ages ago.'

I nod and then remember that he can't see me.

'I'm fine. It's just that I need a lift from Cassie's. Is Dylan still awake? Can you ask him to listen out for Scarlet and Benji?'

'I'm on my way,' says my gorgeous, understanding husband. 'Will I need to bring the sick bowl?'

'That won't be necessary,' I reply in a snippy tone. I hang up and stagger up Cassie's front path, where she is attempting to get her key into the lock and murmuring something dangerous about a little evening snifter before bed.

Chapter 24

It's another long day. My Year Seven class utterly fails to grasp even the most basic rules of the English language and I spend an entire lesson battling to get them to include capital letters and full stops in their work. And then, when I finally get home after spending two hours making notes on Year Nine's Shakespeare essays and collecting Benji from his after-school club, I discover that nobody has cleared up the breakfast things from this morning and that Dogger has obviously had a funny five minutes and has taken it upon herself to destroy all the post. So instead of sitting down with the nice cup of tea that I deserve, I find myself kneeling on the hall floor, jigsawing together mangled pieces of paper and hoping desperately that today wasn't the day that we finally received a large and mysterious cheque in the post. I am ever hopeful of being the recipient of a large and mysterious cheque.

Just as I ascertain that Dogger has only chewed up a gas bill, a request for cash from a charity and what appears to be a flyer for the local yoga group, Dylan crashes down the stairs, his rucksack slung over one shoulder.

'I'll see you tomorrow, Mum,' he calls casually, making his way towards the front door.

I am on my feet in an instant, blocking his exit. 'Where do you think you're going?' I ask. 'I'm cooking supper in a minute.'

Dylan shifts his weight nervously from foot to foot.

'I'm staying over at Zoe's house tonight,' he says. 'I'm pretty sure I told you about it.'

We both know that is a big, fat lie, kiddo.

I tilt my head on one side and pretend to deliberate for a moment. 'Nope. I'm fairly sure that we haven't had this conversation yet. But there's no time like the present.' I gesture towards the kitchen. 'Please. Enter my lair.'

Dylan looks at me pleadingly. 'Come on, Mum. I told her I'd be there by six o'clock.'

I look at my watch. It is half past five. Zoe lives fifteen minutes away.

'Fine. We don't have to talk about this in the kitchen.'

Dylan looks relieved and slightly surprised. 'Thanks! I knew you'd be cool with it.' He takes a step towards the door and I put my hand up, like I'm a New York cop directing heavy traffic.

'Not so fast, sunshine. I said we don't have to talk in the kitchen. We can talk about it right here.'

Dylan sighs exaggeratedly and lets his bag slide off his shoulder before leaning against the wall. 'Okay. Do your worst, Mother.'

I plant my feet apart, adopting a no-nonsense stance. 'Do her parents know that you're going to their house?'

Dylan nods wearily. 'Yes. Her mum is cooking tea which is why I have to be there by six o'clock.' He meets my eye. 'You don't want me being rude to someone's mother, do you?'

It's a nice try, I'll give him that. But my concerned parental inquisition has only just begun.

'Absolutely not,' I agree, amicably. 'I have just a few more enquiries and then you can be on your way, lickety split.'

My skills really are wasted as a teacher. I should have been a detective or a lawyer.

'Just ask what you want to ask and let me go,' begs Dylan. 'And by the way, I am actually eighteen now, remember? If you keep me here against my will then I can have you done for unlawful imprisonment.'

I have no idea if that's true or not, but I am unimpressed with his attitude. I hate it when the suspect gets all prisoner's rights on me.

'Then we'd better make this snappy, hadn't we?' I put my hands on my hips. 'Why do you need to stay at her house tonight? Dad or I can come and collect you if you don't want to walk home in the dark.'

'She invited me to stay over,' says Dylan. 'It's not a big deal, Mum.'

Those six words are the precursor to every single big deal that has ever happened in my parenting life.

The living room door opens and Benji stampedes into the hall.

'When is it teatime?' he bellows. ''Cos I'm literally starving!'

Dylan seizes the moment. 'I'll be off, then.' He picks up his rucksack and Benji lets out a wail of misery.

'Where are you going? We haven't had tea yet and you said this morning that you'd play *Minecraft* with me tonight.'

Dylan pulls a face and bends down to his little brother. 'I'm sorry, mate. I totally forgot about that. But I'll play *Minecraft* with you tomorrow, how about that?'

Benji scowls. 'That's what you said yesterday. Where are you going, anyway?'

'And where are you sleeping?' I add. Benji's arrival is quite timely – he's made Dylan feel guilty and vulnerable and I might actually be able to get some truthful answers out of him if I strike fast.

'I'm going to Zoe's,' he tells Benji. 'And I don't know where I'm sleeping, Mother. Does it matter?'

'Not in the slightest, as long as it's at least twenty-five metres away from wherever she is sleeping,' I say. 'Do not underestimate the power of teenage hormones, Dylan. Maintain a safe distance from her after ten o'clock and you should both be fine.'

Dylan closes his eyes, as if he is trying to transport himself far, far away. 'You are aware that what you've just said makes absolutely no sense, aren't you? You do know that teenage hormones don't magically switch to extreme mode when the clock strikes ten?'

'Are you having a sleepover at Zoe's?' asks Benji. ''Cos if you are, I bet you won't be getting much sleep!'

Dylan and I turn in unison to stare at him, horror plastered across both our faces.

'Now look what you've done,' I hiss out of the corner of my mouth. 'You've robbed him of his innocence.'

'It was you that started it,' hisses back my oldest son. 'If you'd just let me leave then none of this would have happened.'

I lean down next to Benji and put my hands on his shoulders. 'Do you remember when we had that chat about puberty?' I start, ignoring Dylan's whimper of distress behind me. 'And we talked about how sometimes, when people are grown-up, they find other people really attractive and they want to go to—'

'Mum!' explodes Dylan. 'Do you have to do this now?'

I straighten up and turn to look at him. 'Well, from the sounds of it, it won't hurt for you to have a quick recap of the basics. Seeing as you suddenly seem to be sleeping at her house.'

'He won't be sleeping though,' repeats Benji. 'Not if it's a sleepover. When I stayed at Logan's house we didn't get any sleep and his mum had to come in and shout at us because we were talking so much.'

Oh. Right. Thank god for that. The last remaining bit of innocence in the Thompson household appears to still be intact.

'I'm going.' Dylan shakes his head at me, as if I have failed a very important test. 'Thanks a lot for the chat, Mum. It was enlightening.'

I take a few steps and wrap my arms around him. 'I didn't mean to embarrass you,' I say. 'I just want to make sure that you're safe. You know?'

Dylan nods. 'I know. But you need to trust me. I'm not an idiot.'

Yes, you are! You are a raging mess of hormones and you have no clue about cause and consequence. You are the Oxford Dictionary definition of the word 'idiot'.

I stand back and look him in the eye. 'I know you're not. But that doesn't stop me worrying.'

He bends down and gives me a quick kiss on the cheek. 'I'll see you after school tomorrow,' he says. 'And you don't need to stress. Her dad's really strict – I'll probably be sleeping in his garden shed.'

I watch him open the door and head down the path. My first-born, my baby, my little boy. Only he isn't a baby and he isn't little, not anymore, and I know that I have no choice but to let him make his own decisions. And it isn't that I don't trust him – well okay, I don't trust him a *tiny* bit – but mostly it's just that I didn't know it would be this difficult.

Whenever I thought about him growing up, I imagined a scenario where we would all be different; where we would all be *ready*. And he is – I can see that – but I am not. I am not the sensible, logical, mature woman that I imagined I would be. When I waved Dylan off to adulthood I thought I would have perfect hair and possibly be wearing something floral. I would send him on his way with a cheery farewell before heading indoors to prepare a simple yet delicious meal for the sixteen friends that would be popping over for an informal yet entertaining supper. The harsh reality is that I still hate cooking and I *still* haven't found my perfect hairstyle. And Nick and I have never held a dinner party in our lives apart from one time when we invited some friends over and we cooked our signature dish, known as very-hot-chilli-chicken-that-changes-depending-on-what's-in-the-cupboard.

It was barely edible and they got divorced shortly afterwards. We have never quite got over the suspicion that our cooking was the final straw.

I am supposed to be someone different, someone better. Not the same old me that I've always been. Because the same old me doesn't think that she has the strength of character to let her babies fly the nest. Not without a parachute, anyway.

Chapter 25

My inbox pings. I click off the lesson that I'm struggling to plan and into my emails. There's one unread message and it's from my mother. I take a sip of now-cold coffee and open it up.

Subject: Porn

Hannah.

Can you remember what the formula is for working out your porn name?

Mum x

I snort, narrowly avoiding spitting coffee across the keyboard. What the hell?

Nick looks up from his laptop. 'Something the matter?'

I grimace. 'Nothing to see here. Just my normal mother asking me a normal question about how to generate your porn name.'

I look back at the screen and start typing a response.

Re: Porn

MUM!!!!! Do not go sending me emails with PORN as the subject heading!!! The government will absolutely be reading this now …

Anyway, I think you have to use the name of your first pet and the street you grew up on, which if I recall correctly would make you the inimitable Rascal Cavendish. It has a certain ring to it.

Do you have something that you'd like to tell me …?

Her reply pops into my inbox one minute later.

Re: Porn

Was just thinking that it could be your nom de plume.

Or maybe not.

Xxx

My laugh makes Nick close his laptop lid.

'Is your mother going into the adult film industry?' he enquires, with extra emphasis on the word 'adult'. 'Because I'm not sure that I can handle Sunday lunches at her house anymore if she is.'

'Ha-ha.' I close the laptop and yawn. 'She was wondering if that might be a way to work out my writer name. You know, if I ever actually get this book written.'

'Ooh.' Nick's eyes light up. 'Let's work it out, then. What *is* your porn name?'

I think for a second. 'Well, my first pet was a goldfish called Fishy and I grew up on Bush Lane. Urggh – it's not exactly exotic, is it? It's even worse than Edna Tickle, which was her last brilliant suggestion.'

'Fishy Bush. Fishy Bush.' Nick rolls the name around his mouth before shaking his head. 'Sorry, babe. It's pretty bad.'

My competitive side rankles slightly at this. 'Okay then, Mr Sex God. What would your porn name be?'

Nick smirks and I realise that he's already worked it out.

'I am the incredible Mr Big!' he declares. 'Come on, admit it – I totally win!'

I narrow my eyes at him. 'You're lying.'

'I am absolutely not,' he protests. 'You can phone my mum and ask her if you want. When I was four years old I had a guinea pig and his name was Mr Big.'

'Whatever.' I stand up and check the time. Dylan is due back from his shift at the supermarket any time now and I still haven't figured out what we're supposed to be having for supper. 'But even if you're telling the truth, that isn't your porn name. You have to include the name of the street you grew up on.'

Nick's face falls slightly. 'But that ruins it,' he moans. 'Why can't I just be Mr Big?'

I put my hands on my hips and stare him down. 'Those are just the rules, Nick. There's no point complaining to me, is there? I didn't make them.'

'No – you're just the enforcer,' he mumbles.

'I'm waiting.' I tap my foot on the floor. 'Spit it out.'

'Fine.' Nick gives me a glare. 'My *actual* porn name is Mr Big Cook.'

'Ha!' I let out a howl of laughter. 'You sound like a character from that kids' television programme.' I put on my best TV presenter voice. 'And now in the kitchen, Mr Big Cook will be whipping up a storm. His beans on toast are the envy of little cooks around the globe.'

'It's better than Fishy Bush,' Nick snaps. 'Way better.'

'Keep telling yourself that.' I smile sweetly at him and dance across the kitchen, humming a perky tune. 'And this evening, boys and girls, Mr Big Cook is going to be showing his culinary prowess by driving to the fish and chip shop and ordering that well-known delicacy of chips and gravy. Yummy, yummy, yummy.'

'So I take it that your writer name is not going to be your porn name then?' asks Nick, in a pathetic attempt to gain control of the conversation. 'What are you going to call yourself?'

My light-hearted mood instantly dissolves and I start crashing around in the cupboards, yanking out a packet of pasta and some jars of pesto.

'I have no idea,' I admit, filling a pan with water. 'But it can't be my actual name, can it? A writer of erotic fiction needs to have a fitting name. Something glamorous and different. Something that says to the reader, "You are in safe but exciting hands with this author. You can purchase this book secure in the knowledge that you are in for a titillating yet informative read."'

Nick looks doubtful. 'I don't know, Hannah. That's quite a lot to ask from a name, don't you think? And also, I'm not sure that titillating and informative go glove in hand, as it were.'

I dismiss his comments with a flick of my wrist. I'm pretty sure he's got that phrase back-to-front anyway.

'That's where you're wrong. I've done all the research, remember? And I teach English now – I know this stuff. After all, it was Shakespeare himself that asked that well-known question, "What's in a name?"'

'I think his whole point was that the name didn't matter,' points out Nick.

I ignore him. The written word is my domain now.

'No – I need a perfect name that will convey both the provocative and enlightening nature of my book,' I tell him. 'I'll keep thinking about it. The right name will come to me when I'm relaxed and not trying too hard.'

Chapter 26

The kids are all safely at school, Dogger has been out for a walk and I am sitting at the kitchen table, my laptop open before me and my manuscript on the screen. I have decided that tonight, when Nick gets back from work, I am going to run him a hot bath, get him a cold beer and let him read my story so far. He's been on at me for weeks and having talked to Cassie about it last weekend, I feel like I could do with some feedback. And there's nobody that I trust more than Nick to tell me the truth.

I scroll down the screen and read the end of the chapter that I wrote the other day.

> *The more that Bella Rose mulled over the situation, the more confused she became. If only Daxx wasn't so utterly gorgeous, she told herself as she skipped through the paddock.* [Note: what time of year is it? Would the paddock be muddy, in which case she may not be skipping.] *He was clearly damaged goods, and Bella Rose wasn't the kind of insecure, desperate female who thought that she was only good enough to attract the attention of*

messed-up men. But the sight of his rippled six-pack was enough to make her brain splinter into one thousand pieces [note: rethink this phrase – a splintered brain is possibly not massively sexy] *and she found it hard to think straight when she was in his presence. She knew that the things he was suggesting were wrong – but a man like Daxx made wrong seem so right.*

Her mind was made up. Tonight, when everyone else was out at the annual rodeo and the two of them were alone, she would show him exactly what she was capable of. And may the Lord have mercy on her soul …

Cassie said to me the other day that I should write Bella Rose as the woman that I want her to be. She told me to give her some balls; but I don't think Cassie was quite right about that. Bella Rose has got something way more powerful than balls. It's about time that I unleashed her inner diva.

Taking a deep breath and reminding myself that it's only words, I lean closer to the laptop and write the next chapter. The climax that I have been building up to, as it were, where Daxx and Bella Rose finally come together and join in blissful union. I write things the like of which I would never before have dreamt of committing to paper and by two o'clock, when I finally come up for air, I have surprised even myself with the direction that the story has taken.

It is time. I am ready to share this with Nick.

I am more nervous than I thought I would be. Once the kids are home, I cook them an early supper and then bribe them with chocolate to watch a film together in the living room. Nick gets home just after six o'clock and I am ready and waiting.

'Good day?' I ask, greeting him in the hallway. 'Can I get you anything? A cup of tea? A beer?'

He stares at me, suspicion etched across his face. 'It's the car, isn't it? You've crashed it into something again.'

I smile reassuringly at him. 'The car is fine, as are the children and the house and the dog. Everything is fine. More than fine, in fact. Shall I run you a hot bath?'

Nick kicks off his shoes and walks across to me, keeping his eyes on mine. 'Something's up, though, isn't it? I can tell.'

'You are so negative,' I tell him, leading him up the stairs. 'You might want to work on that.' We head into the bathroom and I turn on the hot tap. 'I'm going to get you a beer and then I'll be back up.'

'Did you get much writing done today?' he calls, as I reach the door. 'Is that why you're in a funny mood?'

I hesitate. Now the moment is actually here I'm suddenly doubting my decision. What if he hates it? What if he says that I can't write for toffee and that I'm a big, fat fraud? Or worse – what if he feels like he has to say it's good, but he actually feels sorry for me and my deluded attempts at being an author?

'Do you want to read it?' I whisper, barely loud enough to hear my own voice.

Nick hears me anyway and leaps across the bathroom to sweep me up in a hug. 'I'd love to, Hannah! Do you know how bloody frustrating it is to have a wife who's writing porn and not knowing what kind of kink her fevered imagination is conjuring up?'

He pulls me in for a big squeeze and when he releases me, the beam across his face is akin to his having won the lottery.

'It's erotica, not porn,' I say for the billionth time. 'And promise that you aren't going to judge me.'

'Absolutely no judging,' Nick swears, pressing his hand against his heart. 'I'm proud of you already, Hannah, I really am.'

I smile up at him. 'Okay, well I already downloaded it or uploaded it or whatever. It's on your e-reader.'

'What's it called, then?' asks Nick, unbuttoning his shirt.

'*More Than Sex*,' I tell him, keeping my voice low so that the kids don't hear. 'It's called *More Than Sex*. That's the working title, anyway. I'm deliberating whether having the actual word *sex* on the front cover might be a bit off-putting to the reader.'

'Well it sounds promising.' I can hear the excitement in my husband's voice.

'Don't expect too much,' I warn him. 'It's only a first draft, remember? And it isn't even finished yet. I just need you to tell me if it feels like a *real* book. Does it make sense? Do you care about the characters? Is it utterly rubbish and terrible and a waste of time?'

And then I head downstairs to the kitchen where I pour myself a generous glass of wine and try not to feel like I've just made myself more vulnerable than I have ever been before.

I give Nick twenty minutes before heading back with his beer. When I walk into the bathroom he is submerged beneath the bubbles, his e-reader held high. He barely glances at the beer when I put it on the chair next to him, which I feel is a good sign.

'Where are you up to?' I ask. 'What do you think so far?'

'Daxx just yelled at Bella Rose for recklessly entering a bareback bronco competition,' he answers. 'And Bella Rose is screaming at him and saying that she's been riding bareback forever and that he doesn't own her. To which Daxx is replying that if he did own her, she wouldn't be quite as feral as she clearly is. And then she tells Daxx that she'll show him what real feral looks like if he doesn't start putting the toilet seat down when he's finished having a wee.'

'Ooh, I like that bit,' I say, perching on the side of the bath. 'Have you read the part where Bella Rose catches Daxx making a beef pie for the old man who lives in a neighbouring ranch? Because that's quite a pivotal scene – it shows a softer side to him and makes him more appealing.'

'Hmmm.' Nick keeps reading.

'Do you like Bella Rose? I can't decide if she's kick-ass or annoying or maybe a bit of both. I mean, if I met her in real life then I think that she might be quite a good laugh, but it'd be good to hear what you think. You know, from a male perspective.'

'Hannah. Stop talking.' Nick finally looks up. 'My male perspective cannot think about anything when you're asking me a thousand questions. Just let me read it.'

Chastened, I tiptoe out of the bathroom and sit on our bed, glass of wine in hand. I pick up the book I started reading a few weeks ago from the bedside table, but it's impossible;

I can't focus on anything other than the fact that Nick is reading my words. I strain my ears, desperate to pick up on what he's thinking, but the only sound coming from the bathroom is the occasional splash of water.

Eventually I grow bored with waiting.

'I'm going downstairs!' I yell to Nick. 'Are you going to be in there much longer?'

'I've nearly finished it!' he calls back. 'Give me another twenty minutes and I'll be with you.'

It's actually more like an hour before Nick appears in the kitchen. I'm halfway through the bottle of wine and supper is being delivered courtesy of the local Indian takeaway. I am far too tense to even consider doing any cooking.

'Are we eating anything tonight?' asks Nick, glancing around the empty kitchen. 'I'm starving. And is there any of that left for me?' He sits down opposite me at the table and eyes the bottle of wine. 'Crikey, Hannah! It's only Thursday, you know! What happened to not drinking on a school night?'

'It's called Dutch courage,' I tell him, pushing the bottle across. 'And food is on the way. Now are you going to tell me what you think about my book or not?'

Nick grins and salutes me with his now full glass. 'I think it's great!'

I feel all the air whoosh out of my lungs, where I've obviously been keeping it for the last ninety minutes. 'Are you serious? Do you really think it's okay? Does it sound like a real book?'

He nods and takes a sip of wine. 'You've got a really good way with words,' he tells me. 'I could totally see why Daxx likes Bella Rose and I was wrong about Wyoming. You made me believe that I was actually there on that ranch.'

I feel myself swell with pride. 'I've done loads of research online about what life is like there. For example, did you know that Wyoming is the tenth largest state in America but the second least densely populated? And it's very dry – most of the state gets less than ten inches of rainfall a year.'

'Yes, I read that in your book,' Nick tells me. 'It was surprisingly informative.'

'I think it's important to be realistic when you're writing,' I say, leaning back in my chair. 'I hate it when you're in the middle of a story and the author gets something wrong and it jolts you out of the action. It's totally frustrating.'

Nick puts his glass down and puts his hand on the table. 'I don't think there's any risk of your book not being factually accurate,' he says. 'Parts of it felt like reading a Wikipedia entry. In a good way.'

The doorbell rings and he stands up, scanning the room for his wallet before heading out into the hall. I light the candles that we keep on the table but rarely ever bother to use, and when he comes back in, we decant the delicious-smelling curry onto plates and settle back down.

'This is lovely,' I say. 'We should have more nights like this. So what was your favourite bit of the book? And what do you think should happen next?'

Nick thinks for a moment. 'I liked it when you were building tension between the characters. I thought you did that really well – it kept me wanting to read on, wondering if they were ever going to actually get it together.'

I smile. I don't know why I was so worried about showing my work to him.

'Yep,' he continues. 'There really is a whole load of tension in *More Than Sex*, that's for sure.'

'Tension is the key to good writing,' I confirm. 'I read that in an online article about how to write a bestselling novel.'

'Mmmmm,' mumbles Nick through a mouthful of rice. 'I just wonder if, maybe, the tension needs to actually lead somewhere? Do you want to share some of this naan bread?'

I put down my fork and stare at him. 'What do you mean?'

'This naan bread. Do you want some?' He points to the flatbread in front of me but I am not interested in baked products right now.

'No, Nick. I mean, what do you mean about the tension needing to lead to something? Are you saying that my story doesn't go anywhere? Are you saying that my plotline is *static*?'

'Not at all.' Nick rams more food in his mouth, looking like he's seriously regretting having spoken.

'So what *are* you saying?' I push my plate away. Curry can wait. 'You can't just throw a comment like that out there and then pretend you didn't say it. That's not how constructive feedback works, you know?'

'Okay.' Nick puts down his cutlery and wipes his mouth with the back of his hand. 'I was just wondering if maybe, in a book that is supposed to be pornographic, it might be reasonable to assume that the characters would have actually done something by now.'

'It's not porn!' I howl. 'How many times do I have to tell you?'

'Fine. Erotic fiction or romance or whatever it is that you want to call it.' Nick leans towards me and fixes me with a kind look. 'Maybe it's me, Hannah. Perhaps I've got the wrong end of the stick about what it is that you're trying to do here.'

Trying? What it is that I'm *trying* to do? I have a brief, irrational desire to throw the Peshwari naan at his head.

'Help me out. If I ask you to give me the defining characteristics of porn—' He sees my face and hurries to correct himself. 'Sorry, erotic fiction. If I ask you to describe what erotic fiction is supposed to be, then what would you say?'

I move my hand away from the naan bread. 'It focuses on the relationship between people,' I say. 'It's about how those people feel and the journey that they take together.'

Nick nods. 'Okay. But surely that describes regular fiction too. What makes an erotic story *erotic*?'

'Sex,' I tell him. 'Obviously.'

'Obviously,' Nick agrees, picking up his wine glass. 'And that's kind of where I'm going with this, Hannah.'

I am starting to regret my decision to show Nick my book. I hadn't given enough thought to the fact that he clearly has no clue about this genre. He doesn't know about the complexities of writing good erotica.

'There's no sex in your book.' Nick blurts it out and then starts to laugh. 'You've written twenty thousand words and they haven't had sex yet!'

I stare at him in disbelief.

'What are you on about? Did you even read the part where she's dancing in the bar and he's drinking moonshine out of a jam jar and watching her and she flicks her hair suggestively and he feels a longing that he can't ignore? Or the bit when she gets all mad because he's acting like a chauvinist pig but then she inexplicably wants to kiss him but she's so tiny and he's all manly and tall and so she has to stand on a stool to reach his full, sensuous lips? Or the last chapter where they're in the paddock and Bella Rose says that really interesting thing about sugar beets being one of the main crops that are grown in Wyoming and Daxx quivers and then she puts her hands on his chest and oh—'

I stop, reliving the scene in my head.

'Exactly,' says Nick, wiping his eyes. 'They never actually have sex.'

I glare at him and he holds his hands up in self-defence. 'It's not a criticism, Hannah. Don't go shooting the messenger. I just thought it was probably worth pointing out that you've somehow, quite brilliantly, managed to write a porn book where nobody ever gets it on!'

'Oh shit.' I drop my head in my hands. 'It's terrible, isn't it?'

Nick is out of his chair in an instant. 'No, sweetheart! It's actually really good. It just might need a bit of raunching up if you're intending on selling it as erotica.' He crouches down beside me and gathers my hands in his. I remind myself that I am very, very lucky to have such a supportive husband. 'If you want to avoid falling foul of the Trade Descriptions Act, that is!'

I push him away and stand up.

'It's only a first draft,' I say, in as haughty a tone as I can muster. 'And it isn't even finished yet. There's plenty of time for "raunching it up", as you so eloquently put it.'

Nick nods and returns to his seat. 'And I'm sure you'll do a fantastic job,' he assures me. 'Maybe you should practise now. What's that phrase you're always saying to the kids – "if you can say it then you can write it"? Come on then, give me a taster of the things to come!'

'Not a chance.' I tear off a piece of naan and take a bite. 'I know your game. You'll only laugh at me.'

'I won't!' Nick protests. 'I promise that I will maintain a straight face while you elaborate on the details of Daxx's throbbing member.'

'Ha!' I point my finger at him. 'That shows what you know! Throbbing members are totally last decade. No erotic writer worth their salt would use a description like that.'

'So what *would* you say?' asks Nick, looking genuinely curious. 'Because, no offence, darling – but you're not exactly well versed in dirty talk, are you?'

'I might be.' I raise my eyebrows in a way that I hope looks alluring and a little mysterious. 'I might be an excellent dirty talker. Maybe I'm just not talking dirty to *you*.'

Nick grins. 'Prove it. How would you describe Daxx in his hour of passion?'

He's annoying me now, but I can't back down; and part of me knows that he's maybe got a point. If I'm going to make a success of this book then I'm going to have to overcome my aversion to writing about actual sex.

'Daxx gazed at Bella Rose,' I start, narrowing my eyes at

Nick and daring him to laugh. 'And the more he gazed at her, the more aroused he became. And the more aroused he became, the more his, his—'

I swallow and clench my fists under the table. I am a grown-ass woman. I am not embarrassed by sex or body parts. I am here in my own kitchen, with my husband. It is safe and there is nothing to be ashamed about.

'The more aroused that Daxx became, the more his Daxx Junior twitched.'

I blurt out the words and then slurp the last drops of my wine.

Across the table, Nick blinks at me in confusion.

'Did you just say his "*Daxx Junior*"?' he whispers, as if the very act of speaking the words is causing him pain.

Ha! Who's the prude now, oh darling husband?

I make a valiant attempt to bat my eyelashes. 'I told you that I could do sexy.'

Nick gulps. 'I am indeed blessed among men,' he says. 'You're going to make your fortune, with gems like that.'

'You know it.' I stand up and gather the plates. 'And you'll be sorry that you doubted me when I'm swanning around the world on my superyacht, drinking Mai Tais with cocktail umbrellas and enjoying three hundred and sixty-five days of sunshine.'

Nick starts telling me that he has never once doubted me in his life as we stack the dishwasher and yell at the kids, who have taken advantage of our neglect to watch another film and eat their way through an industrial-size packet of crisps, and then we head upstairs to bed. And the entire time,

I am thinking about how I can take my novel to the next level.

What is becoming increasingly clear is that I'm going to need a little help – and I think I have the solution.

Chapter 27

I go online first thing on Friday morning and order the item that is going to save my writing career. Then I bring my manuscript up on the screen and write like fury, barely stopping to feed the kids or acknowledge Nick's return from work. I write all evening and late into the night, and then I wake up earlier than I have ever voluntarily woken on a Saturday and I keep on writing until I am very nearly at the end of my story.

'I feel like I've barely seen you,' complains Nick, bringing me a cup of tea. 'Are you going to be on your laptop the entire weekend?'

I look up at him, blinking to help my eyes adjust to daylight.

'I'm almost done,' I tell him. 'And I thought that we could have a date night tonight. What do you think?'

Nick's face lights up. 'Why don't I give Scarlet and Dylan some cash to go to the cinema? Then we can actually have some privacy for a change.'

I nod. 'That's a great idea. We could do with some privacy for what I've got planned.'

My husband sighs happily.

He has no idea.

After supper, I bribe Benji with an hour of screen time on the iPad before packing him off to bed. Scarlet and Dylan need little persuasion to take our money, and Nick gives them enough to get a McDonalds before the film starts.

'All the more time for us,' he says gleefully as the front door slams behind them. 'So what's the plan? Shall I run you a bath?'

I shake my head. 'I'm in charge this evening. All you need to do is drink some wine and relax.'

I lead him into the living room, where the scene is set. There are candles flickering on the mantelpiece and music drifts softly on the air. Everything has been chosen to enhance the moment, right down to the sexy playlist that I spent an hour creating this afternoon.

'Good choice,' says Nick, smiling at me seductively as the familiar, husky voice of Marvin Gaye tells us to get it on. 'Dance with me?'

He holds out his arms, and for a second I am tempted. But we're not here to dance, and we haven't got all night.

'You can just sit down there.' I push Nick gently on the chest until his legs hit the sofa and he falls back onto the cushions. 'I told you – all you have to do is relax.'

Nick leans back and eyes me curiously. 'I like the idea of that,' he tells me. 'But shouldn't we slip into something a bit comfier first?'

I glance down at the baggy top and leggings combo that I

threw on this morning. 'No, it's okay. I'm pretty comfortable in this.'

Nick grins. 'Well I'm thinking that you won't be in it for long, so you're probably right. Why waste time, babe?'

I glance instinctively at the clock on the wall. The kids left the house four minutes ago. Time is ticking. I've got a lot to get through this evening.

'Enough talking,' I tell him, snappily. I need this to be as realistic as possible and it won't work if he's chatty. 'Just lie back and listen to the music. I'll be with you in just a moment.'

Dashing out of the room, I head into the kitchen where I pour two glasses of wine. Then I hesitate. Wine doesn't seem right, somehow. Bending down, I rummage around in the cupboard and find a bottle of whisky left over from Christmas; exactly what I need. Sloshing the amber liquid into two fresh glasses, I kick off my shoes and pad back into the living room.

'Bottom's up!' I hand Nick a glass and throw back my drink, wincing as it hits the back of my throat. 'Right, let's get down to business.'

I put down my glass and hover over Nick, who is watching me with what appears to be trepidation in his eyes. 'You need to lie down and put your left leg in the air,' I tell him. 'Straight up, at a right angle.'

Nick frowns. 'I'm not entirely sure what—'

I don't let him finish. 'It's easy.' I grab his glass and set it down out of harm's way, then I put my hands around both his ankles and yank hard until he's horizontal on the sofa. 'Just raise your leg,' I say. 'Simple.'

'But why?' he asks. I realise that I am going to have to work a bit harder than I initially thought.

'Because I want you to,' I tell him, running my hand along his leg. 'Just trust me.'

Behind me, Al Green is crooning, telling me that whatever I want to do is all right by him. 'Listen to the music, sweetheart,' I whisper to Nick, pulling his leg into position. 'Just chill and go with the flow. And do what I tell you to do, okay?'

'I'm trying.' Nick grimaces as I push his other leg onto the floor. 'But this is starting to feel like a dodgy scene from *Pulp Fiction*, Hannah.'

Perhaps 'Let's Stay Together' wasn't such a well-thought-out music choice, after all.

I pause for a second, trying to remember what should happen next.

'Okay, you need to reach out your arms and support my weight,' I say. 'I'm going to crawl on top of you and you should be able to hold me using your core strength.'

I don't give him time to respond as I quickly position myself in a crouch at the end of the sofa. 'Are you ready?'

Nick raises his arms instinctively and I lurch forward, almost as if I am doing one of those weird, starter dives that little kids learn at the swimming pool before they're ready to stand on the edge.

It does not go entirely as I had planned. Nick's arms hold me for two fleeting seconds and then collapse underneath me. I slump down on top of him, hearing all the air leave his body in a massive whoosh, narrowly missing smashing my head into his chin.

I roll to the side and gaze down into my husband's shocked eyes.

'It's okay,' I tell him. 'That one was always going to be a bit tricky. I have others.'

I push off his chest to stand up, ignoring his groans. Then I brush myself down and walk across to the table in the corner of the room, where my new purchase is discreetly placed. I've bookmarked the pages and I turn now to page fifteen, which looks slightly more doable.

'Okay!' I spin round and clap my hands together. 'Let's try something else. This one doesn't need you to be very strong, which is probably just as well!'

Nick sits up and runs his fingers through his hair. 'Firstly, what the hell are you doing, Hannah? And secondly, there's nothing wrong with my strength, thanks very much.'

'Except for the fact that you couldn't hold me up,' I mutter. 'You might want to think about working on your core, Nick.'

'You threw yourself on top of me!' he protests. 'And I think you might have dislocated my right knee, while we're on the subject.'

I narrow my eyes at him. 'Do you want to have a romantic date night or not? Because you're doing an awful lot of moaning.'

Nick stands up. 'I don't know what you're doing, but yes, despite the fact that you are behaving in a bizarre and frankly disturbing manner, I am still keen for a date night with you. But I might need an ice pack for my knee before we go any further.'

'No time.' I prowl across the carpet and peek up at him

through my lowered eyelashes. He clearly needs me to bring out the big guns if he's going to stay, and I need him here. I cannot do this on my own. I've already proven that. 'And you won't be needing your knees for this particular position.'

It's a stupid thing to say, and technically inaccurate, but fortunately my mistress of seduction act appears to be working. Nick reaches out and grabs my hand, pulling me in close before leaning down towards my lips.

I spin round and take a step away. 'Are you ready to have your mind blown?' I ask him over my shoulder, allowing my cardigan to slip tantalisingly to the side to reveal a millimetre of skin.

Nick swallows loudly. 'I think so.'

'Good.' I bend down and peer back at him from in between my legs. 'So, I'm going to move into a handstand position and all you have to do is catch hold of my feet. Then you ease them onto your shoulders and we'll take it from there. Okay?'

Nick gulps. 'Should we – you know – take off some clothes?'

I shake my head and immediately regret it. The blood is already pooling and I know that if I stay upside down much longer then I'm going to start seeing black spots in front of my eyes.

'This is the practice,' I tell him. 'There's plenty of time to do it naked once we've mastered the moves.'

I place my hands on the floor and take a deep breath before elegantly flicking my legs out behind me.

They rise approximately two centimetres before thudding back onto the ground.

I try again.

This time they barely leave the floor.

'How long has it been since you did a handstand, Hannah?'

I can hear the mirth in his voice, but I will not give up. I kick out again, this time with more vigour, but my feet still fail to rise to the desired height.

'I don't understand it,' I say, crouching on the carpet. 'I was excellent at handstands when I was at school. I could do the scissors and the ballerina and the pencil and the one where you had to put one foot against the other leg. I was a handstand expert.'

'That was about thirty years ago, to be fair,' Nick tell me. 'Your centre of gravity has probably changed since then.'

I glare up at him. 'My centre of gravity is exactly where it's supposed to be. I'm just out of practice, that's all.'

'Sweetheart. I have no idea what this is all about but can we please just go upstairs and have regular, vanilla, ordinary sex like the regular, vanilla, ordinary people that we are? Please?'

I flop down onto my backside and stare up at him despondently. 'That's the whole point,' I tell him. 'That's what this is about. Regular and ordinary isn't going to work. Vanilla isn't good enough. It has to be sexy and raunchy and raspberry ripple. Don't you get it?'

Nick moves so that he's sitting beside me. 'Aren't you happy with us, Hannah? Is that what's going on?' He picks up my hand and strokes his thumb across my palm, avoiding my gaze. 'Because if I'm not being enough for you and if I'm not making you happy, then we need to talk about it.'

There's a moment of silence while I work out exactly what he has just said. Then the penny drops and I realise his mistake.

'Not us!' I exclaim. 'I didn't mean that it wasn't good enough for *us*, you numbnuts! It's about Daxx and Bella Rose! Vanilla isn't good enough for them, is it? You said it yourself – erotic fiction is supposed to be sexy – so I thought I'd try to get some inspiration. Look!'

I twist around and reach behind me, pulling the book off the table. 'I bought this online,' I tell Nick, waving it in his face. 'I thought we could re-enact some of the positions and then I might find it a bit easier to visualise what Daxx and Bella Rose might be doing.'

Nick stares at me, his face blank. Then slowly, he reaches out and takes the book from my hand, turning it over so that he can read the title.

'*Kama Sutra: Three Hundred and Sixty-five Positions*,' he reads aloud. 'One for every day of the year.'

'I thought it might be helpful,' I say. 'But it was clearly a waste of money. Those positions we tried were about as sexy as a wet kipper.'

Nick doesn't answer. Instead, he starts flicking through the book, his eyes darting from one image to the next.

'Some of these are a lawsuit waiting to happen,' he murmurs. 'I mean, good god – who in their right mind could possibly think that this one is a good idea?'

He turns the book to face me and I flush.

'That's the one that I was just trying to do,' I confess. 'I thought it looked like it had potential.'

He stares back at the page. 'You weren't doing it right,' he states bluntly.

No shit, Sherlock.

'You didn't need to do a handstand. The man is holding her legs and she's supporting herself by grabbing onto his calf muscles. And then it looks like she has to wriggle up his body and—' He stops and looks at me appraisingly. 'That's not going to work.'

'None of them work.' I sigh loudly. 'How am I supposed to write an arousing love scene if I can't even act it out in the privacy of my own living room?'

Nick flicks through another few pages and then looks up at me, a grin spreading across his face.

'I reckon we could give this one a shot,' he says. 'Come on. It'll be a laugh. If it doesn't work out then we can call it a night and go upstairs – and if it does work then we can still go upstairs and try it again!'

I shake my head. This was a stupid idea.

'Come on, Hannah.' Nick's voice is wheedling now. 'Let's try this one out. What have we got to lose?'

'Our self-respect?' I mutter, but he's already pulling me to my feet. I take the book off him and glance at the page. It does look a little easier than the positions that I attempted, and I can totally imagine Daxx and Bella Rose pulling it off with ease.

One last go, then. I suppose it can't hurt anything more than my pride.

'I'll be here,' Nick says, walking into the middle of the room and standing with his legs planted apart in a wide stance.

'You need to lie down in front of me with your legs in the air.'

I do as he says, holding the book above my face so that I can refer to the instructions.

'Okay, now you have to kneel down by my head,' I inform him. 'How *is* your knee, by the way?'

There's a creaking sound as Nick lowers himself onto the floor. 'It'll be fine,' he says gamely. 'I think we've still got an ice pack in the freezer – I'll pop it on tonight and take a couple of Ibuprofen.'

I look again at the page, rotating the book so that I can figure out exactly what goes where before putting it down on the floor next to me where Nick can see it. 'My legs are supposed to be on your shoulders,' I tell him. 'I think the man is holding onto the woman.'

I make a supreme effort and pull my legs towards me. At the same time, Nick leans forward and grips onto my ankles and between us, we manipulate my lower limbs until they are resting on his shoulders.

'Good job!' praises Nick.

I cannot reply as my thighs are restricting the flow of air to my lungs and I don't want to waste precious oxygen on unnecessary speaking.

'Right, it looks like I now have to move forward and to the side.' Nick takes over as master of ceremonies. 'I think you need to roll back a bit more, Hannah.'

I snarl, and contort my body into a position that reminds me of a turtle. My backside is sticking up and my head is pushed so far forward that I know I must have at least three chins going on. Above me, Nick grimaces as he bends his body so that his face is peering out from beneath one of my knees.

'I'm not sure we're doing it like in the diagram,' I grunt.

'That's because your leg isn't where it's supposed to be,' answers Nick. 'Just shift it a bit and I'll be able to slip into the space.'

'I. Cannot. Move.' My words are punctuated by short, sharp gasps of breath, each intake only a tiny percentage of what my lungs actually require.

'Just clench your arse and roll back a bit,' demands my husband, his face turning puce. 'I'm stuck here now. And don't fart, for the love of god.'

I glare at him. 'I don't fart. You know that.'

He snorts. 'Yeah, okay. So that wasn't you who woke me up last night, letting rip?'

'No, it wasn't,' I snap. 'On account of the fact that *I do not fart*. And get off me. This isn't working.'

'I wasn't kidding, Hannah. I'm stuck here until you move a bit.'

'I can't move!' I howl, feeling my leg muscles start to tremble. 'And I'm about to get a cramp. So if you don't get your stupid face out from between my legs then I'm probably going to crush you to death, anaconda-style.'

Nick's eyes widen but before either of us can do anything to stop my imminent thigh spasm and his imminent death, there comes a sound more terrifying than any I have ever heard before.

The sound of the living room door opening.

We both freeze, which is stupid, because while our teenagers may be self-centred they will still definitely notice their parents entwined like a two-headed beast.

'—least I didn't have to watch that crap film you were suggesting,' Dylan is saying. 'So that's some—' He pauses. Time stands still. 'What-the-actual-fuck?'

There is a tiny gap in between my thighs and Nick's face. I peer through, then wish that I hadn't. Scarlet and Dylan are standing in the doorway, open-mouthed and incredulous.

'Parents.' Scarlet's voice is chilly. Nick stares at me in horror. 'What do you think you're doing?'

'We're practising our yoga moves,' I say, trying to sound breezy.

'Mum lost her wedding ring,' says Nick at the exact same time, his voice only slightly muffled by my leg.

'Is it up her arse?' asks Dylan. 'Because that's where you appear to be looking!'

I close my eyes.

Make them go away. Please, if there is any justice in the world, they will just disappear.

There's the sound of footsteps and I sense our offspring coming closer, circling us like predators assessing their prey.

'Very funny.' Nick makes a valiant attempt to regain some authority, which would possibly be more successful if his face wasn't squashed into my buttocks. 'You can both go and put the kettle on and we'll be through in a moment. Then you can tell us all about the film.'

'Just bugger off,' I add. My spasming thigh muscles are making me tetchy.

'That's not very nice.' There's a creaking sound as Dylan flops onto the sofa. 'And there was no film because the cinema had a power cut. So I think we'll stay here and get a lesson on yoga from you guys. Or was it ring-retrieval? I can't remember now.'

'I don't think it was either,' contributes Scarlet. 'Not if this book is anything to go by.'

Oh for fuck's sake. This cannot be happening.

'Do not look at that book!' I order, making a supreme effort to yank my legs backwards. 'Nick! You have to move!'

I tense my thighs and try to roll back another inch. But this turns out to be a mistake. My muscles scream their objection and instead of releasing Nick's head, I clamp down more ferociously around his neck.

'Argghhh!' he yelps, and when I glance at his face I can see the veins on his neck standing out in angry protest. 'Stop squeezing!'

'I can't!' I yell back at him. 'You need to back off!'

'I can't go back,' he wails. 'I'm going to have to come forward.'

'This isn't even funny now.' Scarlet sounds utterly disgusted. 'Have you seen this, Dylan? Our parents are sex-addicts. We might need to go into care.'

There's a thud as *Kama Sutra: Three Hundred and Sixty-Five Positions* is thrown from the hands of our daughter into the hands of our son.

With a guttural moan, Nick pushes himself towards my head. There is a moment of sweet release as the pressure between my legs abates and I roll down onto my back. And then he lands, half sprawled across my body.

'Get off!' I howl. Nick flings himself to the side, pulling half my hair with him, trapped under his arm. 'Argggh'

'Were you attempting the Coiled Cobra?' enquires Dylan and when I look up, his eyes are dancing with amusement. 'Because I don't want to be rude, but it seems to me that you guys might need a little bit more flexibility to pull that one off.'

'Urgh. I'm leaving.' Scarlet shoots us an evil glare. 'And just so you know, I'll be sending you the bill for any counselling that I might require in the forthcoming months and years. Although I'm sure that allowing me to become Scarlett with two ts would go a little way towards healing my pain.'

'I'll be sending you my bill for all the home-cooked dinners and sleepless nights and endless laundry and unconditional love that I've doled out then, shall I?' I yell back, too exhausted to move. 'Scarlet with *one t*.'

'At least I haven't subjected you to visual displays of my sexuality,' she snaps. 'Yet.'

'We are *fully clothed*.' I feel like it is important to point this out.

She stomps out. Dylan follows her, the sound of his laughter continuing up the stairs and into his room.

I turn my head and look at Nick. 'It's not that big a deal, really, is it? Sex? I should be able to write about it.'

He stares back at me, his eyes sparkling either with humiliation or amusement; it's impossible to tell.

'I think it's the biggest deal,' he says. 'But, yes. You should be able to write about it, Hannah. Just write about what you know. Write about this. It doesn't all have to be Wyoming and perfect, you know.'

Chapter 28

I am staring out of the staffroom window when I see it.
When I see her.

My first thought is to take a step back, just in case she happens to look up and notice me. I cherish these rare moments of observing my children from a distance, seeing them as someone else might. But then my eyes flick in the direction that she is walking and I see the person that she is eagerly waving at. It is Ashley Dunsford. The fact that he is standing almost behind the recycling bins makes me instantly suspicious.

I step back to the glass and watch as my only daughter approaches the school drug dealer. I press my hands against the window as I see Ashley put his hand in his pocket and pull out something, which he then passes to Scarlet. I do not see if she gives him anything in return as I am already sprinting towards the staffroom door, desperate to stop this transaction before Scarlet does anything else incriminating or dangerous.

'Ahh, Hannah. Just the person.'

Miriam is blocking my exit. I quickly debate my options. I could push past her but she'd no doubt have me up on an assault charge before the end-of-break bell has rung. I could tell her the truth. *Sorry, Miriam, I can't stop now. I've just got to nip outside and prevent my daughter from buying illegal substances from a charming young man in Year Eleven.*

My eyes feverishly scan the room. The only other choice that I can see is to crank open the window and abseil down three floors to the ground. It's definitely preferable to telling Miriam what's going on by the bins.

'I wanted to set a good time for your lesson observation,' Miriam trills, like she's inviting me over for a garden party. 'Do you have a preference?'

I shake my head and force a smile. 'No preference at all, Miriam. You come and see me any time you like.' I throw out my hands in an attempt to look casual and relaxed. 'What you see is what you get with me. I have nothing to hide – my lessons are exactly the same whether I'm being observed or not.'

Yes, they're all a bit crap, whispers a voice in my head. I ignore it.

Miriam looks at me and raises one exquisitely plucked eyebrow. 'So you'd be happy to be observed teaching Year Nine, Class C then?'

'Happy?' I laugh, in what I imagine is a mirth-filled manner, although from the expression on Miriam's face, it is possible that I project more manic than merry. 'I'd be delighted for you to watch me teach Year Nine, Class C. Pop on down whenever you feel the urge. Miriam. My classroom door is always open!'

Except when it isn't, which is usually whenever I want to screech at the class for peace or when Vincent or Brody do their twice-weekly storm out, slamming it behind them as they go just in case we failed to get the point.

'Is everything okay, Hannah?' Miriam steps forward and glances around the room. 'You seem slightly agitated.'

That's one way to put it, Miriam. I am slightly agitated *that my sixteen-year-old daughter may currently be overdosing on substances unknown behind the school recycling bins. So if it's all the same to you, I might wander down there and take a little look.*

'Everything is absolutely fine!' I beam, moving towards the door. 'Hunky-dory, in fact. Never been better. Now if you'll excuse me, I have lessons to plan. No rest for the diligent teacher, hey, Miriam?'

I don't wait for her response; I start to run the instant that my feet hit the corridor. Weaving in between groups of chatting kids I speed down the stairs and throw myself through the door at the end of the hallway, erupting into the sunshine like an avenging demon. Or maybe a drug enforcement agent.

'Put your hands where I can see them!' I yell, racing across the concrete yard. 'And nobody move.'

Ahead of me, Scarlet and Ashley break apart and stare at me with their mouths open. Which is preferable to what their mouths were doing a second ago and which my brain is struggling to comprehend.

'Spit it out, Scarlet!' I shout, screeching to a halt in front of them. 'Don't swallow it. Just spit it out, right now!'

My brain has finally caught up with my mouth and I know exactly what is happening here. Ashley Dunsford has somehow, against all the odds, managed to lure Scarlet into his underworld. I saw a television documentary on this very thing, not long ago. He's the kingpin, the drug overlord, and as such he won't ever get his hands dirty. Instead he'll corrupt innocent girls like my daughter and convince them to do his drug running for him.

I should have let Dylan deal with him when his name was first mentioned in our house.

Scarlet's eyes are bulging and the look of horror plastered on her face makes my blood pound in my veins.

'Has he made you swallow a condom?' I demand, grabbing her arm and pulling her out of his reach. 'You need to make yourself sick, darling, otherwise it could burst and the drugs will leach out into your system.'

'Mrs Thompson—' starts Ashley, but I cut him off with a fierce look.

'There will be plenty of time for you to speak when the police get here,' I tell him, but even as the words are leaving my mouth, my mind is whirring with the possible ramifications for Scarlet. Will they believe that she is an innocent victim in this whole thing? Oh god, what if they decide to make an example of her and send her to prison for twenty years? I decide here and now that I will fight to the end to free her. I'll make placards and start a hashtag and camp outside 10 Downing Street if that's what it takes to get my voice heard.

'Mum. What are you doing?' Scarlet finally speaks, which means that she must have swallowed the drugs. I reach for my phone, only to remember that it's in my bag, which is still in the staffroom. We need to call an ambulance, but while we're waiting it is probably best if I stick my fingers down her throat and make her vomit.

'Just stay calm,' I tell her. 'It's all going to be okay. But you do need to tell me what he put in the condom.'

Scarlet shrugs out of my grip and glares at me. 'Will you stop being so bloody weird for one second?' she hisses, casting a glance at Ashley. 'You're totally embarrassing me.'

But the time for embarrassment is long gone. I am no longer a woman who will feel anything as pointless as humiliation or shame ever again, not now that I have known a fear like this.

'You'd better give me the money,' I tell her, holding out my hand. 'It's more evidence for the police when they get here.'

I shoot another harsh look at Ashley when I say this, but he just stares back at me, looking bemused.

Scarlet drags me a few paces away and tightens her grip around my arm.

'I don't know what you're on about but there isn't any money and there aren't any drugs and there sure as hell isn't any condom. So either you are deliberately trying to embarrass me, which, by the way, makes you the world's worst mother, or you're having a nervous breakdown.'

She puts her hands on her hips and glowers at me. 'So which is it?'

I falter for a second, but then remember what I saw.

'He gave you something,' I remind her. 'I was watching you from the window and I saw him hand you a package. Which means that you were either buying his drugs or you're his mule. And honestly, Scarlet, I don't know which one makes you more stupid.'

'It wasn't drugs.' She shakes her head in disbelief. 'And you shouldn't go round spying on people.'

'Well it's a good job that I did,' I say. 'Otherwise you could be out here in a drug-induced stupor and *then* where would you be?'

'At least I wouldn't be standing here letting you ruin my life,' she mutters.

I feel myself falling over the edge of sanity and make a heroic effort to cling on by my fingernails.

'He had his mouth on your mouth, Scarlet!' I snap. 'I saw you. You cannot deny *that*.'

She closes her eyes briefly and when she opens them again, her expression is weary. 'It's called kissing, Mother. Ashley and I were kissing.'

Oh. Right then. I flash my mind back and run the image again. Yes, I suppose it could be construed that way. Possibly.

'So he wasn't making you swallow drug-filled condoms?' I ask, just to be sure.

Scarlet's replying whimper is reassuring.

'So what *did* he hand to you?' I ask. I have to see this through now, it's what any good parent would do.

'It was a poem,' she whispers.

I barely manage to contain my snort. A poem? None of these kids do proper writing anymore. If Ashley Dunsford wants to communicate with my daughter it will be via text or Instagram or Snapchat. He will certainly not be using the handwritten word.

'Show her, Scarlet.' He has moved up behind us and is looking at her shyly. 'It's okay. I know the spelling is bad and everything but I don't mind.'

Scarlet gives him a beatific smile before handing me a piece of paper. I open it and scan my eyes down the page.

It's a love poem. It is messy and confused and Ashley Dunsford wasn't kidding when he said that he couldn't spell. But it is honest and raw and funny.

And I feel like a complete and utter cow.

'I'm sorry.' I hand the poem back to Scarlet and look first at her and then at him. 'I leapt to conclusions and I was very rude to both of you. I really am sorry that I accused you of being a drug dealer, Ashley.'

He has the good grace to blush a bit when I say this. His eyes flick towards Scarlet, who flashes him a quick grin before pulling me towards the still-open door leading back into school.

'I didn't know that you liked him,' I tell her, once we're out of earshot. 'And I really wasn't trying to humiliate you.'

'I know.' She pauses and looks over at me. 'I suppose it's kind of understandable after what I told you about him. You know, the weed and all that. But you don't need to worry, Mum. I can make my own choices about what I want to do, and I don't want to do drugs. And it's not as if he's a massive stoner or anything. Scientifically speaking, it's no different to you having a glass of wine every night.'

Scientifically speaking, I am forty-three years old and not sixteen. Scientifically speaking, I have made my mistakes and I have some idea about the consequences of my actions.

If I tell her now that she can't see him then I'll lose her confidence. She won't talk to me and she won't let me in. And she still needs me, no matter how grown-up she thinks she is. No matter how many times I manage to mess it up.

'Do we need to have a conversation about keeping safe?' I ask as we start up the stairs. 'Because, Scarlet, it's easy to get carried away, and you're a beautiful girl and sometimes boys look at beautiful girls and they forget everything that their mothers have told them, and so you need to be responsible and—'

But my words are drowned out by her howl of anguish.

'Mum! Haven't you caused enough damage for one day?' She drags me into the corner of the stairwell and looks around to check that we're alone. 'First I'm doing drugs and now I'm having *sex*? Are you for real?'

Yes, I am. These things are real. I am absolutely for real.

'I am going to say this once and only once, Mother. And then I am going to pretend that none of this ever happened. I am not doing drugs. I am not having sex. And if you are so desperate to parent somebody then I'd take a look in Dylan's direction.'

And then she's off, taking the remaining stairs two at a time. I rush to catch her, calling out just as she disappears through the doors on the third floor.

'What's that supposed to mean? Is Dylan taking drugs?'

'Try again, Mum!' she yells back. 'Second time lucky!'

Her laughter floats back down to where I lean against the wall, too frazzled to work out whether she's telling the truth or not; too nervous to work out whether I really need to know.

Chapter 29

I am so close to the end of this book that I can almost taste it. The moment that I came home from school on Wednesday I told the kids that they were on survival training and that if they wanted food, shelter or comfort then they were going to have to provide it for themselves until their father got home. Then I shut myself away in my bedroom and wrote as if the hounds of hell were snapping at my heels. Irritating, puglike hounds with Miriam's face superimposed onto their heads.

I only have the closing scene to write. The story is told – for now. Much to my surprise, though, Bella Rose and Daxx don't seem to want to leave, and the more I write, the more ideas I have for what might happen next.

I am not just a writer; not anymore. I am an epic storyteller, bringing forth a tale of sex and love and woe and sex and torment and romance and, above all else, sex.

Bella Rose is a fully formed, kick-ass character, and this is her story. And I feel like I've written something different. There are no pathetic heroines in my book – Bella Rose is a strong, free-spirited woman who has her own weird quirks and fantasies, and if Daxx doesn't know what to do about that then he knows where he can shove his opinion. Not that Daxx should have an issue with Bella Rose's predilections and desires, being the well-rounded, enlightened, twenty-first-century man that he is. This is what I really love about writing, actually. The power. The ability to create personalities and bring forth new lives with only a few taps of the keyboard. When I am sitting at my laptop, dictating actions and deciding outcomes for these characters, I feel like a mighty deity.

It's intoxicating.

And now, the final climax is here, and Daxx has absolutely no idea about what is about to go down. Bella Rose has been revealing more and more of herself. Up to this point, he knows that she's feisty but he still doesn't know the lengths that she is prepared to go to in the name of erotica. Because Bella Rose has been keeping a secret, and I'm about to show Daxx who the queen is around here.

And nobody should mess with an alpha female.

Flexing my fingers, I limber up. Then I start to write.

'Oh, Daxx!' Bella Rose's voice floated softly through the barn. 'Where are you, my sexy hunk of a man?'

Daxx emerged from the hayloft, his bare chest glistening with sweat. He had obviously been working hard, because it was a typical Wyoming April day with temperatures of 55 °F (which is the same as 12.77 °C) and that hardly necessitates the need to go shirtless.

'I am here,' he intoned. Daxx was a man of few words. He preferred to let his rippling muscles and fabulous physique do the talking for him, unless of

course the conversation was about one of his favourite topics, which included world cruelty, animal poverty and cuticle care.

Bella Rose gently guided Daxx towards a conveniently placed haybale, pushing him in the chest with her newly manicured fingernail (because women are allowed to be empowered and independent and *look damn good while they're doing it if they so choose. They can also be all-powerful and look a right state – that's okay too). He resisted for a moment, but she stared at him with her trademark fierce look, and so he sat down obediently and gazed up at her, his eyes hooded and dark.*

Bella Rose stepped back and planted her feet apart. It was time. She was ready. She had rehearsed her moves until she could do them in her sleep. All she had to do now was unleash her inner goddess.

'I thought it was time I showed you the real me,' she purred, slowly undoing the buttons on her brown leather waistcoat. She was naked underneath, and truth be told, the leather was chafing, so it was with a sigh of relief that she eased the item from her shoulders and stood in front of Daxx, showing him all of herself. Well, all of herself from the waist upwards anyway. Bella Rose was not a total strumpet.

Daxx's pupils dilated, which she knew could be a dopamine response or could equally be due to the fact that the sun had just gone behind a cloud, reducing the light inside the barn. Bella Rose was a pragmatist, however, and chose to take Daxx's widened eyes as a good sign. She wiggled her shoulders slightly and stretched out her neck muscles. What she was about to do required flexibility and agility and excellent core strength.

'What's going on?' asked Daxx, not unreasonably. Up to now, Bella Rose, the light of his life, the object of his desire, the wind beneath his wings, had held him at arm's length, granting him only a kiss (and even that only happened when she was in a particularly good mood or when he'd remembered to put the bins out).

'I have come to understand something over these past few weeks,' breathed Bella Rose, prowling closer towards him. 'Something life changing. Something incredibly simple yet astonishingly complex.'

'And what this that, my angel?' gulped Daxx as she reached him. 'What do you now understand?'

Bella Rose put her hands on her hips and stared Daxx straight in the eye.

'It's just sex,' she told him, shaking her head in amazement. 'It's, literally and figuratively, just sex. And if we can call it by its name then we can do anything.'

Daxx's face contorted in confusion for a moment as he struggled to comprehend her words. And then, with a roar of delight and a gleam in his iridescent, blue eyes that seemed to Bella Rose as deep as the mighty ocean, he leapt to his feet and reached out his hand.

Together they fell to the floor, not caring a jot about the dirt and the hay and the unsanitariness of it all. And there, right in the middle of the barn, even though it wasn't actually that comfortable and the only thing that Bella Rose usually enjoyed al fresco was an evening glass of wine, Daxx and Bella Rose finally—

'Muuuuum!'

The cry comes from downstairs and jolts me out of Wyoming and back into my room.

'What?' I yell back. 'It'd better be important.'

'Dylan isn't helping with the supper.' Scarlet's voice is shrill with indignation. 'You said that we both had to do the cooking. And he isn't.'

'So he can go hungry,' I shout. 'And it's not exactly cooking, Scarlet. I told you to make beans on toast.'

'But it isn't fair! He should have to help out too.'

She does have a point. Reluctantly I put down my laptop and ease myself off the bed. I've been up here for so long that my legs have gone dead and my first few steps across the bedroom floor are wobbly, like a newborn foal or someone who has been drinking since lunchtime, which I haven't.

I lean out of the door and look down the landing towards Dylan's room. I've been so engrossed in my writing that I hadn't noticed the loud thudding emanating from behind his door but now I can feel it reverberating through my socks.

'Dylan!' I screech. 'Come out here now!'

There is no reply. I try again and then admit defeat, padding down the hallway and knocking on the door. It's a new thing, the knocking, and not a development that I am particularly fond of. However, now that Zoe seems to be a regular fixture at our house, I am keen to spare all our blushes; and after last week when I barged into his room in search of spare mugs, I am forced to acknowledge that closed doors are there to protect innocent parties. Like mothers.

I bang my fist against the wood. 'Dylan! If you aren't out here by the time I count to five then I'm coming in whether you like it or not. Fair warning.'

I start to count, as loudly as possible.

'One. Two. Three. Four. Four and a half.'

No sign of my son. Damn it – I knew that I should have started with one third.

'Four and three quarters.'

Still nothing.

'Four and seven eighths.'

He is giving me no choice.

'Five!'

I shut my eyes and turn the handle. A wall of sound hits me in the face and I take a tentative step forward, allowing my eyelids to crack open just a tiny bit, ready to clamp back down if the scene before me proves too distressing.

'Hi, Mum!' The music drops and when I squint, I see Dylan standing by his stereo system, grinning at me.

'Hi, Hannah,' pipes up Zoe. She's sitting cross-legged on the floor, fully clothed and surrounded by schoolbooks. I quickly debate with myself what I think about being on casual first-name terms with my son's girlfriend and decide that I like it. It makes me sound approachable and cool. 'We're just getting some revision done before the exams start next month.'

'Very diligent,' I say, casting my glance suspiciously around the room. The smirk on Dylan's flushed face suggests that either a) she is lying or b) he has a newfound passion for algebraic equations. I turn to face him. 'Why aren't you helping your sister with supper, like I asked?'

He shrugs his shoulders. 'I'm living my best life, Mum,' he tells me. 'That's what you want for me, isn't it?'

I shake my head. 'Nope. Not in the slightest. I have no idea where you got that ridiculous theory from. What I *want* is for you to heat up a couple of tins of baked beans.'

Dylan grimaces at me so I smile sweetly and turn to his girlfriend. 'You're very welcome to stay for supper, Zoe. If baked beans tickle your fancy?'

'That sounds lovely. But my mum's cooking a roast tonight and I said that I'd be home by six o'clock.'

'Of course, of course.' I nod at her. 'We'd normally be having something like that. You know, a roast dinner with all the trimmings or a three-meat lasagne with homegrown salad!' I give a little laugh. 'Mealtimes with all the family are the best, aren't they?'

Is her mother actually insane? Who on earth cooks a roast dinner on a Friday night? Friday night is the one night of the week when you are genuinely entitled to feed the kids crap and heat up a frozen pizza to go with the copious amounts of Prosecco that need to be drunk. Why would any mother waste that guilt-free opportunity?

Across the room, Dylan makes a spluttering sound.

'That's a lie, mother,' he says, outing me like the Judas that he is. 'You hate eating meals with us. And you've never grown salad in your life!'

'We grew cress once, when you were at preschool,' I say, a touch defensively. 'Don't you remember? You sprinkled the seeds onto some kitchen towel and we watered them every day. Back when you were a *nice child*.'

Zoe twists round to look up at him. 'My mum said that it'd be fine for Dylan to come back with me. For the roast dinner.'

Dylan leaps into action. 'Excellent. We can continue with our revising after we've eaten.'

'But what about the baked beans?' I ask, standing back as they both move towards the doorway. 'They aren't going to heat themselves up.'

'Scarlet can do it.' Dylan shoots me a smile. 'Zoe's mum is the best cook. You don't mind if I go, do you?'

Yes. I do mind. I mind very bloody much that you'd rather be at her house than at ours and I mind that you've just told me about her mum's culinary prowess. I might not be the world's best cook but I have other skills and I'll probably be able to remind myself of some of them in a minute when I'm not so busy minding.

I look at him. In just a few short months, he'll have gone to university. His room will be empty and I won't know what he's eating or who he's eating it with. And if I want him to come home in the holidays then I'm going to have to play nice.

'Of course I don't mind,' I croon, following them out onto the landing. 'Goodness me no! Why would I mind you going to Zoe's house now that I know just what a fabulous cook her mother is?'

He gives me a quick look and I swallow down my pettiness.

'And honestly, there's no real choice is there?' I grin at him, my pain-in-the-arse heartbreaker of a child. 'I'd choose roast potatoes over baked beans any day of the week.'

It feels like I'm losing him, like he's slipping away and the only thing I can do is smile and wave.

'Thanks, Mum.' He squeezes my shoulder. 'I'll make sure that I'm here all day tomorrow. I'll even cook my world-famous spaghetti bolognese.'

'That would be wonderful. But aren't you forgetting something?'

Dylan frowns, his expression confused.

'Your books!' I point back to his bedroom, where the textbooks are still scattered randomly across the floor. 'You and Zoe aren't going to get much revision done without those, are you now?'

Dylan glances at Zoe and raises his eyebrows. It's a move that is virtually imperceptible to the naked eye, but I am his mother. I know everything.

Quickly, before they can make their escape, I stride into the room. Now that I'm looking properly, I can see what I failed to notice when I first walked in. These aren't books for revision. Dylan is studying Maths and Physics and Biology and as far as I'm aware, Zoe is doing the same three subjects. These books have clearly been swept off Dylan's shelf in the vain hopes of fooling an unsuspecting mother. I pick up the pristine edition of *My First Encyclopaedia* that my mum bought him for his fifth birthday which has never been read. On top of that I pile a large hardback about dinosaurs and a paperback copy of *Five Fail Their Exams as They Are Too Busy Snogging and Generally Getting Up to No Good.*

Or *Five Have Plenty of Fun*, as it is more popularly known.

They weren't up here revising. I knew it. However, I have no idea what I'm actually going to do about it other than to go along with the farce that is unravelling before me.

'Here you go then!' I turn and thrust the books at Dylan, who has reluctantly followed me. 'Thank goodness that I reminded you!'

I bend down and grab another armful of paperbacks. 'Zoe! I think you're going to have to carry some of these too.'

'Very funny, Mum,' says Dylan. 'You've made your point. Can we just go now?'

No. You can't possibly go anywhere. Not now I know that you've lied to me about doing revision. Not until I can sit down and have another chat with you about keeping safe and being respectful and – oh my god, I thought that I'd be cool with all of this but now it's actually happening I am not cool. I am not even a little bit cool.

And then I spot it, lying alone on the bookshelf. The information book that I gave to Dylan when he was thirteen and suddenly started sprouting the occasional lone hair out of his chin. The sunlight glints on the cover and it suddenly takes on all the significance of the Holy Grail. This could be my last chance to do some parenting, no matter how covert.

Dylan sees me see it and his face drops. 'Mum, no!' he mutters. 'You wouldn't.'

I don't want to embarrass him in front of his girlfriend. This can probably wait until tomorrow.

'Dylan, we really do need to head on.' Zoe enters the room,

her glance flickering between Dylan and me. 'I've just had a text from Mum and she's running late so we can get a load of revision done at my house before supper. It'll be super peaceful and we won't be interrupted.'

She gives him a meaningful look and I make a decision. I leap across the room, making it to the bookshelf a fraction of a second before Dylan does.

'Just this one last book for you to take with you,' I say brightly, whirling out of his reach and shoving it into Zoe's hands. 'You're doing Biology, aren't you, Zoe? Dylan has read this book many times – I'm sure he'll be happy to summarise the main points for you.'

Zoe looks down at the book that she is holding.

'*Let's Talk About Sex and Puberty*,' she reads aloud. 'Oh!'

'I'd have thought there are some pertinent points in there,' I say, avoiding making eye contact with either of them.

'Thanks very much, Mrs Thompson,' says Zoe, quickly stashing the book into her bag. 'I'm sure it will be very useful.'

It'll be useful if you actually read it, young lady. I saw the look you gave my son when you told him that the house would be empty. And I'm Mrs Thompson now, am I? It's probably just as well, if we're going to keep this relationship professional.

'I seem to remember page fifty-two having some very helpful guidance on contraception,' I burst out, as Dylan ushers her out of the room. 'You know, just in case it's relevant. To your exams.'

I'm lying, of course. I can't remember if it was page fifty-two or sixty-two. I just want to plant the idea of contraception in their hormone-filled teenage brains.

'See you later, Mum!' yells Dylan, propelling Zoe down the stairs. 'Don't wait up.'

'Have fun, kids!' I call back, as they ram their feet into the trainers that are strewn about the hall floor. 'Not too much fun though, hey? Just the right amount of age-appropriate fun for two eighteen-year-olds. Who happen to be sitting A Levels in a matter of weeks. And who don't want to mess up their entire lives with one daft decision.'

Scarlet heads out of the kitchen, brandishing a wooden spoon.

'Aren't you going to help me cook the baked beans?' she snarls, spotting Dylan. 'That is so typical. Zoe, do you know that you happen to be going out with a complete chauvinist?'

'We're leaving now.' Dylan grabs Zoe's hand. 'I may be a while. And by *a while*, I mean that I'll be back next week when you've all finished being so bloody hilarious.'

I'm not being hilarious. I'm being deadly serious. There is nothing about this that could even vaguely be classed as a laughing matter.

They scramble towards the front door, almost falling over Dogger in their haste to leave our house.

'Make good choices!' calls Scarlet at their retreating figures as they hurtle down the garden path. For once I don't reprimand her for trying to wind up her brother.

Then she turns to me. 'Mum? How illegal is it to say that someone else was driving if you get caught for speeding without a licence?'

I drag my eyes away from Dylan and Zoe and stare at Scarlet.

'Do we need to talk about this?' I ask her. 'Are you in trouble? You can tell me, you know. I won't be angry, I promise.'

I won't be angry. I'll go freaking medieval on you if you have been behind the wheel of a moving car.

She shakes her head. 'No! I was just wondering, that's all. It came up at school today and I wanted to ask you.'

'Have you been driving a car, Scarlet?'

I have to ask.

'Mum! I'm not insane.' She smiles at me sweetly. Every single part of me wants desperately to believe her.

'The answer is: highly illegal,' I say, closing the door and walking towards the kitchen. 'Just like all the other criminal activities that you've been enquiring about, okay? All very, very illegal with a high risk of life imprisonment. And life means life, Scarlet. Do you understand me?'

I'm way out of my depth here. Plus I have a sneaking suspicion that I am lying. I think life imprisonment is actually something like twenty-five years and most people only serve half of that. But I don't want to say anything that might make crime look attractive.

'I understand, Mum! I was just asking!' Scarlet gives me a grin and then heads into the living room, where Benji is watching a film. Arming myself with a glass of cold white wine, I go back upstairs where my laptop is waiting. I am ready to finish this book and then get very, very drunk.

Chapter 30

It is written. I finish the last paragraph on Saturday evening and then spend all of Sunday going through the pages with a fine toothcomb. I'm not entirely sure what the editing process requires but I've made sure that there are no spelling mistakes or grammatical errors and I've tidied up the plot in a few places so that it all makes sense.

I read it for a final time after work on Monday and change a few descriptions of Daxx, just to ensure that his character is well rounded and three-dimensional.

Then I read it once more after work on Tuesday and decide that it could probably do with a few more descriptions of Wyoming and the setting. It's very important that the reader can vividly picture the scene, I know that.

I glance through it again on Wednesday night and realise that some of my sex scenes are possibly a bit much, so I make some notes like a genuine-ass, real writer, and today I've spent hours going over each act of passion and ensuring that it is as romantic and beautiful and accurate as possible. That's probably been my biggest struggle, if I'm honest. It's hard to write about realistic sex and make it sound glamorous. I can't shake the feeling that maybe this is because I'm doing something wrong.

I sit down at the kitchen table and look at the stack of paper in front of me. Eight-four pages. Forty-three thousand words. My very first novel.

I've made a cup of tea and opened a packet of chocolate Hobnobs in honour of the occasion. Everyone is still at school and this moment is mine; all mine. I sit and I sip my tea and I read my book, starting with the title, which was the last thing that I changed before clicking save and printing out the manuscript.

Big in Wyoming.

My debut work.

I read until it is time to collect the kids from school, carefully piling the pages together and putting them on my bedside table. I'm going to get Nick to read it through in its entirety later and then ask his advice about what I should do next. Now that it's actually written I feel a sense of calm about the whole thing. Daxx and Bella Rose will tell their story and my words will be read by other people. And they might like it or they might loathe it and I can handle that.

Because no matter what comes of this whole venture, I will always have Wyoming. Nobody can take that away from me.

The sound of laughter coming from the bedroom makes my heart sink and my stomach churn. I pause outside the door, glass of wine in hand. Maybe Nick is laughing at something totally and utterly unrelated to my book. Perhaps there's a particularly entertaining pigeon at the window? Or maybe he's got bored and is scrolling through humorous videos on YouTube?

If I turn around and go back downstairs, I can avoid any heartbreak. But fuck it – I can't bear not knowing what he thinks. I'm going in.

Nick is sprawled on the bed, pieces of paper spread out around him. He looks up as I enter the room, his eyes sparkling.

'Hannah! This is truly brilliant!' he exclaims and a little bit of me sobs in relief. 'I can't believe you've written all this!'

'Do you really like it?' I perch next to him, feeling oddly shy. 'You don't think some of the sexual descriptions are too shocking? I'm aware that I'm pushing the boundaries of the genre a bit at times.'

Nick sniggers, like I've said something funny. 'I didn't know you had this in you, babe. Seriously. This is golden!'

I allow a smile to spread across my face. 'Honestly? God – I've been terrified waiting for you to read it. I thought you might look at me differently, you know – once you'd read the things that I'm capable of thinking.'

Nick sits up. 'Hannah, I am in awe of you.' He reaches across the bed and picks up my hand. 'You took this whole book in a direction that I just didn't see coming.'

I shrug, trying to act modest. 'It wrote itself, if I'm honest,' I tell him. 'And you helped me out, don't forget. Those Kama

Sutra moves came in really useful when I was describing the incident in the barn.'

'Oh my god, yes!' Nick lets go of my hand and wipes at his eyes. 'The way you had Bella Rose with her leg behind her ear and then Daxx got muscle cramp because he hadn't warmed up – I nearly died at that bit.'

'It wasn't too much?' I ask. 'Too racy?'

Nick removes my glass of wine from me and takes a large gulp.

'Comedy gold, babe. Comedy gold. And the bits where you go into detailed explanations of the weather and the location and the crop rotation cycle in Wyoming are just hilarious.'

A shiver of something cold trickles down my spine.

'Hilarious? Comedy gold? What are you on about?'

Nick clearly fails to hear the warning in my voice because he just laughs. 'You know those Bad Sex awards that are given out every year? I seriously think you could be in with a shot of winning.' He pauses, looking thoughtful. 'Although I think they're actually awarded to serious fiction with terrible sex scenes. Not books like yours that are actually supposed to be funny. What genre is this, anyway? Is there such a thing as erotic humour? Because if there isn't, then I think you just invented it!'

I shake my head, trying to clear the ringing sound in my ears.

'My book isn't funny. It's sexy.'

Nick passes me the wine. 'It's the funniest thing I've read in ages, Hannah!'

I drain the pitiful amount that is left in the glass and stare my husband in the eye. 'Listen to me. It. Isn't. Meant. To. Be. Funny.'

And then I burst into tears.

9.30 p.m. The crying stops. Nick has spent the last hour and a half trying to reassure me and tell me that he was praising my literary efforts and that he truly had no idea that what he was saying was both negative and hurtful. He has also plied me with much more wine.

10.10 p.m. The crying resumes. I curl up on the sofa, clutching a cushion and wailing that I am never going to get the last few months back and that I don't know what possessed me to think that I was the kind of person who could ever write a book. Nick points out that I *have* written a book. I sobbingly tell him that I have clearly written *The Idiot's Guide to How Not to be Sexy*.

10.25 p.m. The ranting begins. I pace the floor while Nick cowers in the armchair.

'Maybe it'll be okay. After all, why shouldn't sex be funny?' I ask, snapping at Nick that I am obviously speaking rhetorically when he tries to tell me that sex with me is often funny.

10.35 p.m. I ceremoniously throw my entire manuscript into the fireplace.

'Burn in hell, you stupid book,' I curse, waving my fist in the air. 'Thanks to you, I will now have to endure another year of Year Nine, Class C. Except I won't because I probably won't even have a job and I'm going to have to become a dog walker and pick up poo for a living.'

10.37 p.m. I start sobbing again. Nick retrieves my manuscript from the empty fireplace and dusts it down before putting it carefully on the table and telling me, quite kindly, that I need to get a grip.

'It's really good, Hannah,' he says, sitting down next to me. 'I think you should get it out there. See what other people think. Otherwise what's the point in having written it?'

'Exactly!' I wail, slumping back onto the sofa. 'What's the fucking point? And I can't let anyone read it because the shackles have been removed from my eyes. It's crap, I know that now.'

'I think it's the blinkers that have been removed from your eyes,' points out Nick. 'I'm not sure that eyes can have shackles.'

'Thank you, oh Wise One,' I howl. 'Why don't you write a bloody book if you're so good with words?'

10.39 p.m. Nick guides me upstairs and into the bathroom where he puts some toothpaste on my toothbrush and tells me to open my mouth. And then he helps me get into my pyjamas and tucks me under the duvet.

'You'll feel differently in the morning,' he whispers, kissing my forehead and turning out the lamp. 'This is just post-writing tension being released.'

I drift off to sleep before I can find the words to tell him that I might be slightly emotional but that I know how I feel.

The book is rubbish and it's still going to be just as rubbish tomorrow.

I'll just be right back where I was at the beginning.

With no prospects and probably no job.

And with absolutely no hope.

Chapter 31

'So, how do you feel the lesson went?'

As opening questions go, it's fairly standard and I'm vaguely surprised. Miriam seems so intent on changing the status quo around here that I was prepared to answer questions on just about anything. But here we are, with an easy starter for ten. I sit back in my chair, relaxing the tiniest bit. I know how to play this game.

'I think it had areas of strength,' I tell her. 'And also some room for development.'

I can't go wrong with that answer. Some confidence in my own teaching ability combined with a little humility. I smile, volleying the ball across to her side of the net.

'And would you say that all the pupils were engaged?' Miriam bares her tiny, white teeth at me. 'Do you feel that they all contributed to the lesson?'

I nod. 'This particular class is very keen.'

'And how do you feel that they have responded to the works of George Orwell?' she presses. 'I know that when I was teaching English I made the decision to stick to slightly less challenging books.'

'Well, as you saw in the lesson, they have a good understanding of the plot,' I bluster.

They do not have a good understanding of the plot. At one point in the disastrous observation, Brody started doing an impression of the animals, chanting 'four legs good, two legs bad' and when Miriam asked him what point Orwell was making with that comment, he scratched his head and then told her that 'it means chickens are evil, innit?'

Miriam's mouth opens and I leap in to stop her before she can get a withering comment in.

'Several of the pupils did extra research in their own time,' I blurt out. 'That's how keen they are.'

'Oh?' Miriam looks surprised. Not that I can blame her. Our school isn't in a catchment where pupils tend to be keen on self-development or self-improvement or self-motivation. They are, ironically, very keen on 'self' though. 'And what form has this extra research taken? Do you have evidence that you can show me? Is there anything in your planning?'

I regret saying anything now. I'm not sure when the teaching profession became as obsessed with evidence as the Crime Prosecution Service but it's a complete pain in the backside. Nothing counts anymore unless you can prove it, which is ridiculous, because some of the best things that have happened in my classroom have been entirely undocumented.

'And the extra research was linked to your lessons on George Orwell, you say?' Miriam looks across at the Head, who appears to be taking the opportunity to have a quick doze. 'Roger? You're quite the Orwellian, aren't you?'

The Head finally opens his eyes. 'Absolutely. And frankly,

I'm rather surprised that you've managed to garner any interest in him from Year Nine. They seem a sadly uninspired cohort.'

Why did I even mention extra research? Miriam's eyes are gleaming and I am getting the sinking suspicion that I am being set up for a very large fall.

'Sadly, Miriam, the work was generated by the pupils themselves,' I say, shaking my head. 'It isn't detailed in my planning.'

I happened to finish an English lesson by telling the class that we would be studying *Animal Farm* the following week and that if any of them felt like getting ahead, they might like to look up the film online.

It was an innocent mistake.

'So how do you know that they actually did the study?' asks Miriam, narrowing her eyes. She's like a super sleuth and I can tell that she won't rest until she's got a satisfactory answer from me. A horrifying thought flits through my brain before I can stop it. *Maybe she already knows? Maybe I should just hand in my resignation now?*

'A couple of them brought in posters,' I say, seizing on the first thing that enters my mind.

The following Monday, I had entered the classroom to find Brandon Hopkins standing at the front, detailing the plot of *Animal Farm* to anyone who would listen, which from the rapt silence appeared to be just about everybody. I stood for a second in the doorway, feeling happily smug that my teaching was finally starting to get results, before the detail of his description hit my ears and I shrieked at him to leave the room.

It transpires that there is more than one film online with

the title *Animal Farm* and, as luck would have it, Brandon Hopkins had managed to stumble upon a version that would have had Orwell turning in his grave.

'I'd love to see them,' says Miriam, leaning towards me with an evil smile. 'We really do want to encourage the pupils as much as possible. If they know that people as important as the Deputy Head will be looking at their work' – she pauses to give a little self-deprecating laugh – 'well, I think they'll be motivated to do even better next time. Don't you agree, Hannah?'

'Absolutely.' Not. These kids couldn't give a rat's arse if Miriam looks at their homework. Not to mention the fact that the posters are entirely fictional and I'm going to have to fabricate some rubbish during my lunch break.

'So, Hannah.'

Overuse of my name. She's definitely going to fire me.

'How do you offer praise and reward in your classroom? These pupils who completed extra study, for example. What did they get back in return?'

I am sweating now. 'Surely learning is a reward in itself, Miriam?'

She frowns and I hurry for something else that might placate her. 'But saying that, I also feel that the home-school partnership is something that cannot be valued enough. So with that in mind, I made sure that I contacted the parents of the pupils who had done additional work and spoke with them at length about their efforts.'

Oh yes, I absolutely did. The instant that the bell rang I was on the phone to Brandon Hopkins's mum. Partly to inform her that her son has access to hardcore porn and that, despite the fact that he is indeed 'a fifteen year old boy and what can you do with him, miss!' this is possibly something that she may wish to monitor. And also to cover my own back in case word got out that I was setting inappropriate viewing as homework.

'I have a question for you.' Miriam leans back in her chair. She's enjoying this, I can tell. 'As you are aware, we are currently reviewing all the temporary contracts. If given the opportunity to teach English next year, would you still choose to use *Animal Farm* as one of your texts?'

It's a trap. She definitely knows. I can feel my armpits prickling with sweat and my cheeks feel like they're glowing. I scrutinise Miriam's face, trying to figure out where she's going with this, but it is unreadable. I make a mental note never to play cards with this woman; her poker face puts Lady Gaga to shame.

What is the right answer? I can't work it out. Should I say that I wouldn't teach Orwell next year? Is that what she wants to hear? Or is she expecting me to confess to the almighty balls-up that I have made of her English class? Does she want her pound of flesh? Does she want me to bleed for this job?

There is only one answer. I don't know if it's right or wrong, but at this exact moment, I have gone beyond caring.

'Yes.' I sit up straighter and give Miriam a smile. 'I'd do some things differently but yes, I would teach *Animal Farm* again.'

Minus any mention of the porn film, obviously, Miriam! Lol.

'I think it has a lot of messages that are worth discussing

with the pupils. If we shy away from the trickier topics then we're failing to do our jobs.' I lean back, satisfied with my reply.

My contract might not be getting renewed but damn, that felt bloody brilliant. I am almost inspiring myself. I should open a Twitter account under the name @toughteacher. I could give talks about how to keep things real in the classroom.

'I see. That's very interesting.' Miriam jots something down in her notebook and finally, after what feels like hours of interminable interrogation, I am released with no further questions.

I trudge down the corridor and down the stairs. I'm not teaching for the rest of the day and I have a pile of books that are waiting for me in my classroom. Outside, the sun is shining and I have a sudden urge to bunk off and escape to the park.

Then my phone beeps and I stop, reaching into my bag to see what latest emergency awaits me. Scarlet has already texted three times today over a variety of crises, including the fact that she appears to have Benji's lunch and therefore will have to starve to death because she refuses to be seen in the canteen with a Pokémon lunchbox.

Only it isn't yet another complaint from my daughter. It's an email from a name that I don't recognise with the subject heading *Submissions/Big in Wyoming*. I open up the message and then freeze in the middle of the corridor, my brain struggling to catch up with the words that leap out at me.

Thank you … sending … your book. After careful consideration … not quite right … wish you … best … placing it elsewhere.

All best wishes,
Jasmine
On behalf of King and White Literary Agency.

What? Somewhere in the distance a bell rings and suddenly doors fly open, releasing dozens of kids into the corridor. I stand very still, an immovable rock in the middle of a river of pupils. I am aware on some level that they are laughing and yelling but it all seems to be happening a very long way away.

Eventually I come to my senses and stagger down the hallway and into the staffroom. Once safely inside, I collapse onto the nearest chair and look again at my phone. None of this makes sense.

'Are you okay, Hannah?' Cassie wanders across the room, looking at me with curiosity. 'You look as if you've seen a ghost.'

I open my mouth but no words come out. I don't even know where to begin.

'Seriously, mate.' She sits down next to me and touches my arm. 'Has something happened? Have you had some bad news?'

I swallow and tear my eyes away from the screen. 'No. Yes. God, I don't know.'

Cassie nods understandably. 'You just had your feedback with Miriam, didn't you? Was she awful about your lesson?'

'It's not that.' I force myself to sit up straight. 'I just opened a really weird email.'

She grimaces. 'Oh no, not you as well? Bloody hell, Year Nine, Class C are getting out of control. You know that Danny has been bombarded with penis enlargement emails? He only figured out that they were behind it when one of the little sods asked him if he'd been getting treatment for his erectile dysfunction when he got back from the dentist last week.'

I shake my head. 'It's worse than that. I think I just got a rejection letter from a literary agency, which is totally insane because I haven't submitted my book anywhere.'

There's a pause while Cassie looks everywhere but at me. I stare at her, watching as her face starts to flush. 'Cassie? What's going on?'

'Nothing!' Her voice is suspiciously squeaky. 'Nothing is going on! And that agency must be stupid to reject it because your book is bloody brilliant!'

'You haven't read my book,' I say slowly, as the penny finally drops. 'I was too embarrassed to let anyone read it once it was finished. The only person who read it is Nick.'

That snake in the grass. That traitor. What was he thinking?

'He gave you a copy of my book and you sent it off? Oh god, Cassie. How could you do this to me?'

Cassie sits on the edge of the seat, as if she's getting ready to run. 'It wasn't me!' she protests. 'It was Nick's idea. Honestly.'

'So now that you've betrayed me, you're going to throw Nick under the bus too?' I ask, dropping my head into my hands. 'I think I'm going to be sick.'

'I haven't betrayed you,' Cassie tells me. I can hear what

sounds distinctly like a smile in her voice. 'And for what it's worth, I agree with what Nick did. He said that you were just going to throw it away, Hannah. All that work and you were just going to waste it.'

'That was my choice to make,' I mumble, closing my eyes. He sent it to a genuine, legitimate literary agency. Someone read it. This cannot be happening.

'He asked me to read it and give him my opinion,' continues Cassie. 'And I know that we should have asked you first but we both knew that you'd only say no.'

'That is not a reasonable excuse for not seeking my permission,' I snap, looking over at her. 'What are you, eight years old? You can't just not ask the question because you know that you won't get the answer you want.'

'I know and I'm sorry.' She is doing a tolerable impression of someone who is feeling a teeny bit contrite. 'But I still stand by what we did. And just because this stupid agency doesn't like it, it doesn't mean that all the others won't.'

Her words hit me like a slap in the face.

'All the others?' I stand up and start pacing the floor. 'Exactly how many agencies did you send it to?'

Cassie shrugs. 'I'm not sure, you'll have to ask Nick.'

I spin round and give her my most evil teacher-stare. 'Oh, don't you worry. I will be corroborating your story with my husband as soon as he has the courage to drag his sorry ass through my front door.'

Chapter 32

I send Nick a text as I'm walking to the car.

Leaving school. Are you home soon?

It is the very first time that I have ever messaged him without adding a kiss at the end. Let that be a warning to him about what exactly is going to go down in our house this evening.

Benji chatters about an argument that happened in the playground at lunchtime as we drive home, but my mind is elsewhere. I manage to make the occasional affirmative grunt but all I can think about is the fact that my book is out there, possibly being read by real people *right at this very moment.*

The thought makes me want to run and hide under the duvet for at least the next six months.

As soon as we're inside the house, I throw my bag into the cupboard under the stairs and storm into the kitchen.

'Hey, Mum.' Dylan is perched on a stool, spooning porridge into his mouth. 'How was your day?'

I pause. This is happening more and more. I will walk into a room and catch a glimpse of him out of the corner of my eye and just for a split second, I will see a glimmer of the man that he is going to be. A man full of honesty and love and consideration and kindness. A man who would never, not in one million years, go behind his partner's back and humiliate them by sharing their most private and personal work.

'It was atrocious,' I tell him, giving him a quick hug before putting the kettle on. 'Promise me that you'll never become a back-stabbing, double-crossing, fink rat narc.'

'What's Dad done this time?' Dylan grins at me. 'Last time you used those words, he'd eaten the last piece of lemon meringue pie.'

'It was *my* piece,' I grab a teabag and slam it into a mug. 'He'd already eaten his and I was saving mine for later. He knew that and he still chose to eat it. What else should I have called him?'

'No, you're right. If anything, your reaction was understated.' Dylan shovels up another load of porridge and I stick my tongue out at him, which makes him splutter most of the oats onto his T-shirt.

We hear the front door opening and a moment later, Nick walks in. He places his bag on the floor and steps towards me, a tired smile on his face.

'I can't believe it's only Wednesday,' he says, reaching out his arms to pull me in for a hug. 'The last few days have been endless.'

'Yes, well, you've been a busy boy,' I say, side-stepping his touch. 'I'm not surprised you're exhausted. It's tiring work, being a double agent.'

Nick frowns. 'I don't know what you mean.' His gaze darts

around the room, as if looking for clues. 'Has someone left a window open? It's freezing in here!'

I fold my arms.

'That'll be Mum's frosty demeanour that you're picking up on,' Dylan tells him. 'Good instincts, Dad. It bodes well for your survival.'

He leaps off the stool and picks up his bowl. 'I think I'll finish this in the living room,' he tells me. 'Then you and Dad can have your sensible, adult conversation in peace. Seeing as you're obviously in a super-mature mood.'

I watch him go and then turn back to Nick, who has taken the opportunity to grab a beer from the fridge and is now leaning against the kitchen counter, eying me warily.

'What's the matter, Hannah? Are you okay?'

I look back at him in disbelief but I don't speak until I've closed the kitchen door. It's bad enough that other people know about this – I don't need the kids to find out too.

'I am not okay,' I tell him. 'I am not even a little bit okay.'

'Are you ill?' Nick's face looks worried. 'Do you need to go to bed? Maybe you'll feel better after some sleep?'

I cackle bitterly. 'Sleep? As if! I can't imagine that I'm going to be getting any *sleep* for quite a while, thanks to you.'

Nick shakes his head. 'You need to stop talking in riddles and tell me what's going on, babe.' He takes a slug of beer. 'I can't read your mind.'

That does it. I stalk forward until I'm standing toe to toe with my husband.

'Newsflash, Nick. You *clearly* can't read my mind,' I spit. 'Because if you could read my mind, you would have asked yourself, *Would Hannah be okay with me doing this?* And the answer would have been, *No! She would not be okay with me doing this.* And then you wouldn't have done it. And I wouldn't be here with my life in tatters and nothing but humiliation ahead of me.'

He reaches out and holds onto my hand. 'Has Cassie said something to you?' he asks as I wrench away from his grip and fling myself down at the table.

'She didn't have to!' I tell him. 'Because I got a delightful email informing me that *More Than Sex* is a pile of crap and I could jog on if I thought it might be worth trying to get it published.' I look up at him. 'All of which I already knew, which is why I didn't want to send it off in the first place.'

'Oh, babe.' Nick sits down next to me. 'I'm sorry that happened. But everyone gets rejections, don't they? I'm sure J.K. Rowling had loads of them before an agent agreed to take her on.'

'I am not J.K. bloody Rowling,' I hiss. 'And I have not written a heartwarming story of wizardry and magic and goblins and people getting on broomsticks, *Nick*. I have written a story about sex and kink and people getting naked. There's a bit of a difference.'

Nick nods sympathetically. 'Which is why we only sent your book to agencies that specialise in adult fiction. Someone will see it for what it is, Hannah, don't give up hope yet. Your book is hilarious – it just needs the right person to read it.'

I am finding it hard to believe that he can be so stupid.

'I am not upset about the rejection. I'm upset because I

don't want to be associated with something like that. Why can't you understand what I'm saying?'

'But you wrote it.' Nick looks confused. 'You worked really hard and you've written something brilliant and different. Where's the harm in putting it out there and seeing what other people think?'

Where's the harm? Where's the fucking harm? I am married to a blithering idiot.

'I'm going to have to go into hiding,' I moan, tipping back my head and trying to think straight. 'I'll have to hand in my notice too – there's no way that I can continue teaching.'

Nick stands up and walks across to the fridge. Thoughts flash through my head – I'll probably have to do all my shopping online in case word gets out. I'll become a total recluse, trapped in my own home for fear of the disdainful and disgusted attention that will surely be coming my way.

'Drink that.' Nick puts a large glass of wine down in front of me. 'And try to stay calm. You're completely overreacting.'

I am too caught up in my own world to respond to this gross allegation. A world where the delights of the supermarket and the pub and the staffroom are all distant memories. I shall probably get a few cats and sit alone all day, gazing out of the window and reminiscing about the life I once had.

'Everybody is going to know what I've written,' I whisper, taking a gulp of wine. 'They're all going to judge me.'

I think I might be in shock. As in the actual medical definition of shock. My palms feel sweaty and my forehead is clammy and my heart is racing crazily like Dogger does whenever we take her for a run around in the park.

'Nobody is going to know,' says Nick, sitting back down. 'And nobody is going to judge you.'

'But people talk,' I tell him. 'Right now, some agent could be reading my book and then later, they might be sitting in their local wine bar, sipping cocktails and nibbling nuts and get onto the topic of what they've read today and they could tell someone else, let's say the barmaid, about this book set in Wyoming with loads of sex and stuff and the barmaid will ask who wrote it and the agent will cast their mind back and say, "Oh, some nobody called Hannah Thompson," and then the barmaid might tell someone else and they'll tell someone else and before we know it, the name Hannah Thompson will be synonymous with raunchy sex and I can't have that, Nick – I really can't!'

'It's not going to happen,' says Nick, in an infuriatingly calm way.

'You don't know that!' I half-sob. 'It could be happening *right now*!'

Nick shakes his head. 'Did you read the email properly, Hannah? Because if you did, you'll have seen that the name Hannah Thompson is not mentioned.'

I put down my glass and stare at him. 'What are you talking about? The agent sent me an email.'

'But not to Hannah Thompson.' He grins at me. 'I'm not completely stupid. I know that you wanted to write under a pseudonym. So when I sent off the manuscript, I sent it under a fake name.'

The only noise now is the clock ticking away on the wall and the muffled sound of a film filtering through the wall between the kitchen and the living room.

'What name did you choose?' I whisper. 'What name, Nick?'

He raises his eyebrows and leans back in his seat. 'I think you're going to be pleasantly surprised,' he tells me. 'I know that you wanted something that sounded a bit more exotic than Hannah Thompson and I remember that you said it should be a name with personal relevance if it was going to be on the cover of your very first book.'

He pauses, obviously hoping to ramp up the tension. There's really no need – if my blood pressure increases any further there is a distinct possibility that I might actually burst a few veins.

'Tell me that you didn't listen to my mother. Tell me that my writer name is not Edna Tickle.'

Nick snorts. 'No way! That's a terrible name. Your pen name is so much better!'

'Tell me.' I force the words out through gritted teeth. 'Who do these agents think that I am?'

'Okay, are you ready for it?' Nick smiles. 'Your name is Twinky Malone!' He throws out his hands, as if he has just offered me a wonderful gift. 'What do you think?'

I ignore his question and push back my chair, half-standing so that I reach the phone in my back pocket. Once I have retrieved it I sit down and turn it on, going straight to the last email.

Dear Twinky Malone,

Thank you for sending us your book, More Than Sex. After careful consideration and review we have decided that it is not quite right for our list. However, we wish you all the very best in placing it elsewhere.

All best wishes,
Jasmine
On behalf of King and White Literary Agency.

He's telling the truth. Other than my rather generic email address, there is nothing to connect me to this manuscript.

'What do you think, Hannah?' repeats Nick.

Twinky Malone is not my name.

That is what I think.

Nick takes my silence as approval, which has always been one of his most irritating traits.

'I remembered that conversation we had about what our porn star names would be,' he says. 'And I know we agreed that Fishy Bush was not particularly glamorous. But then I thought about that cat we found when we moved into our first flat. Do you remember?'

My frazzled brain lurches back twenty-one years to the poky, damp-ridden flat that Nick and I rented when we were fresh out of university. It was advertised as a 'garden flat' although the garden amounted to nothing more than a strip of concrete path running down the side of the poorly built kitchen extension. We attempted to grow some plants in pots, but the sun never reached the ground and after a couple of weeks we got bored with the cold, slimy space and stopped going out there. Occasionally though, I would open up the back door to get rid of the smell of burning toast and it was on one of these mornings that we discovered Twinky. A sad, bedraggled mess of a wild cat who spat and hissed if we tried to go anywhere near her.

Nick made a valiant effort to get her to come inside, but when he got too close she struck out and left claw marks all down his arm. So we told ourselves that she was obviously feral, closed the door and forgot all about her. Until the following day when there was a scratching sound and a faint meowing. When we peered out through the window, she was back.

And that was the start of our non-relationship with Twinky. We would leave bowls of food on the back doorstep and she would hiss and snarl at us if we even thought about taking a step in her direction. Nick named her Twinky because he said it suited her shiny, twinkling disposition.

'So in a way, she was our first pet,' Nick tells me now. 'And we lived on Malone Street, so I thought that would be kind of cool as the surname.'

He looks at me anxiously across the table and I feel my fury start to abate. And by abate, I mean dial down by about one eightieth of a notch. He was trying to help and despite my outrage at the ludicrousness of the entire situation, at least the name Twinky Malone means something to me. To us.

And the honest truth is that now I've calmed down a bit, I can feel a slight thrill at the prospect of someone reading what I've written. I'm not stupid enough to think that anything will come of it, of course not; but I did put a lot of time into Daxx and Bella Rose's story and I guess it being sent off to a couple of agencies isn't the very worst thing in the world.

'Nobody will know that you wrote this book,' he assures

me. 'I just couldn't bear to let you waste all that effort. Not when what you've written is so great.'

'I suppose it was a bit daft to just let it sit there,' I say grudgingly. 'But that doesn't mean I'm okay with what you did, Nick.'

'I know and I'm sorry.' He breathes out loudly and I realise that he's been holding his breath. 'But for what it's worth, I think that Twinky Malone is a brilliant name.'

I take another sip of wine and mull over his words in my head.

'It could be worse,' I agree. 'And that's the best I'm prepared to offer right now.'

Nick stands up and stretches out his arms. 'I'll take it,' he says. 'But if one of these agents actually offers to represent you then I'm expecting a full apology.'

I grunt. 'I'm not sure that there's much of a market for comedy erotica or whatever you called it. But in the unlikely event of me getting an agent, then I will happily apologise to you.'

'I'm already looking forward to it.' Nick opens a cupboard door and looks inside. 'Maybe you can repay me with a date night.' He glances back over his shoulder. 'You know, a proper one, not a fake one that's purely for the purposes of research. It'd be a shame to let that Kama Sutra book you bought go to waste.'

'Maybe.' I give him a faint smile, not prepared to let him off the hook just yet. 'But I wouldn't hold your breath.'

Chapter 33

So. It's a new day and I am feeling good. The birds are singing, the sun is shining and everywhere I look, people are laughing and smiling and generally making merry.

If my life were a film, at this point the soundtrack would screech to a halt to signify that something is not right. Because actually, despite my best efforts at positivity, I am *not* feeling good. I am feeling low and flat and possibly just a little bit depressed.

My book is a flop. My career is in tatters. Dylan is leaving for university in a matter of months and I can't rid myself of the mental image of Nick and me abandoning a helpless baby in a rowdy hall of residence.

Downstairs, it is the usual mid-week scene. Benji and Dogger are playing an enthusiastic game that appears to involve Benji balancing on a chair while trying to convince Dogger to jump through a hula hoop. Scarlet is storming around the kitchen, angrily slamming toast onto her plate and sticking her knife into the jam as if she's about to kill something or someone. Dylan has his headphones rammed over his head and is oblivious to everything.

'Mum!' Benji gives me a chocolatey smile. I consider telling him off for eating chocolate spread on a Wednesday when everybody knows that it's only for weekends, but I decide that I really can't be bothered. If chocolate spread is what's getting him through the day then he can have it. Maybe I'll try some and see if it can work its magic on my mood.

'There isn't any cucumber in the fridge.' Scarlet looks at me accusingly. 'I specifically asked you to buy more cucumber.'

There has been an uneasy truce between us since the Ashley Dunsford incident. I invited him here for tea, but Scarlet told me that the idea of him being subjected to our family was horrific and abusive and that it would be a cold day in hell before he darkened our doorstep. Something along those lines, anyway. I could tell that she was pleased that I'd asked, though.

I shrug. 'And I specifically haven't been to the shops yet. I'll get some tomorrow.'

Scarlet's face starts to redden. 'But I wanted cucumber sandwiches today,' she moans. 'My friends and I all agreed that we'd bring in cucumber sandwiches for lunch.'

I nod at Nick and gratefully accept the cup of coffee that he is holding out to me. 'Well, you've got two choices,' I tell her. 'You can take regular old cheese sandwiches or you can go to the shop yourself.'

'There's no time.' Her voice is sulky and I can feel myself starting to get cross. 'All I wanted was a cucumber sandwich.'

'Well you're not the Queen,' I snap. 'So you're just going to have to cope without cucumber today.'

'Did you know that sea cucumbers can shoot out their innards to put off anything that's trying to eat them?' adds

Benji, stepping off the chair. 'How cool is that? If there's any danger then they just pop out their intestines and whatever is trying to attack them is so grossed out that they run away.' He pauses. 'Or swim away.'

'You are disgusting,' snaps Scarlet, turning to me. 'Why do we have to let him speak when we're eating? He should be banned.'

'That is an excellent idea, darling,' I tell her. 'I think we need a new house rule that says anyone under the age of nineteen must be mute during mealtimes.'

'I concur,' agrees Nick, raising his coffee cup towards me. 'Starting from now.'

'If I can't have cucumber then can I—' starts Scarlet.

I hold my hand up to silence her. 'No speaking, remember?' I whisper. 'Just lovely, cucumber-free peace while I drink the rest of my coffee.'

'You people are ridiculous.' She slams her plate into the dishwasher and shoots me a glare. 'When I'm an adult, I'm not going to behave like you both do. I'm going to treat my children with respect and courtesy and I'm going to give them names that are properly spelt.' She stomps towards the door before turning to deliver her parting shot. 'And there will *always* be cucumber in my fridge.'

'That sounds like an ancient proverb,' Nick calls after her. 'May your fridge be forever well-stocked with cucumber.'

The muffled sound of her frustrated scream goes a little way towards thawing my cold, miserable heart. But not much.

I trudge into the staffroom. The first thing I see is the white envelope sticking out of my pigeonhole and I know instantly what it is. Of course it is. I couldn't be feeling much worse right now so obviously, today is the day that Miriam informs me that my contract will not be renewed. Part of me considers turning around and heading straight back out of the door, but I have nowhere to go unless I'm planning to visit the local Jobcentre, and I don't think it's open on Wednesdays. Or Mondays. Or Thursdays.

'All right?' Cassie approaches from the other side of the room. We haven't spoken much since the day that I received the rejection email but she's sent me a few texts and I've replied. I don't blame her for going along with Nick's plan, but I'm still feeling embarrassed that she read the book and despite my protestations, the rejection is stinging.

I nod back at her. 'Looks like Miriam has left me a missive.' I pick up the envelope and turn it over in my hands. 'Guess I'm going to be looking for another job for September.'

'You can join me at Pizza Parade if you like.' Kurt comes up behind Cassie. 'I'm going to need reliable members of staff to work the phone and the till. I think you'd be great, Hannah.'

I smile at him, momentarily warmed by this display of friendship. 'I might take you up on that,' I tell him. 'But I'll need a lot of shifts. Dylan's student loan isn't going to go very far when he goes to uni.'

Kurt beams at me. 'No problem. And you'll get the staff discount on pizza, obviously. Twenty-five per cent off, Hannah! That's not to be sniffed at is it? Not when a family-size Americano costs twelve pounds. That means you'd only be paying ...' He falters and Cassie and I watch as he tries to work out the amount. 'You'd only be paying ... ermm, well – it's a big deduction, I know that!'

I take pity on him. 'I think it would be three pounds off, Kurt. So the pizza would cost me nine pounds, which is indeed a bargain.'

Kurt looks at me admiringly. 'That's why I need you on the till,' he tells me. 'You're very quick with tricky sums.'

He wanders off and I turn to Cassie.

'Bloody hell! I knew he was a bit rubbish but seriously?'

Cassie grins. 'I think Miriam's doing him a favour actually, getting him out on incompetency. He's going to be a whole lot happier running Pizza Parade than he is here, teaching Maths and doing "tricky sums"!'

I look back at the envelope. 'Which is what she probably thinks about me. Best to put me out of my misery and get rid of me, before I actually do some real damage.'

Cassie puts her hand on my arm. 'You're not like Kurt,' she says quietly. 'You've been thrown in the deep end and made to teach a subject that you knew nothing about. It's been a hell of a year, Hannah – but look at what you've achieved.'

Oh yes. My list of successes is quite astounding. I managed to get an entire class to write the rudest word of all time in their English books. I have traumatised the same class by exposing them to the plot of the most notorious and foul hardcore porn film that exists in the history of the universe. And unbeknownst to anyone here except Cassie, I have written an abysmal book that was supposed to be raunchy and provocative but has ended up being a tragically unsexy version of a *Carry On* film.

I cannot think of anyone less qualified to inspire the next generation about the joys of the English language.

'Are you going to open that, then?' Cassie's face is concerned.

I shake my head. 'No. Why bother? Miriam hates me and she hates what I've done to her beloved English class. I know she'll have leapt at the chance to finally get shot of me. She's probably going to replace me now and make me teach something truly lame like PE for the rest of the year.'

And then the bell rings and I walk away.

Because the world obviously despises me, I am teaching Year Nine first lesson. We're part way through reading *Lord of the Flies*, a book I have always found to be engrossing and thought-provoking. That is, until I had the pleasure of sharing it with the members of Year Nine, Class C.

'Piggy is a loser'; 'Jack sounds like a proper boss'; 'why don't they just phone for help when they get stranded on the island'? Just some of the more intelligent comments that I have been forced to deal with. I have tried to convey the horror of the boys' situation, but my attempts have fallen on deaf ears.

I wait for most of the class to be sitting down before I embark on my usual, futile questioning. 'Who has read chapter nine?'

Brandon Hopkins pulls back Brody's chair, just as Brody is about to lower himself into it. There is a crash as Brody's backside hits the floor, followed by a howl of rage.

'You fucking dick!' he yells at Brandon, who is sitting back in his own seat looking smug. 'I'm gonna kill you for that.'

Brody struggles to his feet and makes a move towards Brandon, but I get there before him. If nothing else, teaching this class has improved my reflexes.

'Enough!' I shout, holding out my arm to keep Brody out of striking distance. 'There will be no unsanctioned killing in this classroom today.'

'But he pulled my chair!' screams Brody, his eyes wide. 'I'm not gonna let him get away with that.'

'Annihilate him, Brody!' whoops Vincent from across the room. 'Do it!'

I am too tired and too furious to put up with this crap for another second. Whipping my head around, I fix Vincent with a steely gaze.

'Do not push me, Vincent. I am not in the mood today. Understood?'

Vincent gives me a nod and sinks back into his seat. He obviously has just enough sense to recognise a woman on the edge.

I turn back to Brody. 'Sit. Down,' I mutter. 'I will deal with this, but if you make one more sound I will not be held accountable for what happens next.'

Not my most professional moment, but it works. With a last snarl at Brandon Hopkins, Brody wrenches away from me and grabs his chair before lowering himself cautiously onto it.

'It was an accident, miss,' smarms Brandon Hopkins. My fury runneth over.

Leaning over, I place both hands on his desk and move forward until I am right in front of his face.

'If you ever pull a stupid stunt like that again, I will make sure that it's the last thing you do,' I hiss at him. 'I will end your time at this school and you will have no choice but to go cap in hand to Mr Jenkins and beg him for a job at Pizza Parade. And he will give you a job because he is a nice man, who happens to believe in second and third and fourth chances. But because of your lack of a decent reference and the fact that you are a bully and a coward, he will offer you the position of toilet-cleaner and floor-mopper and you won't even be given the staff discount of twenty-five per cent off all pizza until you have proved your worth.'

I pause for breath. 'What you just did was cruel and infantile and dangerous. You could have given Brody an injury that lasted for months and I speak from experience, Brandon Hopkins, because when I was sixteen years old, a horrid little bully called Jason Jones did exactly the same to me. I landed smack down on my coccyx bone and I was in agony for over a year.'

I pause, to allow for inevitable sniggering at the word 'coccyx', but the room remains silent. I am clearly more terrifying than I thought.

'*One year,* Brandon Hopkins! And where is that little scumbag Jason now?'

Brandon Hopkins shakes his head. 'I don't know, miss. Is he in prison?'

I scowl back at him. 'More than likely. More. Than. Likely.'

I'm lying. Last time I Facebook-stalked Jason Jones, he was in the Bahamas, honeymooning on his yacht with his third and incredibly beautiful wife. But Brandon Hopkins does not need to know that.

'Consider this your final warning,' I tell Brandon Hopkins. 'And unlike Mr Jenkins, I do not believe in second chances.' I turn and glare around the room. 'One more incident involving any of you and I'll be forced to ask someone else to teach you English.'

Might as well get ahead of the inevitable. For all I know, my replacement is on their way down here as I speak.

I walk back to the front of the class. 'Although no doubt that would give you all great pleasure.'

It was supposed to be a subtle aside to myself but the words come out louder than I'd intended and they hear me.

'I'm sorry, miss.' Brandon's voice stops me in my tracks. 'And I'm sorry, Brody. I didn't mean to hurt you and I don't want us to have another teacher. I like your lessons, miss.'

'Me too,' adds Brody and then there is a half-hearted murmuring from the rest of the class as they add their agreement.

I turn and stare suspiciously at Brandon Hopkins, but his face is remarkably smirkless. If I didn't know better, I'd say that the boy almost appears genuine. It's obviously time that I leave this job – I'm clearly losing all sense of reality.

'Right, let's try again.' I pick up my copy of *Lord of the Flies*. 'Who has read chapter nine?'

The room goes still. I learnt a while ago that the quickest way to gain silence is to ask them a question.

'It was set as homework at the end of last lesson,' I remind them. 'You should all have read it. Elise? How about you?'

'I had to visit my nan in hospital,' she tells me, her face flushing red. 'There wasn't time.'

'Well, what about you, Vincent?' I turn to look at him. 'What's your excuse?'

Vincent looks awkward. 'I was going to read it,' he says quietly. 'But my mum needed me to help her and then it got late and—'

'Okay, that's fine,' I say, remembering too late that Vincent's mother is often to be seen coming out of the off-licence in the middle of the day. 'Well, perhaps we'll start this lesson with me reading the chapter to you.'

The shuffling of bodies and the contented sigh that ripples around the room take me by surprise.

'I used to love it when teachers read to us,' says Wayne and there isn't even a hint of sarcasm in his voice. 'You know, when we were little. Nobody does that anymore.'

For some reason, this makes my throat constrict. I look around the room as Year Nine, Class C make themselves comfortable and I think about the bedtime stories that I used to read to my children. Maybe I've been going about this in the wrong way, treating these kids like they're mini-adults when all they really want is to be looked after.

At the back of the room, Brandon Hopkins has kicked off his shoes and in the row in front of him Brody is leaning back in his chair as if he's sunbathing at the beach. And instead of doing what I would usually do and yelling at them to look like they're paying attention, I open the book and I start to read.

The silence when I finish is unlike any silence that I have heard in this classroom before. It isn't awkward and it isn't empty. This silence isn't because nobody has anything to say – instead it is humming with the thoughts and questions of twenty-six fourteen-year-olds.

'They killed him,' whispers Elise, eventually. 'They actually killed Simon.'

Her words unlock everyone else and the classroom is suddenly filled with raised voices and exclamations. I hold my hand up.

'One at a time,' I say, pointing at Brody. 'What did you want to say?'

Brody is looking at me with an expression of disbelief on his face. 'Why did they do that?' he asks. 'They didn't have to kill him, did they?'

'That is an excellent question. Who's got any ideas about why the boys killed Simon? Yes – Brandon Hopkins?'

'They were scared?' he offers, sounding unsure. 'They thought he was the beast?'

'No way!' calls Vincent from across the room. 'They knew he wasn't the beast. They just wanted to make themselves feel better.'

I walk across to his desk. 'Okay, that's an interesting point of view. How could killing a person make you feel better?

'It made them powerful!' calls someone from the back.

'It made them part of a team,' shouts someone else. 'Them against the beast.'

'But why kill Simon?' I push, heading back to my desk. 'What had he done to deserve that?'

'He knew who the beast really was,' says Elise quietly. The rest of the class stop talking and turn to look at her. She flushes a little but continues. 'Simon knew that the beast was *them*. The boys. The evil was inside them and not some scary creature lurking on the mountain. That's why they had to kill him.'

I have been trying to get them to see that William Golding was telling a story about much more than some stranded private school boys on a remote island. In just a few sentences, Elise has done what I have failed to do in weeks.

I have never felt prouder as a teacher in my whole life.

'Man, that's dark,' mutters Brody, shaking his head. 'People can be bloody horrible.'

'How does it finish, miss?' Wayne's voice has a tinge of concern. 'Does it all work out at the end? Will you read us the rest, miss?'

I think of the rest of the story. The death of Piggy and the hunting of Ralph. The unsatisfactory ending where the boys are rescued but nothing will ever be the same again. And then I look around the room, at this group of disorganised, disrespectful kids who are all looking at me and waiting for my answer.

I can't leave them yet, not when there's still so much pain to come.

I just can't.

No matter how much I hate this job.

Chapter 34

I open the front door and step inside the empty house. The white envelope from Miriam is lying on the kitchen table but I still can't bring myself to open it. I need to plan next week's lessons and I want to find a way to engage Year Nine, Class C. I'm not going to be able to do that if I've read Miriam's letter.

Pushing it to one side, I open up my laptop and open a new file. I had an idea at about three o'clock this morning for a lesson using drama techniques to get inside the minds of Piggy and Jack and Ralph and I actually think the kids will love it. It's not the kind of thing I'd have even contemplated doing before but right now it feels like I've got nothing to lose. I know in my heart that I won't be teaching these kids in September so I might as well enjoy the final few months of term.

When the doorbell rings, I've finished planning the first lesson and I'm partway through the second. For a moment I consider ignoring the door. Maybe whoever it is will go away and leave me in peace. But then I hear the letterbox flap open and my mother's voice booming down the hallway.

'Hannah! Coo-ee! I know you're home, darling!'

Reluctantly, I close the laptop lid and heave myself out of the chair. I am not especially in the mood for my mother's enthusiasm today but even I can't leave her standing out there on the doorstep. And with any luck she'll have brought cake with her.

'I knew you were in!' Mum breezes past me, throwing me an air-kiss as she marches towards the kitchen.

'Out of interest, how could you be so sure?' I ask, trailing behind her. 'I could have been out.'

Mum laughs. 'Darling, you're never out! Unless you're at work, of course. Or at the supermarket.'

She isn't saying it to be unkind but it still irritates me.

'I go out all the time,' I mutter, taking the flowers that she is proffering and dumping them in a vase. 'I do things.'

'Of course you do.' My mother is oblivious to my sullen tone. 'Now I'm not stopping – I've got a hair appointment in half an hour and if I'm late that new man at the salon punishes me by giving me a very severe style. Tell me quickly about what's going on with you.'

'Apparently nothing.' I'm not prepared to move on from her insult yet. 'Unless you want to hear a detailed account of the two-for-one offers at the supermarket?'

Mum smiles at me and perches on the edge of a chair to show me that she's not intending on staying. 'I've brought your favourite – lemon cake!'

I'm not prepared to hold a grudge if there's lemon cake up for grabs so I swallow my injured pride and walk across the room to put the kettle on. My phone beeps with an incoming email but before I can reach for it, Mum starts talking about why she's really here.

'Scarlet's worried about you,' she says, launching right in. 'She thinks you're not coping. Apparently you aren't keeping the fridge stocked with the food they need – the poor girl had to text me to request that I buy her some cucumber. Is everything okay, Hannah?'

I sigh and glare at my mother.

'For god's sake, Mum! You should know better by now. Scarlet is behaving like a complete diva at the moment and you pandering to her is only making her worse.'

'So you're absolutely fine, then?' Mum gives me a piercing stare. 'Because you do seem a little pent-up, darling.'

I take a deep breath. 'I am only as pent-up as any mother of teenagers. I've got a sixteen-year-old daughter who appears to be on the verge of actual juvenile delinquency and an eighteen-year-old son who can't wash his own socks so how he's supposed to fend for himself when he leaves home is a mystery to me. And Benji asked me yesterday to buy him some hair gel and it's only just dawning on me that before I know it, I'm only going to have teenagers and young adults as children and I don't know how I feel about that because teenagers are really, really hard work and exhausting.'

I pause, gasping for air. 'And I'm going to lose my job which sucks because I actually almost liked it for approximately three seconds yesterday, although I'm highly aware that my change of heart is probably just because it's going to be taken away from me, like the time that I was going out with Jimmy Gordon and I dumped him and then Tracey Evans said that she liked him and I suddenly realised that he wasn't that bad after all.'

Mum laughs. 'You were fourteen when you went out with Jimmy Gordon,' she reminds me. 'I feel like you've possibly matured somewhat since then, Hannah.'

'But I haven't!' I moan. 'I'm going to have no job and I don't even care because I hate teaching stupid English but I need to make money and I don't know what to do. And I finished writing my book but apparently it's rubbish and everything is just too hard.'

'So what do you actually *want* to do?'

I stop ranting for just a second. What did she just say?

What do I want to do?

Nobody ever asks me that.

I don't ask me that.

Mum leans forward and scrutinises my face. 'You might need to be a bit brave, Hannah,' she tells me. 'If you want something different then maybe it's time to embrace the change and work out exactly what it is that you're looking for.'

She stands up abruptly. 'I'll leave you the lemon cake,' she tells me. 'But you're only allowed to eat it when you start being honest with yourself.'

I see her to the door and then walk slowly back into the kitchen. She doesn't know what she's on about. I am always excruciatingly honest with myself.

I am terrified about what is inside that envelope. That's why I haven't opened it. I am truly scared that my job is about to disappear.

Fine. So I'll open the letter and deal with the consequences. I can do that. I can be brave.

And I am gutted about my book being rejected. Ever since I found out that Nick had sent it off, I haven't been able to shake the thought that I could be more than me. That just maybe I could actually be Twinky Malone.

I have absolutely no idea where *that* came from. I sink into a chair and put my head in my hands.

I am not Twinky Malone.

I can never be Twinky Malone, that's been made abundantly clear to me by the six rejections that I have received over the last few weeks. I keep begging Nick to tell me how many agents he contacted with *More Than Sex* but he claims to have forgotten.

And I'm over it. Or at least, I thought I was.

Daxx and Bella Rose. They can fade into the background as if they never existed, along with Twinky Malone, because there is absolutely no future for me in being an author. I gave it a go and I was rubbish and that's okay because we all have an inventory of things that we're really crap at and now I know that I can add writing to that list. It's good to know your areas of weakness, apparently. This whole experience has probably been really useful and self-improving. Even if it feels more like character assassination than character building.

Twinky Malone is dead and gone and Mum is right. I have to figure out what I want to do next.

I lean across the table and pull Miriam's white envelope towards me. I will read the words and accept my fate. No, not accept my fate. Embrace the change, that's what Mum told me. In the name of empowered females everywhere, I am going to woman-up and move on.

And also, I really, really want to eat that lemon cake and my mother will know if I've cheated.

Before I can hesitate, I rip open the envelope and pull out the single sheet of paper that is inside, my eyes skimming the words. But it doesn't say what I'm expecting it to say and I have to stop and start again, this time reading slowly from the very beginning.

When I reach the end, I fold the letter up neatly and pull the plate of cake towards me. Then I take a huge bite, allowing the lemon tang to explode onto my tongue. I haven't planned for this outcome and I don't have a pre-prepared response to hand.

> *I have looked at your English books and there is evidence of progress and deeper thinking. I have spoken to the pupils and they are enthusiastic about your lessons. I am pleased to offer you a permanent contract as an English teacher – hours to be confirmed.*

I take another bite, tentatively allowing myself to explore how I'm feeling. A few weeks ago, this letter would have been a slap in the face. I would have said that a permanent contract teaching English was worse than a death sentence. And I know that I was starting to enjoy it, but now? Now that I know it's mine, I have to decide if I still want it.

This calls for more cake.

Chapter 35

When Nick arrives home, I have made up my mind.

'Fuck it,' I tell him, showing him the letter. 'I'm going to accept. A part-time job is better than no job, and it means we don't have to completely freak out about helping Dylan out financially next year. And you never know, I might learn to tolerate teaching English.'

Nick grabs me round the waist and gives me a hug. 'I am so proud of you,' he says. 'We should celebrate! Do you fancy Chinese?'

I nod, grinning back at him. 'The kids are all out for the evening. We can actually have a date night.'

'For real?' Nick looks at me hopefully.

'For real,' I agree. 'But you need to order the takeaway soon before they get inundated.'

There's only one Chinese restaurant in our town and on Friday nights it's the busiest place in a twenty-mile radius.

'Have you got the number?' Nick starts scanning the noticeboard. 'I can't see it up here.'

'Phone ordering is totally last year,' I tell him, nudging him out of the way so that I can open the fridge. 'It's all about online ordering now.' I gesture behind me. 'You can use my laptop.'

I pull out a chilled bottle of white wine and start unscrewing the lid. I'm feeling weirdly calm now that I've made a decision. These last few months may have been fun, playing about with pretending to be a writer and developing my story but I know that I've got to leave all of that daftness behind and throw myself one hundred per cent into being a teacher. And actually, it's a little bit embarrassing that I ever believed I could write something that anyone else would want to read.

Maybe Scarlet was right. Perhaps it was a kind of mid-life crisis.

But now I know where I'm going. I can start afresh in September, ready to inspire a whole new class of pupils. Maybe I could be like Michelle Pfeiffer in *Dangerous Minds*, delivering edgy and alternative lessons that cut through the crap. And maybe, one day, I'll discover that one of my pupils has written a book and dedicated it to my wonderful, inspiring teaching.

'Hannah. Have you read your emails today?' Nick's voice has a strange ring to it that jolts me out of my daydream.

'No, I don't think so,' I tell him, pouring the wine. 'Why? Is there something important?'

I wonder if I could get away with wearing a black leather jacket to school? I might buy a whole new wardrobe entirely in black. Nothing screams edgy like a teacher who refuses to wear floral skirts.

'You might want to come and look.' Nick takes a step back and stares at me. 'And it's probably a good idea if you bring your wine with you.'

I groan. 'It's not another complaint about Scarlet's school uniform, is it? I swear when she gets out of the car in the morning that her skirt is regulation length. What am I supposed to do if she insists on rolling it over at the top the instant that she's out of my sight?'

'It's not from school,' Nick tells me. 'Just read it.'

I walk across the room and bend down to peer at the screen. My emails are open and I can see five blue dots showing the unread messages. I scan down. An email forwarded from Cassie with a very rude subject heading. Another from a shop where I once made the rookie error of signing up for a store card and am now inundated with stupid messages inviting me to members-only shopping events, which sound hideous. I don't think either of these would be reason for Nick to get so insistent.

And then I see it. The third email down the list with the now-familiar subject heading *Submissions/More Than Sex*. My heart falls. Not another one. Not when I'm making a real effort to embrace my inner Michelle Pfeiffer.

I'm about to step back and close the lid when something makes me look again. This email is different to the others; I can only see the first two sentences, but they aren't what I expected to read. My hands are shaking as I click on the screen and the whole message opens up in front of me.

Dear Twinky Malone,

Thanks for letting me see your manuscript, MORE THAN SEX. It is not often that I read a submission this quickly but your opening lines had me hooked and I read the whole book in one sitting. Since then, it has been passed around the office and has been thoroughly enjoyed by the rest of the team. You have a very engaging voice and we feel that MORE THAN SEX *could have a strong future as a breakout book in the genre of Erotic Fiction/Humour. We are very keen to represent both you and your debut novel.*

I am out of the office for the rest of the day with clients, but will phone you later this evening if that is okay? Then perhaps we can chat about the direction you are hoping to take the book and any ideas you have for a sequel. I can talk to you about our vision and the publishers who, we feel confident, will be interested in BIG IN WYOMING.

Very much looking forward to speaking with you,

Persephone Andrews

Bluebird Film and Literary Agency
London

I stop reading and look up at Nick in disbelief.

'Is this a joke?' I ask. 'It has to be a joke?'

'It must be.' Nick looks just as shocked as I feel. Part of my brain registers this as being slightly insulting, seeing as it's him who keeps going on about how much potential my book supposedly has.

'If this is Cassie, I'm going to kill her,' I mutter, throwing back a mouthful of wine. 'I know I said I didn't care about writing anymore but still. It's not funny.'

And then the phone rings.

I freeze.

'Did you put our phone number in the submissions emails?' I whisper at Nick, as if the person calling might be able to hear me.

He nods. 'Cassie read an online article about what submissions are supposed to include,' he whispers back. 'And then she told me what I needed to send.'

Fuckety, fucking fuck. My heart is beating so fast that I think there's a very real possibility of it pounding right out through my mouth.

'Answer it.' I hiss at Nick.

'It isn't for me,' he hisses back. 'You need to answer it.'

'Well it isn't for me either,' I snap. 'According to this email, they're expecting to speak to Twinky Malone.'

We stare at each other for a few, long seconds. And the phone keeps ringing.

'What have you got to lose?' Nick asks. 'Just pick it up and say hello.'

'Fine! But it's probably Scarlet demanding a lift home.' I tiptoe the three steps needed to reach the phone and put my hand on the receiver, not taking my eyes off my husband.

We both know that it isn't Scarlet.

And then I take a deep breath, like I'm about to go underwater for the longest time, and yank the handle off the phone base.

'Hello.'

I listen to the voice on the other end as she introduces herself. Nick stands very still, as if movement of any kind will break the spell that we appear to be under.

'Yes.' I gulp and then I stand up straight, pushing my shoulders back and my chest out. 'Yes, it is. My name is Twinky Malone.'

Across the room, Nick exhales and raises his glass of wine high in the air, and I can see in his eyes what he is telling me. He is saluting Hannah Thompson, part-time English teacher. He is saluting Hannah Thompson, wife, mother, daughter, and friend.

And he is saluting Twinky Malone, unwitting writer of erotic humour.

Twinky Malone is not dead and gone.

Twinky Malone is only just beginning.

Acknowledgements

Writing this book has been a whole new adventure for me and it would not have been possible without the help of a few (very fabulous) people. So a huge thank you to Kerry, Lizzy & Polly who have been there every step of the way, always ready for a raucous conversation and a cackling session, either over a cup of coffee or several glasses of wine. Thank you to Edie E for taking the time to read an early version and offer advice. I also need to thank my long-suffering kids (whose names have been changed to protect the guilty) and my highly understanding husband. Adam, your enthusiasm and support is never-ending and I hugely appreciate your help with the research element of this book ...